W9-AVB-347

Home at Last

Center Point
Large Print

Also by Shirlee McCoy and available from Center Point Large Print:

Home with You
Home Again

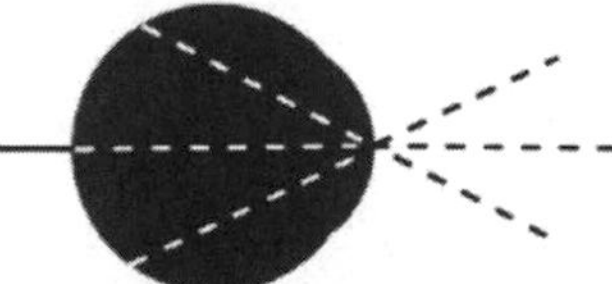

Home at Last

The Bradshaws

Shirlee McCoy

CENTER POINT LARGE PRINT
THORNDIKE, MAINE

This Center Point Large Print edition
is published in the year 2019 by arrangement with
Kensington Publishing Corp.

The text of this Large Print edition is unabridged.
In other aspects, this book may vary
from the original edition.
Printed in the United States of America
on permanent paper.
Set in 16-point Times New Roman type.

ISBN: 978-1-64358-366-2

The Library of Congress has cataloged this record
under Library of Congress Control Number: 2019944969

CHAPTER ONE

Sunday Bradshaw was out of breath by the time she made it down the stairs. Panting and sweating like she'd run a marathon when all she'd done was descend fifteen steps.

Fifteen!

Her legs were shaking, her heart thumping. She'd have sat right there at the bottom of the stairs and stayed until dawn, but she was afraid Rosie would find her, sound the alarm, and mobilize everyone in the house to help "Poor Ms. Bradshaw."

Good Lord! She hated being called that.

She hated hearing it whispered when she was limping through the five-and-dime with one of the kids or moving at a snail's pace down the aisle at church. She hated hearing Rosie tell Matt's brothers that "Poor Ms. Bradshaw" just needed a little more time.

As if that would ever be enough to get over losing her memories, her independence. Losing Matt.

Losing the world they'd been creating together.

The world you'd been creating, that voice in her head said. The one that had been speaking loudly ever since she'd been released from rehab.

She tried not to listen, because there was no

sense holding on to old disappointments. She'd already lost enough, and she didn't want to lose her joy with it.

Not that she had much of that left either.

She shuffled down the hall and stepped into the living room, the old furniture well-worn and comfortable, hand-me-downs from the days when she'd lived there with her parents.

Life had been a lot simpler then.

A lot less stressful and busy.

She might have lost days and weeks and months and years of her memories, but she knew that.

She crossed the room and settled into the old recliner. It was true she spent too much time sitting there, listening to the kids play outside or watching as they read books on the couch or love seat. Every day, she told herself she should be reading to them. She told herself she should be outside in the cooling days of late summer, laughing as they cartwheeled and blew dandelion seeds into the air.

She also told herself she should make dinner, wash the kids' clothes, go to the school to see what teachers they each would have in the fall. She told herself a lot of things, and then she sat in the recliner and let others do what she used to.

It was the path of least resistance, and she was embarrassed that she kept taking it. Before the accident, she'd hit the ground running. Every morning, she'd been up before dawn, making lunches and doing chores. If she had enough courage for it, she'd spend time going through the farm's books, trying to organize receipts that Matt left in the bottom drawer of the file cabinet. Piles and piles of receipts. Matt liked to buy stuff. He liked to give stuff away. That hadn't bothered her as much before they'd had kids. After . . .

Well, she'd spent a little too much time worrying about finances the last few years.

Funny how she could remember that, but she couldn't remember what Matt had been wearing the night of the accident. She couldn't remember where they'd gone to eat dinner. She could remember the lights, though—high beams coming straight at them.

She saw those lights in her dreams, woke with a scream dying on her lips.

But like so many other things, the rest of the night was lost to her.

She blinked, rubbing suddenly sweaty palms over worn yoga pants. She was afraid. At night, when the house was asleep, she could admit that. If she could have gotten away with it, she'd have spent the rest of her life inside. She'd have kept the children there too. Playing board games on the floor nearby or reading quietly as she rested her eyes. They'd be safe there. No drunk drivers coming at them in the dead of night. No strangers lurking in the shadows hoping to steal them away.

No heartache from being betrayed by the only person they'd ever loved.

She winced away from the thought, because dwelling on it wouldn't change anything.

That was another irony—remembering the betrayal when she'd forgotten so much. She'd have preferred to forget. It would have made life a little easier.

Or at least a little less sad.

There was a photo on the mantel. One she'd spent hours staring at these past few weeks. Even in the darkness, she found it easily, lifting the ornate crystal frame and carrying it to the window. The curtains were closed, and she pulled them open, letting moonlight filter in. In the grayscale world it created, she could see herself as she'd been on her wedding day—glowing in the 1920s lace dress that had been worn by three generations of brides before her.

And there was Matthias, handsome in his tuxedo.

She touched his face, her finger sliding across cool glass instead of warm flesh.

She'd loved him the first time she'd seen him—a mischievous dark-haired six-year-old late for his first day of first grade. She'd loved him all through elementary, middle, and high school. She'd loved him the day they'd married.

Even after she'd learned the truth about all

those business trips to Seattle, she'd loved him.

She liked to think they'd have made it. That they'd have survived his affair and grown closer and stronger and gone on. Not for the sake of the kids, but for the sake of the love they'd always had for each other.

She'd never know for sure, though.

She set the photo down, her arm shaking from the weight of it. She went to physical therapy three times a week. She was supposed to be getting stronger. Maybe she was, but life was a lot harder than it used to be. Simple things like walking down stairs or showering or making an egg on the old gas stove had to be planned out, and when she finally completed a task, she was too tired to start another one.

What had happened to the cheerful, chipper, energetic young woman she'd heard about? Where had the Sunday Bradshaw who could raise six kids, keep a house clean, balance impossible-to-balance checkbooks, plant lush gardens and make beautiful magazine-worthy meals gone? Well-meaning friends came to visit and listed all Sunday's amazing accomplishments. She wasn't sure if they were complimenting her or trying to motivate her. Either way, they were failing.

She didn't want to be complimented on the woman she'd been.

She didn't want to be motivated to be that woman again.

Mostly, she just wanted to be left alone.

Trying to remember names and faces of people she should know well was exhausting. Trying to keep track of those she hadn't known well was nearly impossible. Traumatic brain injury did that to a person. Lost synapses and misfiring neurons. The neurologist assured Sunday that things would improve.

Sunday spent a lot of time thinking that might happen too late.

Too late to regain her life.

Too late to make up for the fact that she'd missed out on so much of her children's lives.

By the time things "got better," the kids would be happy in lives that barely included her.

She hated that, and she was trying to change it.

But every day she failed in a dozen different ways.

Just yesterday, she'd heard Heavenly ask her uncle Sullivan to take her shopping for a dress she needed for a state choir competition. She'd already asked Sunday three times. Three times, Sunday had promised to take her and forgotten. That's what Heavenly had told Sullivan. There'd been just enough bitterness in her voice to break Sunday's heart.

"At least they have your brothers. Right, Matt?" she whispered into the silence.

No answering whisper from Matthias.

Not that she'd expected one.

Even if Matt could have found a way back from Heaven, she doubted he'd have returned to the farm. He'd have had bigger fish to fry. Places to explore. New sights to see. All the things he'd pretended not to care about while they were married.

Maybe if she'd known the truth . . .

But she hadn't.

At least, she didn't think she had.

Her memories weren't sharp or clear, and lately she wondered if everything she remembered about her relationship with Matt was a fantasy she'd concocted to make herself feel better about his betrayal.

Betrayal*s*? Maybe. Probably.

That was another thing she didn't want to think about.

Tears burned the back of her eyes.

She forced them away.

She couldn't waste hours and days thinking about what had been or mourning what would never be. She had six children, for God's sake. They were depending on her. She had to figure out how to move past the emptiness, the lost memories, the sorrow. Step into this new life she'd been given. God was the God of second chances, right?

And this was hers.

She didn't want to waste it.

She walked back through the hall and into the

kitchen, passing the 1920s stove and the old farmhouse sink. She loved the old appliances, the creaky floor, the nicked table where the kids did their schoolwork. Matt had talked about nicer things. She was certain of that. She could almost hear his cheerful voice listing all the wonderful new things they'd have once the farm was up and running. A brand new stainless-steel stove. A larger refrigerator. A new dinette set. She'd thought he was just thinking aloud, wanting nicer things for her sake.

I still love you. You know that, Sunday.

She thought he'd said that the night of the accident. She could picture him sitting across the table from her, a glass of wine near his elbow, his blue eyes filled with remorse and concern.

Only she wasn't sure if the memory was real or if she'd conjured it.

And, she wasn't sure if his love were a better thing or a worse one. Because, she couldn't understand—no matter how hard she tried—how it was possible to love someone and still hurt her so deeply.

All she knew was that she'd loved him enough to go to dinner that one last time, to give him a second chance he hadn't really earned.

That willingness had cost him everything, and her a lot.

Her chest ached with the thought, her heart throbbing painfully, the panic that was always just beneath the surface, trying to bubble up and take control.

She stumbled to the back door, shoved it open, and stepped outside, gasping for air that didn't seem to want to fill her lungs.

She'd been prescribed anti-anxiety medicine, and she'd taken it for a while. Now, she tried to rely on the techniques her therapist had taught her.

Breathe in. Breathe out. Find your grounding. Focus on the here and now—the late summer air, the kiss of moonlight above the trees, the soft rustle of leaves and grass as nocturnal animals moved through.

She limped down the back steps and shuffled through freshly mown grass. The moon was high and bright and beautiful, illuminating the path from the house to the gate. Not that she needed light to navigate. She'd walked this way hundreds of times. Maybe thousands. Even if her memory failed, her feet knew the way. She didn't have to think about where to step or how. She didn't have to worry about tripping over roots or wandering in the wrong direction.

This she knew.

This was easy.

She opened the gate and walked through. Fields of corn stretched as far as the eye could see. Beyond them, the Spokane River flowed sluggishly. There hadn't been much rain this year, but Matt's brothers had kept the crops growing. There would be a good harvest for the first time since her father's death. Ten years. Or was it eleven?

Time was as murky and misty as her memories tended to be.

She crossed the country road, knowing exactly where she was heading. She didn't allow herself to think about it. She didn't question her reasons. She picked her way down the steep hill that led to the riverbank, followed the silvery flow of water to the footbridge that had been stabilized by Matt's brothers. Listened to the soft sounds of country life as she crossed from one side of the river to the other.

Water lapped against the rocky shore. An owl called from its perch somewhere in the grove of pine trees that stood watch over the river. A gentle breeze rustled the grass and sent spent leaves skittering across the pebbly beach. The night was exactly as it should be. Except that she was alone.

How odd to be single after so many years of being part of a couple.

Matt and Sunday. Sunday and Matt. Everyone in the small town of Benevolence talked about them as if they were one unit, one entity.

Only now Matt was gone.

She stepped onto the bridge, grabbing the hand-rails on both sides as she made her way across the river. Boulders peeked above the surface of the water, the soft splash of waves a sweet familiar melody.

She knew this place better than she knew herself.

She knew the curves of the riverbank, the dips and rises of the land. She knew the heartbeat of the earth and the whispered breath of the towering pine trees.

She'd thought she could teach it to Matt and the kids.

She'd thought that if she put enough time and effort and love into her family and the farm, everything would be okay.

This was far from okay—her painstaking trip across the bridge that she should have been able to run across. Her hobbled steps as she headed toward the path that led to the old family cemetery.

Forgotten shopping trips and missed opportunities and kids growing up while she sat in a chair and watched life pass by weren't part of the life she'd planned to build.

She had been left behind to finish the work she and Matt had begun together.

And, she wasn't doing a very good job of it.

That was the worst part of all. She was failing, and she didn't know how to stop the freefall, put on the brakes, change directions.

She sighed, picking her way up the hill that led

to the chapel her family had built over a century ago. For a while, it hadn't been much more than ruins. Just a few months ago, the kids, her brothers-in-law, and her friend Clementine had rebuilt it, creating a beautiful, peaceful place for those who needed it.

She needed it.

She needed a lot of things.

Mostly, she thought she just needed to learn how to live this second-chance life.

Behind her, an animal yipped. A coyote, maybe. Or a fox. Whichever it was, it sounded like it was in distress. She scanned the area, walking back the way she'd come, following the sound because she could never leave an injured animal to fend for itself.

She reached the riverbank. The sound was louder there, carrying above the soft gurgle of water sliding against rocks. The yipping turned to frantic barking, and she finally found the source. A bedraggled puppy sat on the slopped surface of a boulder in the middle of the river, its paws scrabbling against the wet rock.

"How'd you get there?" she called, and the puppy howled, prancing a little in its enthusiasm.

"You can swim, you know," she continued, taking an unconscious step forward, forgetting for just a moment that she wasn't the woman she'd been, that walking on slippery rocks might not be the best choice.

“Come on, buddy,” she encouraged, taking another step and another. The water was cold, but not winter-cold. Just cool enough to make her shiver as it seeped through her yoga pants.

“Sunday!” someone shouted, the voice so much like Matt’s she spun around. Too quickly. Her balance too tenuous. She was down before she realized she was falling, water splashing up around her belly and back and shoulders. Her head glanced off a rock. Not hard. Just enough so she knew it had happened.

She lay there, winded, staring up at the night sky and the sparkling stars, thinking about Matt and that voice. Wondering who had called her name and if she’d imagined it.

And then he was splashing into the creek, running toward her, lifting her out of the water, and . . . of course . . . it wasn’t Matt. It was his brother Flynn. Taller. Darker hair. Broader shouldered.

“What in the heck were you thinking?” he asked, one arm firmly around her waist, the other on her wrist.

“About the dog,” she responded, but she didn’t think he heard. He was too busy slogging toward shore.

If Flynn Bradshaw had been one to curse, he’d be doing it now. Long-dormant phrases that he’d learned from his father filled his head and were right on the tip of his tongue. But, of course, he'd given up cursing and yelling years ago.

"Sunday, what were you thinking?" he repeated as they reached shore. His arm was still around her waist, his fingers curved into the sopping fabric of her T-shirt, his thumb resting against her bottom rib. He could feel it through the soaked fabric, jutting out from her too-thin frame.

"The river might be low, but it can still be dangerous," he continued, easing his grip because he was afraid he'd hurt her. He was used to reining in horses and wrangling cattle. He was not used to being gentile with fragile women.

"I know, and I told you," she responded, stepping away, her eyes too-large in her gaunt face. "I was thinking about the dog."

"You don't have a dog," he replied, studying her face, searching for some truth that she wasn't speaking or some hint of the confusion that he thought she must be suffering.

His brothers had said she continued to have memory lapses. He hadn't been around enough to notice much more than her frailty and her obvious continued pain.

He'd worried about both those things.

But, the confusion was alarming, the fact that she'd left the house in the middle of the night and crossed the river filling him with fear and frustration. The kids had already lost their father. They couldn't lose Sunday, too.

"Don't look at me like that," she said, a slight snap to her voice.

"Like what?"

"Like I've lost my mind."

"You're mistaking my look of concern for one of judgment," he replied, keeping his voice calm and easy. Prior to the accident, Sunday had been the calmest person he'd ever met. Low-key. Unflappable. He'd visited the farm two or three times a year, because family should be important, and his nieces and nephews mattered. He'd never heard her raise her voice to any of her children or to Matt.

Since the accident, she still didn't raise her voice. Not to her children. Not to Flynn or his brothers or to the many people who came to visit.

But, something in her had changed. Her placid, unflappable, soul-deep peace had been replaced by anxiety and fear. He could see it now, plainly written on her face and in her eyes, and he didn't want to make things worse by upsetting her.

"I'm a grown woman, Flynn," she said. "No one needs to be concerned if I walk to the river by myself."

"It's the middle of the night, Sunday," he pointed out.

"And, I'm still a grown woman, and there *is* a dog in the middle of the river." She pointed, her hand trembling.

Sure enough, there *was* a dog sitting on a rock.

Right in the middle of the river.

If he hadn't been so focused on keeping Sunday from drowning, he'd have noticed before. "Most dogs can swim. The river is low. He could walk across easily, if he wanted to."

"Probably," she agreed, "but, sometimes we're trapped by our own fear. Sometimes, things that other people think are easy look really hard to us."

"Here, boy!" she called, walking to the edge of the river, water lapping up across her bare toes.

No shoes.

No coat.

Just yoga pants and a T-shirt.

And, that alarmed Flynn, too, because it was late summer, and autumn was cold in this part of the country.

He slipped out of his coat and dropped it around her shoulders. "We need to go back to the house. It's cold, and you're soaked."

"So is he."

"He's a dog."

"He's scared," she replied, moving away from his hand, her eyes dark in the moonlight, her skin pale. "Wait here. The water isn't going to be much deeper than my knees, and I'm already wet. A little more isn't going to make a difference."

She'd have stepped back onto the slippery river rocks, if he hadn't grabbed her arm and stopped her.

"I'll get him," he muttered.

And, she smiled, her eyes crinkling at the corners, her face easing into the soft sweetness he recognized from his visits before the accident.

"Thank you," she said, the smile still in place.

"You can thank me by not coming down to the river in the middle of the night again. Or, at least, not wading into the water," he responded more gruffly than he intended. He'd been looking for glimpses of the old Sunday for months, searching her face and her posture every time he was in town, trying to find hints of the person she'd been. He'd found them. Here on the riverbank where her children couldn't see, and his brothers couldn't breathe sighs of relief.

But, at least, he'd seen them, and that gave him hope that things would be back to normal one day; that Sunday would regain the pieces of herself that the accident seemed to have stolen.

That the children would have their mother.

She would have her life.

Things could go back to what they'd been before. When Flynn and his brothers hadn't had to carry the responsibility of their brother's choices.

He frowned, wading into the river, the cold water sloshing into his work boots, and then up to his knees. The dog stayed right where it was, barking excitedly as Flynn approached. He extended his hand, let the dog sniff his fingers and lick his knuckles.

Obviously, this was not an attack dog or a fearful animal that might bite.

"Alright, buddy. Let's go," he said, scooping the dog into his arms. It was a bag of skin and bones, its big paws huge on its spindly forelegs. A gangly puppy that would turn into a large dog. Its curly fur reminding him of Patricia's miniature poodle, Tilly. His ex-wife had loved that dog. Probably more than she'd loved anyone or anything else.

It had taken him a long time to realize that.

He carried the puppy to shore and set it down near Sunday. She crouched, wobbling as she held out her hand and crooned something inane and sweet. *Little pupper* or *Darling little pupper*.

Flynn didn't hear the words, but he saw the joy in her face, and he decided not to remind her that the house already had enough chaos without adding a puppy into the mix.

The puppy sniffed her fingers, licked her hand, then moved in for the kill, lunging for her and knocking her backwards as he bathed her face with kisses.

She'd have fallen if Flynn hadn't grabbed her shoulders, holding her upright.

She was laughing, the sound a little rusty, as he urged her to her feet.

"He's adorable, isn't he?" she asked, laughter lingering in her eyes and easing some of the lines of tension and pain that usually creased her fore-head.

"If you're into floppy-eared dogs," he responded, and she met his gaze, that sweet smile still curving the corners of her mouth.

"Let me guess: You prefer . . ." Her voice trailed off, and the joy faded from her face.

He knew she'd lost the words.

That somehow whatever dog she'd planned to name was trapped in her accident-damaged brain.

"Working dogs?" he offered, hoping to ease the tension.

But, the moment was gone, and she seemed discontent, anxious, worried again.

"I guess," she replied, her attention on the puppy who was staring at her longingly, his tail thumping the ground.

"This guy," he continued, scratching the puppy behind his ears, "is more the frou-frou variety."

He'd been hoping to distract her from her frustration, but it didn't seem to be working. She looked . . . sad and a little defeated, and that made him want to fight harder to give her whatever it was that would heal the hurts.

Which, he supposed, was his Achilles heel.

He wanted to fix things, and sometimes that meant he wanted to fix people. Or, at least, help them solve their problems. It was one of the few traits he'd inherited from his mother. He considered it to be one of his greatest strengths and his biggest weaknesses, because some people wanted to be helped. Some didn't. Some wanted to solve their problems. Some preferred to dwell in them.

"Sunday, people forget words all the time. I know the accident made things difficult."

"Let's not talk about the accident, okay?" she murmured.

"What would you rather talk about?"

"The fact that you're here. I thought Sullivan said that you'd be in . . ." Her voice trailed off. Another word lost, and he could feel her tension hanging in the cool crisp air.

"Texas?" he offered.

"Right," she agreed. "He said you'd be there until October or November. Something about horses."

"Cattle," he corrected gently, because she'd known all this before.

"Cattle," she agreed, that one word filled with a thousand disappointments and frustrations.

"Spring and autumn are our busiest times at the ranch. I planned to stay in Texas through October, but Porter and Clementine really want a fall wedding, and it didn't feel right to expect them to wait. They've already done more than—" He stopped, because he didn't want Sunday to feel guilty for what his brothers had sacrificed. They'd given up their time, their money, their homes. They'd left lives in other places and created lives in Benevolence, Washington. All for the sake of Matt's kids and for the farm those children would one day inherit.

And, for Sunday, because she'd loved them all so well and so selflessly.

None of them had put words to that, but Flynn knew he and his brothers felt an obligation to Sunday. Not just because she was Matt's widow, but because she'd opened her home, over and over again, to three brothers-in-law who only made appearances when it was convenient.

"You can say it," Sunday said quietly.

"There's no need to say what we all know," he responded. He'd always been a straight-shooter and honest to a fault, so he wasn't going to pull punches or pretend things that weren't true. But, the truth was, he'd shirked his responsibility after Matt's death. He'd had a ranch to run, and he'd made that his excuse, because it was difficult to see six kids suffer and hard to watch Sunday struggle to recover. "But, if you need me to, I will. My brothers have been here while I've been in Texas. It's my turn to be a good uncle to the kids."

"That's a very kind way of saying that I'm not pulling my weight around the farm," she said, turning away and heading up the hill that led to the family chapel.

"You aren't yet, but you'll be back to it eventually."

"So, people keep telling me."

"You don't believe it?"

She met his eyes, and he could see the truth

she didn't speak. "I'm not sure it matters what I believe. People are depending on me to get better, so I will."

"Or, you'll pretend?"

"A parent does what she has to, right?" She smiled, but there was no humor in her eyes or her face.

The puppy was trotting along beside her, and she seemed content to let him. Based on the looks she kept shooting in Flynn's direction, she'd rather he not.

"You can go back to the house," she said, proving that he wasn't nearly as bad at reading women as Patricia had once claimed. "I won't go back in the water. I promise."

"Not even if the mutt jumps in?"

She glanced at the dog. "I might have to make an exception for that."

"Then, I guess I'll hang around until you're ready to go back."

"I came out here to be alone," she said pointedly, still trudging up the hill at a pace just a little slower than Old Blue—the twenty-year-old retired Coon hound his ranch foreman owned.

"At this time of night, you could have been alone in the house."

"I could have been," she agreed, not making any excuse for her late-night walk, not offering any explanation.

He admired that. Admired the gumption that

kept her moving up the hill even when he could see that her legs were trembling. There was defeat in the slope of her shoulders and the agonizing slowness of her pace, but she seemed determined to keep going.

Who was he to discourage that?

After all, he'd come to town to help, but he'd also come with the express purpose of encouraging Sunday to be more independent, to get more involved in her children's lives, to take part in the running of the house and the farm again.

Because his brothers were worried.

Truth be told, he was worried, too.

But, he wasn't going to tell her that, so he matched her pace and continued walking up the hill.

CHAPTER TWO

Once upon a time, she'd wandered the farm without supervision. She'd wake in the middle of the night, her head filled with worry, her heart pounding frantically, and she'd ease out of the bed, pull on her old robe, slide her feet into the boots that sat by the back door and walk outside. She'd meander through the yard and the fields, the stars glittering in the blue-black sky. She'd listen to the silence and be filled with the kind of peace that only home could bring.

She had no clear memory of it. Just vague feelings that she'd wandered the farm alone at night. Vague thoughts that Matt had never come to find her, and that, sometimes, she'd wished he would.

Alone was a pleasant thing until you longed to be with someone who longed to be with you.

At some point in their marriage, she and Matt must have lost that longing for one another. There was no other way to explain what had happened. All she had were vague feelings and vague thoughts and vague memories of spending a lot of time alone.

Now, everywhere she went, someone followed.

It didn't matter what time of day. Early morning. Afternoon. Evening. If she got up from the old easy chair or the couch, someone followed. Either one of the kids or one of her brothers-in-law or the housekeeper, Rosie.

Usually, they tried to be unobtrusive, leaning against a fence and pretending to look at text messages, peeking into rooms, guarding the doors as if she might somehow escape and never return.

At night, if she were quiet enough, she could have time to herself, time when she wasn't being watched and worried over.

Tonight, though, Flynn was sticking to her like glue, following her over the apex of the hill and into the grassy expanse beyond. The chapel was just ahead, rising from the nearly-flat landscape, its white steeple gleaming in the moonlight.

Maybe Flynn thought she was heading there, or maybe he knew she planned to visit Matt's grave. Either way, she didn't want him to follow her.

"You can wait here, if you want," she suggested, stopping and turning to face him. He had a broader, sturdier build than any of his brothers, his shoulders solid and thick with muscle, his biceps straining against his flannel shirt. He owned a ranch in Texas. Cattle. Not horses. She needed to write that down when she returned home. If he planned to stay for a while, she didn't want to forget the details.

"What if I *don't* want?" he asked, and, for a

moment, she was confused. Not sure what he was asking, his words tumbling around in her head, disjointed and incomprehensible. She grasped them. One at a time. Piecing them together like a jigsaw puzzle.

By the time they finally formed a sentence, by the time she finally understood its meaning, she felt slow and stupid and frustrated.

"I . . . You . . . Waitress . . . Waiting . . . Wait . . ." Like his question, her answer refused to form easily in her mind. Her cheeks heated, the warmth spreading down her neck and to her throat and chest.

He was watching her, his gaze steady and unflinching.

Unlike some of the people who visited and watched her wrestle with words or memory, he didn't seem uncomfortable or embarrassed by her struggle.

He just . . . waited.

She took a breath. Tried again, taking the words one at a time and putting them into an order that made sense. Slowly. Painstakingly. "I would appreciate it if you wait here. I need some time alone."

There.

The words were stiff and formal, but the sentences made sense.

"Okay," he nodded, still watching her steadily.

"Okay?"

"Are you surprised that I'd agree?" he asked, scratching the puppy between the ears as he continued to stare into her eyes.

"Maybe," she admitted. "Your brothers watch me like hawks. I don't think I'm ever very far out of their sight."

"I'm not my brothers, and, as you've mentioned, you're a grown woman. If you want time alone, you have a right to it. I'll wait here with the puppy until you're ready to go back." He pulled the collar of his coat close around her neck, his knuckles brushing the underside of her jaw. "Keep this on, okay? It's chilly tonight."

She nodded, because she couldn't speak.

Her thoughts were on the quick brush of rough warm skin against hers. She'd been touched a million times since the accident. By nurses and doctors, friends and family. Most of it impersonal, therapeutic or comforting. None of it making her think of the past, of the way it felt to have warm hands slide along bare skin, sweet kisses pressed into the crook of her neck, the hollow of her throat.

She turned away, appalled and alarmed, annoyed with herself and the fickle way that her bruised and traumatized brain functioned. Because that quick split-second thought about warm hands and smooth flesh could only be a product of the injury she'd suffered in the accident.

She was too damaged for it to be anything else.

She walked into the chapel, inhaled the cool damp air. She just needed to center herself, find that sweet soul-space where peace and contentment had always dwelled. She dropped onto the nearest pew. A varnished wood bench that had been salvaged from a church in Seattle. Soft with time and use. Silky smooth from decades of dresses and slacks brushing against its surface. Gouged and nicked from Sunday after Sunday of children's dress shoes scraping against the surface as they shifted and moved, bored and trying to behave.

Suddenly, she could see Moisey as she'd been the first time she'd attended service at Benevolence Baptist Church. Her gleaming patent leather shoes buckled around her ankle socks. Her dark eyes gleaming with enthusiasm. Three years old and new to the country and the family, but not afraid. Not at all.

"I wish I had your courage," she murmured, picturing her daughter's impish smile, trying to remember if she'd said good night to the seven-year-old, given her a hug and kiss. Told her she loved her.

It bothered her that she didn't know.

Something jumped onto the pew beside her, and she screamed, her heart in her throat as the thing took shape in the shadowy darkness. A dog. *The* dog.

"What are you doing here?" she asked with a shaky laugh, running her hand over his still-wet head and neck.

"He refused to listen to reason, and insisted on following you inside," Flynn said, taking a seat beside her.

"You used reason on a dog?"

"I told him you wanted some time alone," he replied, grinning at her through the darkness.

"Apparently, he's not concerned about my need for personal space. Or, maybe, you're just using him as an excuse to follow me in here."

"That's a possibility, too. My brothers are worried about you, Sunday. If they are, I am."

"Why are they worried?" she asked, but she knew why. As much as they tried to encourage her to be more involved in the lives of the children, she couldn't seem to get into the swing of things. The muscle memory that carried her from place to place on the farm, didn't carry her from moment to moment of motherhood. Nothing about her kids felt familiar. Not their likes or dislikes. Not their personalities. Not their needs and desires. Every interaction she had with them felt stiff and unnatural, forced in a way that made her feel guilty.

"They think you're too hard on yourself," he responded. "That your expectations are too high. You're early on in your recovery and beating yourself up because you can't do as much as you'd think you should, is only causing you frustration."

"So, they're spying on me and reporting back to you?" she replied, the sharpness in her tone surprising her more than it seemed to surprise him.

"No one is spying on you," he said calmly, gently. As if she were a wild colt that needed taming.

And, that only made her feel worse.

"That didn't come out the way I meant it to."

"What way did you mean it to come out?"

"A lot less accusatory," she replied, and he smiled again.

"I don't guess I'd feel happy if a bunch of near-strangers were calling the shots and running the show for me. This is your place, Sunday. Your farm. Your kids. Your family. If you're feeling smothered, you just have to say it. We'll back off."

"I'm not." That was the truth. She didn't feel smothered. She felt lost.

"No?" He was staring into her eyes, watching her in a way she couldn't remember anyone ever doing. Not before the accident when she'd been the busy mother, rushing from place to place. Not after when she was the invalid, lying in bed or sitting in a chair or limping her way through stores and up the aisle at church.

This was the kind of look that asked questions.

The kind that demanded answers. The kind that wanted to see beyond the surface truths to the deep ones.

"No," she said, because she couldn't explain without fumbling for words and struggling to express herself.

"Okay." He nodded, stood, stretched to his full height. "But, if you ever decide that you do, let me know. I'll make sure things change."

He lifted the dog from the pew and walked away, his feet nearly silent on the old wood floor.

And, then she was alone again, the small chapel still and quiet. She leaned forward, resting her forearms on the pew in front of her. There were windows at the front of the small room, flanking a cross hewn from salvaged wood. The place was as beautiful as it had been when the family had built it. Snapshots taken by traveling photographers nearly a hundred years ago depicted the same rough-hewn style cross and tall windows. The rehab had been done with care and with attention to detail.

Sunday hadn't been involved. She'd been attending daily rehab, going through intense therapy that had worn her out. She hadn't watched the progress, but she'd seen pictures snapped on cell phones. The twins hammering nails. Moisey standing on a pew wearing a tutu, a tiara, and work boots.

Those were the images she remembered.

She knew there had been others, but the rest were lost to her.

She walked to the front of the room, ran her hand across the small pulpit that stood there. Another salvage from a church in Spokane. Or maybe Seattle or Portland. She didn't remember. It was smooth with age. Just like the pews.

A cool breeze blew in through the window openings, carrying the scent of water and summer grass. No glass to keep fresh air from circulating. No shutters to keep out the wind or rain. This was the way things had been a hundred years ago—simple. The floor swept and dried by the family after storms. Leaves and debris removed before Sunday service. Fresh air and sunshine the only incense needed.

She walked to one of the windows, listening to the world's night song. The hush of rustling grasses. The burble of water over rocks. No traffic this far from town. No voices. Nothing but nature playing its stunning symphony.

She climbed out the window without thinking, her bad leg catching on the window ledge and almost sending her to the ground. Thanks to dozens of hours of physical therapy, she managed to catch her balance and right herself. Dry grass swished against her legs as she moved through it and headed around the side of the building. She could see the cemetery from there, the old grave markers shimmering in the moonlight. It didn't take long to make her way to the gate and walk through it. Four generations of family members had been buried there, and now Matt was too.

She settled onto a spiky blanket of grass a few feet from his grave. His brothers had chosen the spot. They'd chosen the marker. They'd contacted the pastor and arranged the funeral and done everything they could to make things easier on the children. They'd taken them to Spokane and bought the boys suits and the girls dresses. They'd let them choose the flowers that would be placed on the casket during the service, the songs that would be sung, even the scripture that would be read.

She knew, because she'd been told the story by friends and church members, by the pastor and his wife. She'd heard it so many times, she might never have forgotten it, but she'd written the details in her journal. Just in case. She'd wanted to remember that her children hadn't faced their father's death alone. That their uncles had been there when she couldn't be.

She sighed, pulling her knees up to her chest, ignoring the twinge of pain in her leg and the ache of discomfort in her ribs.

"Hey, hun," she said, running her hand over the marble headstone. "I miss you."

If he'd been alive, he'd have pulled her in for a hug, told her that he missed her too.

He'd been good at telling her what she'd wanted to hear.

She had notes and cards to prove it, written words that she found herself pouring over in the middle of the night when she couldn't sleep, searching for clues to the truth about who Matt had been, what he'd really thought and desired.

"The kids start school soon," she continued, forcing herself to stop thinking about what she might have missed.

Because, Matt was gone.

The fact that she'd discovered his infidelity just a few days prior to his death didn't change the other truth: They'd been married for a decade, had been raising children together as a team. A team that had worked well.

Most of the time.

"The twins are going to be in the same class this year. Remember how we talked about whether or not they'd do better together? The principal thinks they will, so I agreed," she murmured, hoping she was getting the details right.

Just in case he could hear.

Just in case it mattered somehow to a man who'd been dead for nearly a year and who'd been thinking about walking away from his family when he died. She had that, too—the email that had given away the truth, that had proven what she'd probably suspected long before she'd confronted him.

She'd read the email as many times as she'd read all the love notes and poems and letters he'd written to her. She'd studied the words, trying to make sense of it all. She couldn't remember discovering the email. She couldn't recall printing it. She only knew she had. She'd never been one to snoop. She'd trusted Matt. Too much. So, she guessed that he'd left his laptop open, that maybe he'd wanted her to see the note he'd written to his lover. The one that professed his love and his desire to leave his family and make a new life in Seattle.

But, of course, she could only guess.

She remembered his betrayal. She had no idea how she'd learned of it. She just had the email. Printed out and folded neatly, hidden in the packet of written missives she'd collected during their nearly twenty years of friendship and love.

They'd been babies when they'd met.

First graders. Younger than Moisey.

And, maybe, that had been the problem. Puppy love wasn't really meant to last.

She touched the cold stone again, tracing her fingers through the carved letters of his name. "Heavenly has a choir competition coming up. You were right about her voice. It really has been her pathway to friendships. You wrote that in last years' Christmas letter. Remember?"

He didn't respond, of course.

And, she felt the futility of what she was doing. Sitting at his grave, trying to connect with him. Trying to find some reason or meaning that would help her make sense of what happened.

She pressed her forehead to her knees, wanting to pray. No words came. No thoughts. No longings or dreams. Everything she'd wanted had been tied up in her family, and now that was slipping through her fingers.

A wet nose pressed against her cheek, and she realized the puppy was there. Fur still wet, body shivering. He was cold, and she was too.

It was time to get up and go back home, but she felt too tired to move and too defeated to care.

"It's going to be okay," Flynn said, suddenly at her side, reaching down to slide his arm around her waist and help her to her feet.

"What?"

"Whatever it is that's making you cry."

"I'm not crying." But, maybe she was. She could feel moisture on her cheeks, and she would have wiped it away, but he was already doing it, his palms warm against her cold skin.

"So, these are just fairy kisses slipping down your cheeks?" he murmured, his voice as gentle as the first spring rain and as soft as the kiss of a butterfly's wing.

"Fairy kisses?"

"That's what my mother used to say when I caught her crying," he replied. "*They aren't tears. They're fairy kisses. Just like the dew on the roses in the morning*."

"Your mother was a poet."

"She was an artist. A good one. If she'd been married to a different man, she'd have probably become a book illustrator." He shrugged. "But, she wasn't, and all her illustrations were created for me and my brothers."

"Matt never told me that." At least, she didn't think he had.

"He might not have remembered. He was very young when she died."

"Yes. He was."

"He loved your mother. Both your parents. He used to tell me that. About how he married you and finally got the family he'd always wanted."

A cool breeze ruffled her hair and seeped into her damp clothes, chilling her. Or, maybe it was his words that had done that. She'd kept journals all her life—diaries filled with accountings of thoughts and dreams, her friendships, her interest. She'd read through them since the accident. She knew how much Matt had loved her parents, and she'd wondered . . . because why shouldn't she? . . . if that had been part of the reason why he'd fallen in love with her.

"My parents loved him, too. He was the son they never had," she said, because it was true, and because she had no intention of talking about her suspicions and her insecurities.

"I know he wasn't always easy, Sunday," Flynn said quietly as they walked back to the river, his words so surprising, she stumbled and would have fallen if he hadn't still had his arm around her waist.

"What do you mean?"

"It was obvious to me and my brothers that he hadn't been doing his part around the farm."

"He had a lot of big dreams," she responded, defending him the way she always had.

"And, that didn't leave a whole lot of room for pursuing the smaller ones? Like keeping the farm financially stable? Making sure the house you'd inherited didn't get sold out from under you?"

"He wanted to sell it," she admitted. "He had dreams of moving to Seattle or Portland. Maybe even Texas."

"Texas?"

"He talked about you a lot. About your ranch and all the things you'd accomplished."

"He sure as heck wasn't going to own a place like mine, and I don't think he'd have been happy in Texas. Matt hated wide-open space and dirt." He laughed quietly.

"You're right. He did."

Matt had hated the country. He'd hated rural life.

He'd longed for high-rises and busy streets.

How is it that she hadn't learned that until it was too late?

She pressed her lips together, sealing in words she couldn't say. Not to Flynn or to anyone. Enough people had already been hurt by Matt's death.

She didn't want to compound the injury.

She wouldn't.

They crossed the bridge silently, the puppy trotting along behind them. When they reached the house, Flynn held the back door open with his foot and lifted the puppy in his arms.

"I don't suppose you have a plan for this guy?" he said.

She didn't.

She hadn't thought beyond rescuing him from the river.

"I guess he can stay in the house for the night."

"Not in your room," Flynn responded. "He's got too much energy, and you need your sleep. I'll keep him with me."

"Are you sure you want to do that?"

"As sure as I am that adding a puppy to the household mix is a good idea." He said it deadpan, but there was just enough humor in his eyes to make her smile.

"I know it's not a good idea, but the kids have wanted a puppy forever."

"It's your house, Sunday. It's your decision. Can you make it up the stairs yourself? Or do you need help?"

"I've been getting up the stairs by myself since before I turned two," she responded, flicking on the light in the mudroom.

"That was before you broke your femur," he responded, his gaze dropping to her thigh. She knew he couldn't see through her leggings, but she had a feeling he was looking straight at the scar that curved down her leg.

That made her wonder if he'd seen the wound while she was in the hospital. She'd been in a coma for a few months, had nearly died enough times that people still mentioned it. She had no memory of anything that had happened before she'd woken in a rehab facility.

"My femur is as good as new," she murmured. "But, thanks for your concern."

He smiled. "Then, you go up to bed, and I'll go get my bag."

"You're staying at the house?" She didn't know why that hadn't occurred to her before.

"Would you rather I didn't? I can stay in town with Porter, but I plan on doing some work on the farm. Staying here will make it more convenient."

"Of course, you should stay here. It's just, Rosie is in one guest room, and Heavenly has taken over the other. She thinks she's much too old to have to share."

"I can sleep on the couch."

"It's not very comfortable."

"I've slept on worse."

"Do you know how many kids have jumped on those cushions? And with how much vigor?"

"Like I said, I've slept on worse." There was a smile in his voice. "I'm going to grab my bag and try to get some sleep. It's been a long day of travel, and I'm beat."

"Alright. Good night," she responded, because what else could she say? That she'd rather he stay with Porter? That she found his presence oddly unsettling?

"Good night." He closed the door, and she walked through the mudroom and into the kitchen, floorboards creaking and groaning under her feet. A draft seeped in through the windowpane above the sink, the air felt musty with damp and cold.

The place was old.

Just like Matt had said.

She'd written about it in her journal last year. Yesterday, she'd underlined the entry three times. Because she'd wanted to remember that he'd been hinting at his unhappiness, that she'd ignored the hints because she hadn't wanted to believe he'd loved their life less than she did.

She'd always been prone to optimism.

That was another thing she'd written about in her journals—the hope she'd had for the future, her determination to make things work. The farm. The parenting. The marriage.

But, no amount of effort could change another person's heart.

No amount of trying could make someone want what they didn't.

And, no amount of wishing could change the past.

• • •

If he could have changed the past, Flynn would have.

He'd thought about that a lot these past few months. Thought about how he'd tried to be the cool uncle who'd flown in a couple of times a year for a quick visit, the easy-going brother who hadn't demanded or expected anything other than warm welcomes and a few phone calls a year. Maybe if he'd been more present, more available, more demanding, Matt would have made better financial and business choices.

But, the past couldn't be changed.

All Flynn could do was try to be there in the present and in the future.

No matter how inconvenient that might be.

He set the puppy down. It loped after him as he rounded the side of the house and opened the trunk of the SUV he'd rented. He glanced at his cell phone before he grabbed his bags. Just to make sure there weren't any emergencies. His foreman had left a couple of texts. Just as Flynn had expected, things at the ranch were fine. There'd been five new calves dropped, and one of the mothers had rejected her baby. It was being bottle fed and kept in the nursery.

Typical ranch-day stuff.

The kind of stuff Flynn knew plenty about.

What he didn't know was how to step into Matt's world for longer than a few days.

He lifted his suitcase and carry-on from the back of the vehicle. He'd packed light. It wasn't like he was in the African savanna or the Mohave desert. He was right outside Benevolence, Washington. There were stores in town, and what he couldn't find there, he could find in Spokane.

If he had to stay longer than a week or two.

And, he'd been hoping he wouldn't.

He'd been thinking that he might arrive and discover that Sunday wasn't struggling nearly as much as his brothers had claimed.

It hadn't taken him long to realize she was.

Not just because she'd fallen in the river, but because of the sadness and desperation he'd seen in her eyes. First at the river, then in the chapel.

And, there'd been the tears.

He hadn't known quite what to do about those.

Patricia hadn't cried. She'd screamed. Cursed. Yelled.

So, he'd been undone by the tears he'd seen on Sunday's cheeks. He'd come to the farm with the hope of pushing her just a little harder than his brothers had, giving her the pep talks and the rah-rah speeches that would bring her closer to recovery. The goal, of course, was to have her take over the operation of the farm once it became profitable.

Heck! It already was profitable. With the help of his brother's fiancé, Clementine Warren, once-fallow land was now lush with produce. They'd been selling to local stores, to visitors and to residents. This fall, there'd be a corn maze, a petting zoo, hayrides. They'd be selling homemade jams and jellies from their produce stand and teaching classes on pulling and dyeing wool.

But watching Sunday's slow, laborious journey to the chapel had made him wonder if she'd ever be capable of running the place. She'd looked fragile, broken and worn down.

And, for the first time in a while, he'd seen her the way his brothers and her friends did.

Changed.

He set his suitcase down next to the puppy who sniffed it enthusiastically. He doubted there was any remnant of Tilly left on it. Patricia had preferred to use colorful luggage, and she'd taken it all with her when she'd left seven years ago.

He hadn't cared about the suitcases. He hadn't cared about the silver tea set, the old coin collection, or the half of their savings account she'd taken with her when she'd gone.

He hadn't really cared that she'd gone.

They'd been married five years.

He'd loved her, but she'd been high maintenance, greedy in a way that had frustrated him.

More had been her motto. Contentment had been his.

In the end, they'd just been too different to make it work.

He didn't dwell on that, and he didn't know why he'd thought about her so many times since he'd arrived. The puppy with its curly coat, he'd guess. Reminding him of a past he'd walked away from without regret.

He rolled his suitcase to the back door, the puppy jumping and pouncing beside him.

"Come on, boy," he called as he stepped inside.

The puppy scampered after him, sniffing the ground and following a scent trail from the door to the empty slop bucket. He sniffed it for a few seconds, before putting his nose to the ground and following a scent trail from the mudroom to the kitchen trash can.

He wasn't dumb. Flynn would give him that.

He also hadn't been fed much recently. He was about as scrawny as a dog could be—his furry coat patchy from malnutrition, his ribs showing clearly through his fur.

He needed some food, and then they both needed to sleep.

Flynn opened the fridge, looking for something the puppy could eat. He found sliced turkey and offered the puppy several pieces, then filled a plastic cereal bowl with water and set it on the floor.

The puppy lapped it up, his tail thumping happily.

At least he was uncomplicated, the solution to his problems easy to solve.

"That's it, pup. Tomorrow, we'll go to the feed store and get some puppy chow. Right now, we're hitting the hay." Flynn walked into the living room, dropped his luggage on the floor near the couch, and grabbed the old throw from the rocking chair in the corner.

He didn't bother with a light. Just pulled off his flannel shirt, kicked off his boots, and dropped onto the couch.

God, he was tired.

A few hours of sleep wouldn't be a bad thing.

When he woke, he'd be more clearheaded and more able to figure out exactly what needed to be done to get Sunday further along on the road to recovery.

That was the point of this extended visit.

Not to take care of a puppy or supervise a farm that was already being well managed. Sure, he wanted to give Porter and Clementine a chance to plan their wedding and enjoy some much-needed alone time.

Mostly, though, he was there to get Sunday from where she was to where she needed to be. Maybe it would take longer than he was hoping, and he'd have to stay in Benevolence longer than he'd like, but he'd put things to right. Not because fixing problems was what he did, but because he and his brothers were a poor substitute for a mother. The kids needed Sunday. She needed them. And, somehow, in this big mess that Matt's death had created, they seemed to have lost each other.

CHAPTER THREE

She heard the kids whispering, their voices drifting through the floor vent that had been installed when centralized air conditioning was added to the house. Had that been before or after she'd married Matt? It was unimportant, the memory one she hadn't missed until she'd realized it was gone.

But, she still wanted it back.

She still wanted to be able to pull it out and look at it, study the details and then file it away again.

Memories didn't seem important until they were missing.

Then, the holes their absence left took up way too much space in the mind.

She sat up, shoving the covers away and crossing the room in bare feet. The old alarm clock sat on the dresser, turned away from the bed so that she couldn't watch the glowing numbers change while she was trying to sleep.

She turned it so that she could read the time.

Six o'clock. Early for the kids to be awake and plotting, and she was certain plotting was what they were up to. There was something about the cadence of their conversation, the frantic edge to their whispers that seemed to warn of dastardly deeds and nefarious plans.

So, what she was doing?

Hiding in her room, waiting for someone else to make sure the kids didn't get themselves into trouble.

Or, die trying to.

She frowned. She didn't need a good memory to imagine all the ways a few young children could get hurt on the farm.

She shoved aside the blankets and got to her feet, but she didn't run downstairs like she thought she probably would have before the accident.

Somehow, she'd been diminished by what had happened to her, pieces of her heart and soul seeming to have disappeared with the memories she'd lost.

Diminished . . .

She glanced at the palm of her hand, saw the word scrawled there in Twila's neat handwriting, the black ink on pale white flesh the only way Sunday seemed to be able to remember the word of the day.

Diminished was yesterday's.

Today there'd be a new one.

Twila would wipe the old one away with baby wipes, fan the skin to dry it, then write the next word. It was a new game. One Twila probably didn't realize Sunday understood. It wasn't just a little bookworm fun. It was a desperate attempt to bring the old Sunday back. The one who'd ruled the Scrabble board and crowed with delight when the kids had to look up the word she'd used. The old Sunday had a big vocabulary, filled with words she'd wanted to share with her children.

The new Sunday struggled to remember simple words and to put them together in cohesive ways.

That upset Twila, and Sunday knew it.

Not because her mother's intuition had finally kicked in. Not because she suddenly had regained all the insight that she seemed to have lost the night of the accident.

Because, she'd read the short story Twila had written for her fourth-grade class. Twila's teacher, Anna Johnson, had been one of Sunday's high school friends. She'd been worried and trying to be helpful when she'd stopped by the house and given a copy of the story to Sunday.

She'd wanted Sunday to see herself through her daughter's eyes. Not just her new self. The old one. The woman who'd brought a little girl from China to the United States and taught her how to speak lavishly.

Lavishly had been Thursday's word. Or maybe Wednesday's.

In Twila's story, Sunday was a caped heroine who flew from one side of the globe to the other, rescuing the broken and the wounded and the lonely. Until she was struck by a bolt of lightning and was no longer able to fly or rescue anyone.

Then, all those people she'd helped, swooped in and rescued her.

Sunday had kept the story. She'd tucked it into the old hope chest at the end of the bed, hiding it away with the letters and notes Matt had written. Every few days, she took it out and read it. She didn't need mother's intuition to feel the sorrow that seeped through her daughter's words.

She didn't need to be a genius to know the story reflected all the sorrow the real-life accident had brought. And, she didn't need to understand that sorrow to know that the word-of-the-day was Twila's attempt to bring the old Sunday back.

She glanced at the calendar that hung on the wall near the door. Heavenly had put an x through every day that had passed. Today was Saturday. Rosie's day off. That was written neatly in today's calendar square.

Usually, Rosie left late Friday night and visited her sister for the weekend, returning early Monday morning to start the coffee and get the kids ready for the day.

If she wasn't around, saving the kids from themselves was Sunday's responsibility.

So, she needed to do it.

Now. Before someone got hurt.

She opened the door and walked into the hall, surprised by the quiet. During the week, the house bustled with activity. Her friend,

Clementine Warren, stayed at the ranch house at the edge of the property, but on weekdays, she was at the house before dawn, pouring coffee from the pot Rosie brewed. Her fiancé, Porter, was usually there, too. The second oldest of the four Bradshaw brothers, he'd taken a job with the sheriff's office a few months ago and lived in town in the house he and his brothers had inherited from their father. Sullivan and his wife, Rumer, lived with him, splitting their time between Benevolence and Portland. Sullivan was an art history professor, and still taught classes at the university.

Sunday had written the details in one of her notebooks, and she reread them often, trying to commit them to her faulty memory.

So far, today seemed to be a good day. She remembered almost everything, but she didn't remember why the house was so quiet. Even on the weekends, it usually bustled with activity. Probably, Sullivan and Rumer were in Portland. Porter might have traveled back to California. He did some consulting work for a security firm there.

Sunday had probably been told all the details and written them in one of her notebooks. She couldn't remember, though, and she tried not to think about that as she descended the stairs, barefoot and wearing the old sweats and tank top she'd changed into after her fall in the river. Both were too big. She'd tried to convince herself that they'd belonged to Matt, but she knew they were hers. That she'd once been muscular and strong. Small but fierce, her father used to say.

She remembered that and the way it had felt to muck stalls and saddle a horse.

Yeah. Today was a good memory day.

She followed the sound of the kids' voices through the hall. Found them in the kitchen, gathered around the table. All of them. Huddled together. Dark hair. Light hair. Straight. Curly. Baby Oya was the only one who noticed Sunday standing on the threshold. She wasn't a baby now. She was a year old with chunky thighs and dimpled knuckles that were gripping the collar of Heavenly's shirt.

A cropped shirt.

Sunday could see two inches of skin above the waistband of Heavenly's skin-tight jean shorts.

"I hope you're not planning to go out like that," she said in a mother voice that she hadn't realized she still possessed.

Five sets of eyes turned toward her.

Blue, brown, green, nearly black.

Some wide with surprise, some filled with pleasure.

Heavenly's, though, were filled with disdain.

"Are *you* going out like *that?*" she responded in a voice that could have come from any rebellious sixteen-year-old.

Only Heavenly hadn't even reached fourteen. Her birthday was looming, a mark on the calendar placed there by Twila.

"No," Sunday responded, digging through the muddy wreck of her memories, trying to remember how they'd been before the accident.

She couldn't picture any interaction, had no idea except for what she'd read in the journals. Most of the things she'd written had been about wanting Heavenly to know she was loved.

She'd go with that. Still and always. Even if she never remembered meeting her daughter or making the decision to adopt her.

"Thank God for that," Heavenly said, tossing her head as if she still had the long hair Sunday had seen in family photos. She'd cut it after the accident and wore it in a shaggy pixie that suited her.

"I'm sure God appreciates your gratefulness," Sunday said, trying to keep a firm edge to her voice. "Just the same way He'll appreciate you putting on a shirt that covers your stomach."

"God doesn't give a da—"

"Heavenly Bradshaw!" she snapped, and she knew the voice was one she'd used with the teenager before, because Heavenly's eyes widened, all the haughty indifference sliding from her face.

"I'm sorry," she muttered, hiking Oya a little higher on her scrawny hip. "I'll change my shirt before I go out."

"School is starting soon," Sunday said. "We can go clothes shopping together, if you want, and pick out some nice new clothes to enter eighth grade in."

"Rumer said she'd take me," Heavenly replied. There was no resentment in her voice, no disappointment. Nothing in her face that would tell Sunday how she really felt about that.

"Well, I'd like to go with you, too."

Heavenly shrugged. "Whatever."

"What does that mean?"

"It means she's thirteen and has an attitude," Moisey offered, her dark eyes boring into Sunday's. "But, let's not worry about that, okay? We have a problem, Mom. A big one."

"All of you?" Sunday asked, crossing the room and trying to read the expression on each child's face. She'd known before how to do that. How to read lies and honesty and mischief and sadness and joy.

She knew she had.

Now she could only see wide eyes and tousled hair and the twins hanging back just enough to make her wonder what they'd been plotting with their siblings.

"Don't say," Maddox hissed. He and Milo were identical except for their scars. They'd joined the family three years ago. They'd been five and tougher than any kindergartener should have to be. She knew that from the journals and from a vague memory of watching them run through the yard, blond hair to their shoulders, tangled and baby fine, the wounds on their faces and arms still raw.

"What don't you want her to say, Maddox?" she asked, taking a seat, because her bad leg ached. She'd walked too far earlier, pushed herself too hard.

"Milo," he corrected, and she almost believed him, but she'd spent hours at night pouring over the journals and the photos. She knew the curved scar beneath his left ear and the jagged one beneath his jaw.

"Maddox," she said calmly, feeling the weight of all her children's stares.

Her children.

She had to remind herself of that every day.

Her children. Her responsibility.

"You're right, Mom." Milo smiled happily, and she felt like she'd won a battle she hadn't known she'd been fighting. "You never make a mistake with us. Not the way the uncles do."

"She's your mother, dweeb," Heavenly said with just enough affection in her voice to make it an endearment rather than an insult.

"Tell me what you're worried about, Moisey," Sunday said before she forgot that the kids were hiding something, and that Moisey was about to break their confidence and give away their secrets.

"No!" Maddox barked, but Moisey loved to tell stories, and she'd already started talking.

"I woke up really early this morning," she whispered, moving close and leaning against Sunday's shoulder. She smelled like coconut and flowers and that brought a memory of a trip to the mall in Spokane, walking into a store filled with lotions and soaps, picking one that Moisey loved.

"Sunday on a Beach," she said aloud.

"You remember my favorite lotion," Moisey crowed, and Sunday felt it again—that feeling that she'd won something she hadn't realized she was fighting for.

"We went to the mall to pick it," she continued. "You said it smelled the best and had the prettiest name."

"Like you!" Moisey cupped her cheeks and stared into her eyes. "You remember, and I didn't even have to tell you. It's good you're coming back to us, Mom, because we have a problem."

"A dilemma," Twila corrected. "That was our word on Monday."

She touched Sunday's arm. Tentatively. As if she were afraid of overstepping her bounds.

"I remember." She didn't. Not really, but Twila didn't need to know that. Just like she didn't need to know that Sunday didn't remember traveling to China, didn't remember the adoption ceremony or the trip home. Didn't remember anything but a few random snippets of time—glimpses of Twila as a somber toddler, her dark eyes focused on the ground.

"What's the dilemma?" she prodded, and Twila's somber expression eased into a half smile.

"Moisey got up early, and she got herself cereal."

"There's nothing wrong with that."

"Mom," Moisey said, tugging at her hand, demanding her attention. "I was going to eat in the living room."

"You're allowed." She thought. But maybe she was wrong. Rules had never been as important in their home as structure and love. She knew that without reading the journals.

"Uncle Flynn was in there," Moisey stage-whispered, the loudness of it making Sunday smile.

"He got in late last night."

"He had something with him." Moisey was nearly bouncing now, her curls dancing around her beautiful face.

"A puppy," Milo nearly shouted.

"Shhhh!" Heavenly growled. "You're going to wake the whole house up."

"We are the whole house," Milo pointed out. "Rosie left last night, and Mom is already awake."

"You're going to wake *him,* and then he's going to wonder what happened to his da—"

Heavenly's gaze cut to Sunday. "Dang dog."

"The puppy is gone?" Sunday asked, confused, bewildered.

Tired.

Exactly the way she always felt when she was around all the kids.

She should feel excitement, amusement, joy.

She should feel happy to be included in their plots and plans.

But she wanted to go back to bed, hide under the covers, and let them figure it out on their own.

"That's the dilemma," Twila explained. "Moisey was so surprised when it jumped off the couch, she ran into the kitchen and out the back door."

"Because I thought it was a wild animal. Like . . . a rabid coyote or mountain lion."

"Uncle Flynn would have been dead if it were any of those things," Milo pointed out reasonably.

"It could have been a wild animal," Moisey responded. "And, I was doing the safe thing and getting out while the getting was good. But, the puppy followed me. I tried to catch him and bring him back inside, but he was too fast. He hid, and I couldn't find him." Moisey's lower lip trembled. A sure sign that she was going to cry.

Tempted as she was, Sunday didn't glance around to see if another adult was there to comfort her.

She was it.

She knew that.

"It's okay, honey. We found him near the river last night. He's probably gone home."

"You were at the river at night?" Twila's eyes were wide, her expression one of pure shock.

Don't go to the river after dark.

Don't go alone.

She'd told the children that dozens of times. She was certain of it.

"I'm an adult," she reminded them, but they were having none of it.

"Sunday, you could have gotten hurt," Heavenly chastised. Suddenly an adult in a scrawny teenage body. "Please don't ever do that again."

"Flynn was with me," she said as if it were the complete truth, and as if she needed to justify her actions to a child.

"And you found a puppy and brought it home for us?!" Moisey inhaled joy and exhaled enthusiasm and lived and breathed a life of stories and lore.

That was a direct quote from the journal.

Written a month before the accident.

"We found the puppy and brought it home, but he's probably headed back to wherever he belongs."

"I don't think so. I don't think that's the truth." Moisey was bouncing again. "Animals find the people they're meant to love. They might seem like they're lost, but they never are. They're searching for the soul they belong with. When they find that soul, they never leave. Never! I read all about it in a book Heavenly got me at the library."

Heavenly brought you a book from the library? Sunday meant to say, but Moisey had run for the back door, thrust it open as if God Himself had ordered her to do it.

"You found us, puppy! We'll be together forever!" she cried as she ran outside.

A mass exodus followed. Kids darting after her, nearly flying in their rush to freedom.

All of them out in the great wide world with all kinds of trouble that could happen to them, and Sunday was still at the table, staring at the open door.

Waiting for someone to do something.

Only she was it.

The person responsible.

No Rosie rushing to call the children back. No Sullivan or Porter or Rumer or Clementine shouting for order or attention.

Just . . .

Sunday.

She tried to spring to her feet, but she only managed to move slowly. Unbending from her seated position. Straightening. Shuffling to the door and outside, the sounds of Moisey's joy filling her ears as she slowly made her way down the stairs and into the yard.

One thing Flynn had learned young—if you fell off a horse, the best thing to do was get right back on. Waiting gave fear a chance to take hold, and fear was a very hard thing to let go of.

Fear of falling again.

Fear of failing.

Fear of some unknown force sweeping you into danger.

Emmerson Riley had taught him that. He'd owned an equestrian farm on the other side of the river. In its heyday, the place had produced some of the soundest horses in the greater Northwest. By the time Flynn had found his way to the farm, the place had been run-down, the stables filthy. Emmerson had been seventy-eight. Suffering from arthritis and emphysema, abandoned by his only son after money started running dry and the work got too demanding.

There'd been an ad in the *Benevolence Times*. Just a little snippet about a farmhand being needed. Only experienced horse people needed to apply.

Flynn had been twelve. Tall and strong for his age. Tired of listening to his father rage and watching his mother suffer. Tired of being a punching bag and a doormat.

Tired of being bullied and mistreated.

Already planning his escape, but he'd been too young to get much work in town, so he'd walked the five miles to Emmerson's farm, knocked on the door, and stared into the weather-worn face of a man who'd looked about as kind as a hot desert breeze. When Emmerson demanded to know why he was there, Flynn hadn't stammered and he hadn't glanced down. He'd offered a prepared speech about being a hard worker and a fast learner who needed a job. Either Emmerson had felt sorry for him, or he'd been desperate. Maybe a little of both.

Flynn had worked there after school and on the weekends for nearly six years. He'd cleaned out the stables. He'd patched fences. He'd fed livestock. He'd saddled horses for Emmerson and for himself. He'd learned. Just like he'd said he'd would, earning a pittance, because it was all Emmerson could offer. They'd produced one more horse on that farm. A stunning filly that Emmerson had sold three months before he'd died.

He'd left the house and land to his son.

But he'd named Flynn as beneficiary of his life insurance policy. Two hundred thousand dollars.

By that time, Flynn's mother was gone, his brothers were doing exactly what he had—planning their escape. They'd encouraged him to take the money and go before their father found a way to hold him back and keep him prisoner.

He'd gone with their blessing, and he'd sent money to help each one make his own escape. One at a time until it was Matt's turn.

Yeah. The money had helped, but it was the learning that had been most important. All the lessons taught by a man who hadn't been his father but who'd acted like one.

You fall off a horse, you get back up. Right then, before you even have time to feel pain. You get up and you ride until you know what you're doing again.

He could hear Emmerson's voice as he walked outside and watched Sunday follow her children into the yard.

The car accident had been a heck of a lot more traumatizing than a fall off a horse, but that didn't mean the lesson didn't hold true. That being the case, he was stepping back, letting her solve the dilemma that Moisey had been so passionately telling her about, because that's what she'd have done before the accident.

Sure, he could have rushed into the kitchen when he'd heard her with the kids. He could have offered to search for the puppy with them. He could have allowed Sunday to stay where she was while he took over a role she'd once coveted.

He knew how much she'd wanted children.

Hell, he'd been the one to fund the trip to China to adopt Twila. Sunday didn't know that. She'd never know it. But he'd stepped in financially when Matt asked—*begged*—for help in making Sunday's dreams come true. They'd been married three years and were still childless, and she and Matt had thought adoption was their best option. They'd seen Twila's face on an adoption website, and they'd fallen head over heels.

That wasn't something Flynn had understood.

He worked with rationality and reasonableness. He let his head rule and his heart stay mostly quiet. Life was easier that way, but he'd loved his brother, and he'd liked Sunday, and the ranch had been doing well. Financially, he'd had no worries, and with Patricia out of the picture, his bank accounts were healthier than they'd ever been.

He'd agreed to help, and he'd agreed to not tell Sunday he'd been asked. Later, he'd learned that Matt had claimed he'd borrowed the money from an old friend.

It had been a strange and unnecessary lie. One that may have said something about Sunday and Matt's relationship. It hadn't been Flynn's business.

At least, that's what he'd told himself.

Now he wondered about it. Wondered why Matt had felt compelled to hide such a simple truth. Wondered why Sunday hadn't pushed to know more. Had they paid back the debt? And if they had, where had that money gone? Certainly not to Flynn. He had given Matt the money, and he hadn't expected a return on the investment.

Although, he had to admit, he enjoyed being an uncle.

He watched from the porch as the kids raced around the yard searching for the missing puppy. Sunday was doing her part, shouting “Here, boy!” with almost as much enthusiasm as the kids.

That’s what he’d been hoping for.

He knew what she’d been before the accident, and it was his goal to bring her back to that. Let her feel the joy she’d once lived with so that she could live with it again.

She was afraid.

He sensed that every time he visited. Afraid to be hurt, afraid she might shatter, probably afraid she’d fail her kids and herself.

The only way to get over that was to do.

This and a bunch of other things.

According to Emmerson, anyway, and he valued that old man’s opinion more than just about anyone else’s. Including the therapists who’d been working with Sunday. They had good ideas. They did. He’d listened and agreed with a lot of what had been said during conference calls while she was still in a coma and still in rehab. Now, of course, the therapists were closemouthed about treatment. Sunday was awake and capable of making her own decisions regarding recovery. He and his brothers had backed out of the equation, and they’d been waiting for her to take control.

Only it seemed like she hadn’t.

At least to Flynn.

Then again, he hadn't been here day in and day out in the first weeks after she'd been released from rehab. He'd only had a small glimpse of her struggles, and he hadn't gotten into the mindset of viewing her as damaged or fragile.

He watched her now, limping across the yard, her left foot dragging just enough for it to be noticeable. Trying to run but not quite able. Her body still not as coordinated as it had once been. It took years to recover from traumatic brain injury, and sometimes, a person never did. Not completely. He'd been told that the day after the accident. He didn't remember a heck of a lot about what he'd been told, but he remembered that.

Just like he remembered the flight, the feeling of numbness and shock and grief. He'd flown all day and arrived so late the hospital had been nearly silent, the nurses' station run by a skeleton crew of exhausted professionals who were doing everything they could to keep their ICU patients alive through the night.

He'd entered Sunday's room knowing Matt was dead, and that she was the last parent his nieces and nephews had. Sullivan had been there, standing beside the bed, his eyes red-rimmed with fatigue and tears.

He'd been there within hours of the call, arriving from Portland and stepping into a role he'd never prepared for. Thank God for the church family that had swooped in and helped with the kids and the house and the farm.

Flynn remembered that.

He remembered how terrible Sunday had looked, pale and lifeless, her face bruised, her head shaved. Her leg swollen.

Now, she was moving. Slowly. Maybe painfully. Obviously, awkwardly. Trying to catch up with Oya, who'd toddled toward the driveway, her chubby legs brown from the sun, her blond hair spiking out around her head.

"Oya! Wait," Sunday called, a hint of panic in her voice. The other kids had spread out through the yard and even into the fields, calling for the puppy. Usually Heavenly stayed close to the baby, but even she had wandered away, heading toward the orchards that were just hinting at a fall harvest.

"Oya!" Sunday called again, and this time she sounded frantic. He wasn't sure why. The baby was fine, toddling across the gravel driveway, heading toward some flowering bushes that Clementine had planted.

"Stop!" Sunday shouted, trying to sprint after the toddler, who'd stepped between two bushes, her hair gleaming in the morning sun. Happy and carefree, the way a kid should be. Learning the world through experience and exploration.

Sunday tried to follow, but her foot caught on the narrow plank of wood that separated the gravel driveway from the flowerbed. She flew forward, landing with a thud inches from her daughter, skidding forward a few feet and lying there. Still. Maybe dazed.

Flynn ran to her side, scooping Oya up on his way. "Hey, you okay?" he asked, touching Sunday's shoulder.

She lifted her head just enough to scowl in his direction. "I couldn't even do that right."

"I don't know about that. It was a pretty spectacular fall." He offered a hand, but she ignored it, pushing to her knees and then her feet. There was a hole in the knee of her old sweatpants, blood on her pale skin. He could see it and a glimpse of the ridged purple scar from surgeries to repair her leg.

"It's not funny," she panted, taking Oya from his arms.

"I'm not laughing."

"You're joking." She hugged the baby tightly. A little too tightly judging from the way Oya pushed against her.

"Sometimes a joke is better than tears," he replied, taking her arm and helping her out of the flowerbed.

She didn't seem impressed by his effort.

If anything, she looked pissed. Something he'd never observed in her before.

"Sometimes, silence is better than either," she responded, and she sounded so much like the old

Sunday he looked at her. Really looked. Took in the dark circles beneath her eyes, the paleness of her skin and lips, the jutting edge of her cheekbones.

She didn't look much like the young woman who'd married Matt over ten years ago—smiling and happy and soft with youth.

She'd been a kid then. At least, that's how he'd thought of her. Eighteen and too much of a child to understand what she was getting into. Just like he imagined his mother had been all those years ago when she'd married his father. Filled with hopes and dreams and not much practicality. He'd seen his parents' wedding photo, and he'd always wondered at the relaxed young woman his mother had been. She'd seemed ancient by the time she'd died of cancer, worn down and faded, despite the fact that she'd only been forty when she'd died.

"You're right. Sometimes, I open my mouth before I think things through."

"No, you don't." She walked to the other side of the driveway and put Oya down on the grass, then dropped down beside her as if she were too tired to stand any longer.

"Why do you say that?"

"You're careful and smart. You're quiet and insightful." She sounded like she was reciting a script.

He settled down beside her. "Who told you that?"

"My journals."

"I didn't know you had them, or that you'd written about me."

She offered a quick smile. "I did, and I wrote about everyone. Thank God. I don't know what I'd do about the kids if I hadn't. Speaking of which"—she pushed to her feet, wincing as she straightened her legs—"I need to round them up and get them back inside."

"Why?" he asked.

"Because . . ." She shrugged. "It seems like the motherly thing to do."

"Letting kids play outside is also a motherly thing to do."

"Look how far they're going." She pointed to the twins, who were halfway between the house and the closest cornfield.

"I went farther when I was their age."

"Things were different then."

Not really. There'd always been danger in the world. His had just been closer to home. Much closer.

"I'll bring them home," he said, even though he should let her do it. Even though he knew she could. Because that was what he'd come for, right? To get her back to a place of independence, to help her realize what no one else had been able to—that she could do this without a network of willing hands and feet.

Yet there he was. On his feet, moving across

the yard, ready to call the boys back, yell for the girls, go hunt them all down so that Sunday wouldn't have to worry.

He was stepping into the same pattern his brothers had. The pattern Sunday's church had. The pattern Rosie had. Caretaker of Sunday's kingdom and treasures.

No matter how much his brain was telling him to stop, he just kept moving.

"It's okay, Flynn," she said, a hint of unease in her voice, maybe a little fear or self-doubt. "If you watch Oya, I'll get the others."

He stopped where he was. One foot on the gravel driveway, the other on the grass, his eyes still fixed on the towheaded boys who were darting toward cornstalks. He was faster than Sunday, for sure. He could run there and be back before she made it halfway across the field.

It would be easier, quicker, less painful for everyone.

He turned back anyway, taking Oya from Sunday's arms and watching as she walked away. Staying where he was, because sometimes the hardest things were the best ones.

Emmerson had taught him that, too.

CHAPTER FOUR

She should have let Flynn handle things.

That's what Sunday was thinking as she picked her way through brambles in bare feet and sweatpants. The sun rose languidly in the distance, hovering just above the highest mountain peak. Soon, the days would shorten, but now, the sun came up early and went to bed late.

"Maddox! Milo!" she called as she walked, trying to get the boys' attention. They moved nonstop when they were awake. They had from the very first day. Always busy. Always in motion. Always looking for something to occupy their minds.

"Too smart" is what she'd written in her journal. She'd written other things, too, but none of them really captured the essence of the twins. Funny, intelligent, loyal, determined.

Everything they should be, she decided as she called them again.

This time, they must have heard. Both darted toward her, white-blond hair gleaming, legs churning.

"Mom!" they shouted in unison as they approached. "What are you doing?"

"Coming to get you. You're going too far."

"No, we're not," Maddox said, his face

scrunched in consternation. “Uncle Sullivan said that we can go all the way to the cornfield. We just can’t go in it.”

“He did?” she replied, surprised that rules had been set by their uncle. A little more surprised that they were obeying them.

“Yes. Because we went down to the river once. When you were in the hospital, and we just about got our heads chewed off.” Milo sighed. “It was his idea.” He pointed at Maddox.

“It was not.”

“Yes, it was.”

“No, it—”

“Let’s not argue, boys. It’s much too pretty a day to be cross,” she interrupted.

They were surprised enough to stop bickering.

“Cross?” Twila walked out from behind a clump of overgrown azaleas. “That’s a very good word, Mom.”

“Thank you,” she replied. “Have you seen Moisey?”

“She’s near the garage. She thinks the puppy went there to find food.”

“Why would the puppy look for food in the garage?” Milo asked, and Twila shrugged.

“I don’t know, but Moisey does.”

“You three go back to the house. I’ll find your sisters. Then we’ll have breakfast.”

“And then go to buy the puppy some food? That’s an important thing. All living creatures need to eat," Twila said, as if Sunday needed a reminder.

"I'm aware of that."

"Yesterday, you forgot about lunch. Rosie said you'd fade away to nothing if she didn't remind you to eat."

"Honey, I'm not in danger of fading away, and I didn't eat lunch because I wasn't hungry. Not because I didn't remember."

That was true.

She was never hungry.

She wasn't sure if that had happened because of the accident, or if she'd been having the problem before it.

She'd lost weight prior to her tenth anniversary. She knew that. She'd written about needing to buy new clothes in one of her last journal entries.

"Well, you have to eat, Mom. Because you're too skinny. Ms. Myers says so," Milo said, eyeing her critically enough to make her cheeks warm.

"Ms. Myers?"

"Our Sunday school teacher?" Maddox prodded, apparently hoping to spark her memory.

She racked her brain but couldn't put a face to the name, and she couldn't recall any journal entries about the woman.

"I'm sure Ms. Myers understands that I've been . . . ill."

"You nearly died. Everyone knows it." Maddox pulled something from the pocket of his shorts and pressed it into her hand. "This is for you. I'll make pancakes, and you can eat when you get back to the house."

He sprinted away, his twin close on his heels.

"I had better supervise," Twila said, darting after them.

And she was alone, watching them go, something clutched in her hand.

She opened her fist. A small heart-shaped rock lay in her palm. White. Sparkling with minerals. Smooth from eons of water running across its surface.

It was a child's offering, and it was perfect enough to bring tears to her eyes.

She didn't have pockets, so she held it as she walked around the side of the house and found her way to the garage. Just as the other children had predicted, Moisey was there, on her hands and knees near the trash cans.

"Moisey, what are you doing?" she said, trying to crouch nearby. Her legs wouldn't have it, and she fell on her butt instead, the rock falling from her hand and skittering across the packed earth.

She grabbed for it, but Moisey grabbed it first, lifting it to the sky and eyeing it with appreciation. "A heart! Where did you find it, Mommy?"

"Maddox gave it to me."

"Where did he find it?" she demanded to

know, the sunlight dancing across her skin and bestowing golden kisses on her dark curls.

"He didn't say."

"It's from Dad. It has to be," she announced.

"Does it?"

"Of course. Dad always signed his cards with hearts, remember?"

She hadn't. Not until that moment.

"Yes, but—"

"So it has to be from him. He put it right where Maddox could find it and bring it to you. It's like a kiss from Heaven. Which is good, because the puppy is really gone. I looked everywhere. I was even pretending to be a dog and think like a dog, and he still didn't show up. Maybe we aren't his soul people, after all."

"There will be other puppies, Moisey," she said, but Moisey was having none of it.

She shook her head. "He was special."

"Don't you think every puppy is?"

"That would be like saying every mom is special. Or every dad. Maybe they are to someone, but not to people who already have a mom or dad. We had Rembrandt, and now he's gone. There will never be another dog as special as him."

"Rembrandt?"

"That's his name."

"Do you know who Rembrandt was?"

"Of course I do. Uncle Sullivan talks about art all the time. He's an artist. And a professor."

Moisey added the last as a side note. It was a pattern with her. Adding bits of information to make things easier on Sunday.

For some reason, that hurt.

Maybe because Moisey was only seven, and she shouldn't have to worry about things being easy on her mother.

"I remember what Uncle Sullivan does," Sunday assured her.

"Okay. I was just making sure." Moisey handed her the rock. "The kiss from Heaven is nice, but I kind of still want Rembrandt."

"We can go to the shelter next week. I'm sure they'll have a puppy you'll love."

"I want a puppy that finds me. Just like in the story. Plus, you'll forget about the shelter, and we won't go."

Ouch.

That hurt worse than Moisey's careful recital of facts.

She tried not to let it show, because it wasn't Moisey's fault. She was being honest, and honesty was a good thing.

Even when it hurt

"Your brother is making pancakes," she said, sidestepping the issue, because it wasn't something she could put words to. Or wanted to.

"Last time he tried that, he almost burned the house down." Moisey skipped away.

Sunday didn't follow. Twila was supervising

the boys, and she always took her jobs seriously. If there was trouble, Sunday would know before it got out of hand.

Of course, she probably should have gone back to the house and made pancakes herself. That would be the motherly thing to do, wouldn't it? Make a batch of pancakes and serve it with warm maple syrup and pats of room-temperature butter?

She was certain she'd done that dozens of times. Maybe even hundreds. Sunday morning breakfast? Or Saturday mornings? Lazy days with pancakes and sausage or bacon?

Or maybe she was remembering her childhood, the weekend breakfasts that her mother had prepared. She'd learned to cook on rainy Saturdays, standing over the old gas stove and stirring pots while her mother supervised.

Had she done that with her kids?

She hadn't written about it in any of the journals, and she couldn't recall.

"You're frowning," Flynn said, his voice so unexpected, she jumped.

"I startled you," he continued, walking across the grassy yard, Oya in his arms. "I'm sorry."

"Don't be. I'm jumpy since the accident." She smoothed her fingers over the heart-shaped stone, her heart thudding painfully in her chest. Because she'd been surprised, and because, for just a second, she'd thought his voice was Matt's.

"I think most people would be."

"Not Matt. He'd probably already be over it." She wasn't sure why she said that. Maybe because he was on her mind—his handsome face and charming smile dancing just at the edges of memory.

"Not if you weren't around."

"I need to find Heavenly," she murmured, changing the subject because she didn't want to talk about the accident, and she didn't want to talk about Matt. She certainly didn't want to think about whether he'd have missed her if she were gone.

"I sent her back to the house. Apparently, the boys are making pancakes."

"Twila planned to supervise," she offered, and he smiled, a slow, easy curve of his lips that drew her attention to his jaw and the dark stubble there.

He had a rougher look than his brothers. Tougher. The kind of look earned from years of working outside in the cold and the heat, the rain and the sun.

"She told me that she'd take care of things, but those boys are . . . creative when it comes to cooking. It's probably best if we're there, too."

"Creative?"

"You didn't hear about the French fry incident?"

"I . . . don't think so."

"It went like this." He cupped her elbow, and she found herself walking along beside him. No rush. No hurry, their pace like his smile—slow and easy. "You were in the hospital. People were distracted. The boys were tired of casserole, and that was pretty much what the church had been providing. One night, they decided they'd make French fries, but they didn't think it would be a good idea to do it on the stove."

"Thank God."

"Yeah. So they dug a firepit in the backyard, started a fire, and tossed a bunch of potatoes in."

"Whole potatoes?"

"According to Milo, they were afraid they might cut their fingers off if they tried slicing the potatoes."

"But they weren't afraid of burning themselves, the yard, the house and, maybe, the entire town down?" she asked, appalled at the thought of the twins striking matches and tossing them into a pile of twigs and leaves and paper. Maybe with an accelerant added for good measure.

That's how Matt had started fires. Lighting fluid poured over the wood, a quick strike of a match.

The image was there, the memory clear and crisp. Their first camping trip in the fall after they were married. It had been cold, and she'd been shivering. Matt had dug a firepit and prepped the fire, insisting that he didn't need her help.

Stay in the sleeping bag and keep warm. I'll take care of this.

She'd let him. Even though doing it herself would have been quicker and easier. Because she'd known those kinds of things had been important to Matt—being able to make the world work the way he thought it should for the people he loved. He'd never wanted Sunday to be unhappy. He hadn't wanted the kids to be. That desire had led to lies and cheating and all kinds of deeds done in darkness.

Sunday would have preferred the painful truth to the hidden betrayal.

She shivered, and Flynn squeezed her elbow. "Cold?"

"A goose walked across my grave," she responded, and he must have understood the old phrase, because he didn't ask again. Just kept the same careful unhurried pace, silently now, Oya resting her head against his shoulder, her chubby fingers curled in the ends of his hair.

She looked away, trying not to imagine Matt there, holding their daughter, carrying her back home.

"What happened?" she finally asked. "With the fire, I mean?"

"Someone driving by saw smoke and called the fire department. Half the fire brigade showed up, thinking the house was on fire and . . ." He stopped, but she thought she knew.

"They were afraid I'd lose my kids and my home after already losing my husband?"

"Maybe the story isn't as cute as I was remembering," he said, his hand still on her elbow, his stride still matched with hers.

"It's cute. If they aren't your kids, and it isn't your house. Or if dozens of years have passed and all the kids have survived their childhood. And really, it is cute. Even though they are my kids, and I still have a long way to go before I stop worrying about them," she admitted, offering a smile as reassurance, because Flynn meant well. Just like his brothers. Like Clementine. Like Rumer and Rosie and all Sunday's friends.

They wanted things to be like they had been.

They wanted her to move on and be okay.

They wanted to imagine that life wasn't changed forever.

That, eventually, things would go back to being the way they'd been.

She couldn't blame them. She didn't. She wanted to believe all those things too. She wanted to think that one morning, she'd open her eyes, and she'd feel like she'd felt the day she'd married Matt. Certain and happy and filled with hope.

But things wouldn't be the same.

Not just because Matt was dead.

Sure, that was the biggest part of it, but there was the other part. The secrets that she'd keep forever because voicing them would only hurt the people who'd loved and admired Matt.

It was her last gift to him, the final sacrifice to their relationship and their family.

The pancakes were good.

That was Flynn's first surprise of the day. Despite the fact that the twins had found the recipe, mixed the batter, and cooked the pancakes, nothing was burned, no one was hurt, and everyone left the breakfast table with a full belly and a smile.

Even Heavenly seemed content after the meal, her normal taciturn expression replaced by pleasure.

That was Flynn's second surprise of the morning.

His third surprise?

Clementine and Porter were taking the kids to the county fair. This year, it was being held three towns over. A long ride for a bunch of kids, and Porter had found a hotel that could accommodate the group. A full day, a night and they'd be back after church tomorrow.

It sounded good.

So good even Heavenly seemed keen on going, her enthusiasm as contagious as her siblings'. Clementine bustled from room to room, her long cotton skirts swishing as she supervised overnight bag packing. Porter was washing breakfast dishes, looking a little too domestic for Flynn's peace of mind.

He'd never known his brother to care much

about home-cooked meals or hand-washing dishes. Up until a few months ago, Porter had been a sought-after security expert who made big bucks protecting high profile clients. He'd had a high-rise apartment in Los Angeles filled with chrome, sleek furniture, and modern art. Now his home base was the old house they'd been left by their father.

House?

Mansion.

Not that Flynn had ever thought of it as either of those things.

Prison was more the word he'd have used to describe it.

"You want to come with?" Porter asked, setting the last plate in the drying rack and turning to face him. Like the rest of the Bradshaw men, he was tall and dark-haired. Unlike Flynn, he was polished. Dark jeans. Button-down shirt opened to reveal a blue T-shirt. Expensive watch. Expensive haircut.

Expensive taste.

He was the most like their father in looks and in lifestyle, but he had an even temper and an easy outlook on life.

"To the fair?"

"That is where we're going," Porter responded dryly. "For better or worse."

"I'm guessing it wasn't your idea?"

"You're guessing right. I have a few days off,

and I was thinking Clementine and I could go canoeing, maybe have a nice dinner together. Alone."

"She had other plans?"

"She wants to look at the booths, see if anyone is selling hand-pulled and dyed wool. Next year, she wants the farm represented there, and she's trying to decide what products will sell best and attract the most interest. Plus, school is starting soon, and she wants the kids to have a fun day away from the farm." He shrugged. "Once she explained it all, I decided to jump on board. If things go the way I'm hoping, I'll be setting up an office in town this fall, starting a new business, and the county fair may be a good place to make some security connections."

"Security connections?"

"It takes a lot to make sure a venue of that size stays safe, and I'm thinking of launching a security business here. I like working for the sheriff's department. Don't get me wrong. But, I'm used to a more high-stress faster-paced job," Porter responded.

"You could go back to LA," Flynn suggested, and Porter shook his head.

"No. I couldn't. This is home now."

"I thought that, for you, home was always going to be the big city," Flynn said, feeling a jolt of surprise at Porter's words. Maybe, even, unease.

He knew his brothers, and he'd thought he knew them well.

If he'd been asked before the accident, he'd have said that Sullivan and Porter were happy with their lives, and there wasn't anything that would bring them back to Benevolence for good.

Obviously, he'd have been wrong.

If he was wrong about them, maybe he was wrong about himself, too, because if anyone asked him right now at this very moment if he were happy to be back home, he'd have made it really clear that home was Texas, home was the ranch.

The little town he'd grown up in? It wasn't even close.

"Goals and dreams change," Porter said.

"They do," Flynn agreed. "I guess I'm just wondering how much business a company like yours will find in a town like Benevolence."

"Not just Benevolence. We'll be taking clients all over the Northwest."

"We?"

"I've got some people willing to relocate. If things go as planned, I'll open the office after the new year."

"You've convinced other people to come to Benevolence to work?" He sounded surprised, because he was.

He hadn't thought much about the town he'd grown up in. Not while he was living there and not after he'd left. Sure, he'd come to visit Matt and his family, but Benevolence wasn't the kind of place he imagined anyone relocating to.

"You sound shocked."

"It's a small town on the edge of nowhere," he pointed out.

"Your ranch is in the middle of nowhere and look how successful you've made it. I'd better go get Clementine and the kids moving. Otherwise, we'll miss half a day of adventure. Sure you don't want to come along?"

"As sure as I am that I want to take my next breath," Flynn responded.

Porter laughed as he walked out of the room.

He sounded . . .

Happy.

And that was as surprising as the rest of the morning had been.

Floorboards creaked above his head, feet pounding against old flooring as kids raced through their bedrooms gathering stuff. He could have followed his brother, helped get things organized, but he didn't think he'd be much of an asset. He had no idea what a child might want to bring on an overnight trip and only a few vague notions about what would be necessary.

His time would be better spent on the land, checking fencing, feeding whatever livestock Clementine had purchased. Last he'd heard, there were a couple of pigmy goats, an old cow, a donkey, and a pig.

He'd only ever seen the pig. A behemoth named Gertie who ate her weight in kitchen slop.

He walked into the living room to grab his hat and gloves.

Sunday was there. Sitting in the easy chair, staring at the wall. Nothing in her hands. No book. No phone. No magazine, paper, or pen. She had a blanket over her legs and a sweater wrapped around her shoulders. She looked like an invalid—weak and sapped of energy, and for some reason, that pissed him off.

"There are a lot better views," he commented as he crossed the room and unzipped his suitcase.

"Pardon?" she replied, turning her attention in his direction. Slowly. As if it were too much of an effort to move.

"There are more interesting things than a wall to spend the day looking at," he replied, yanking his work gloves out and shoving the hat on his head.

"You have a point," she said, a hint of amusement in her voice.

"Then why are you staring at white plaster?"

"It's cream," she corrected, shoving the blanket aside and standing. She seemed shaky, and now that he thought about it, she hadn't eaten more than a bite of the pancakes Milo had piled on her plate. "But you're right. I should be helping the kids get ready instead of sitting here staring at a wall."

"Clementine has things under control."

"I know, but they're my children. They still need me, right?"

It should have been a rhetorical question, and he shouldn't have felt the need to answer. He heard the heaviness behind her words, though, the weight of her fear. She'd lost Matt. Maybe she was afraid of losing her children, too. Afraid that the accident would take more than it already had.

"They still need you," he repeated, and she smiled. Bright. Fake. Faux happiness at its finest.

"So I'll go help." She was across the room and stepping into the hall when footsteps pounded on the stairs.

"We're ready to go, Mom!" Moisey shouted, bounding through the hall and throwing her arms around Sunday. The force of the hug threw her off balance and nearly knocked them both off their feet.

Flynn put out his hand to stop the backward momentum, his palm settling between Sunday's narrow shoulders. For a split second, she was leaning into it, her weight too light, her bones too fragile.

Then she righted herself and laughed. "You're getting so strong, Moisey!"

"That's from working outside. Clementine says farmwork makes kids tough."

"Clementine is right," Sunday agreed, pulling her daughter in for a hug and pressing a kiss to her forehead. "Have fun at the fair, honey. Behave. Be careful."

"I always behave," Moisey responded.

"Really?" Sunday asked, raising an eyebrow.

Moisey giggled. "Mostly, but this time I will for certain, because I want to make you proud."

"You always make me—" Sunday began, but Moisey was bouncing away, joining her siblings near the front door, grabbing a bright pink pack from the floor.

"Sunday?" Clementine called as she descended the stairs, Porter just a few steps behind her. They both looked happy. They both looked enthusiastic. Neither looked like they felt tortured by the thought of a few hours in the car with six kids. "You're coming with us, right?"

"I . . . didn't realize I was invited," Sunday said, her gaze darting to her children.

"Invited?" Porter responded, stepping up beside Clementine and sliding an arm around her waist. "Why would you need an invitation. We're family. Everyone is going."

"I didn't pack."

"That will only take a minute. Come on, hun," Clementine said, holding out a hand. "Heavenly and I will help, won't we?"

She glanced at the teen.

Heavenly sighed but set her bag down. "I'll do it myself. You stay here, Sunday. Otherwise, it'll take too long."

Sunday winced. Just a tiny little tightening of muscles that Flynn would have missed if he hadn't been watching her so carefully.

"No, that's okay," she called as Heavenly started up the stairs. "I . . . have other plans."

"You do?" Heavenly, Clementine, and Porter said in unison.

"Well"—Sunday's gaze darted from her oldest daughter, to Clementine, to Porter, and then to Flynn—"Flynn and I are going to the east side of the river today. To talk about setting up tents for the fall festival."

"I thought you wanted to wait until next year to host a festival?" Porter asked, obviously not buying the story.

"I do. I did. But I've been thinking about it, and I'm feeling so much better. Plus, it looks like the pepper harvest is going to be good, so we'll be able to make pie and jams to sell."

"Pepper pies?" Milo asked, elbowing his twin.

"You mean apple?" Clementine corrected gently, and Sunday's cheeks went three shades of red.

"Of course. Sorry. Apple pie and jams. And . . . other things. People will love that, so we should do it this . . . August . . . Augus . . . autumn." She was stammering now, fighting for words the way she had in the first days after she'd woken from coma.

The kids noticed.

They probably felt her frustration and embarrassment.

Flynn sure as heck did.

"So I was thinking about that, and the stuff you make, Clementine. All that beautiful . . . stuff. We can sell that, too. And maybe we can get the kids something to ride." She pressed her lips together, stopping the flow of words, and Flynn had the absurd urge to hug her, to tell her it was okay, that everyone understood.

"You mean . . . like a horse?" Heavenly asked, her voice breaking through the uncomfortable silence. She sounded . . . sweet and kind. Nothing like the bratty teen who'd been huffing up the stairs moments ago.

"That's what I was thinking," Sunday said, her voice devoid of emotion. "You wanted a horse. You told me that the day we brought you to the farm."

"I still want a horse," Heavenly agreed, the look in her eyes and the gentleness in her tone speaking of a maturity Flynn hadn't realized she possessed. "I'll stay home with you and Uncle Flynn. We can plan things together. I'll write everything down for you, okay?"

"I'll stay home, too," Twila agreed, dropping her navy blue backpack near the steps and throwing her arms around Sunday. "We'll have fun today, Mommy. You'll see."

"You can't—" Sunday began, but the kids were

all dropping their bags, rushing to her side, acting excited about touring the farm and discussing a fall festival that might not even happen.

Clementine and Porter looked . . . confused. Maybe a little lost.

And, Sunday looked devastated, her face pale, her eyes glittering with what Flynn was afraid might be tears.

She didn't want the kids to give up a fun trip.

She didn't want to go with them and slow the group down, maybe put a damper on the fun.

He figured that was her choice.

He also figured it would be good for the kids to get away for a while. To just be kids without having to worry about slowing their pace to match their mother's.

"Hold on," Flynn said, trying to break into the cacophony of voices.

The kids just kept talking.

"I said," he repeated, "hold on. As in stop. As in quiet."

Still no response, so he pulled the whistle from his pocket. The one he used to signal herding dogs. He blasted it twice. A signal for attention.

To his shock, the kids shut up.

Their mouths gaped open, their gazes were glued to him.

"Guess this isn't just good for dogs," he said as he tucked it back into his pocket. "Now, here's the deal. You kids and Clementine and

Porter have plans. Good plans. Your mother and I have plans too. We're all going to have fun doing the things we had planned. All of us." He met Heavenly's eyes, was pretty certain he saw mutiny in her gaze. "Meaning everyone standing in this foyer."

"I understand what 'all' means," she muttered, but leaned in to kiss Sunday's cheek. "I'll go, but tomorrow, can we talk about the horse?"

"We can talk about anything you want," Sunday assured her. She said good-bye to each of her children, thanked Clementine and Porter for taking them, waved at the departing group from the front porch.

Her hand was still in the air until the beat-up Chevy passenger van was out of sight.

Then it dropped to her side. Her shoulders slumped, her fake-happy expression fell away.

Flynn watched it all, a voyeur to a scene that he'd rather not be privy to.

"They'll have fun," Sunday whispered, and he wondered if she'd forgotten that he was standing on the porch.

"Of course they will."

She met his eyes, and he realized hers were deep purple-blue. The color of bluebonnets at sunset.

"Thanks."

"For?"

"Helping with that." She sighed, brushing a strand of light brown hair from her cheek. It had grown since the accident, the buzz cut giving way to a soft flyaway style that danced just above her shoulders.

"You don't have to thank me."

"Thanks anyway." She smiled. Another fake expression of happiness.

"You don't have to pretend, either" he commented as she opened the storm door and stepped inside the house.

"What?" She stopped but didn't turn to face him.

"You don't have to pretend to be happy, Sunday. We can all handle the truth. Whatever it is."

"Good to know," she murmured, and walked away.

He could have left things like that.

She'd earned the right to have negative feelings. Lots of them. And she'd earned the right to hide them, if that's what she wanted to do. He, on the other hand, had earned the right to be alone. Not just earned it. Worked dang hard for it. He preferred solitude to the messiness of relationships. He'd spent his childhood watching his father destroy his mother, watching his mother push aside her feelings to create the best life she could for her sons, watching his brothers become as stoic as she'd been.

He'd vowed to never marry because he hadn't wanted to hurt or to be hurt. He'd wanted one thing, and he'd planned to always have it—peace.

And then he'd met Patricia his second year at Texas A&M. He was on scholarship, heading toward a degree in agricultural engineering. She'd been studying the same. They'd bonded over homework, and they'd been a couple all through their junior and senior year.

They'd married after graduation, because he'd loved her, and because on paper it all worked. They had similar views, beliefs, and values. They had similar ideologies. They both were interested in agriculture and in sustainable living.

Until Flynn had taken a job as a ranch hand for one of the biggest cattle operations in Texas, things had been great. But that job had changed things. Flynn had wanted to learn ranching from the bottom up. He'd wanted to use his degree to fix real-world problems on a working farmstead. Eventually, he wanted to own land and cattle, make a name for himself the way ranchers had done decades ago.

Patricia had wanted a job in the city, designing farm equipment for John Deere, making big bucks and using it to entertain high-society friends.

They might have still made it work if she hadn't gotten bored and restless. If she hadn't cheated on him.

If she hadn't left with everything they'd saved, her dog, and the only nice set of dishes they owned.

He frowned.

Water under the bridge and not something he spent much time thinking about. Patricia had been out of his life for longer than she'd been in it. She'd tried to resurface after the *Houston Chronicle* ran a story about Two River Run. Flynn bought the successful ranch when the previous owner retired. He'd doubled its profit in the first three years of business, and people in the business were interested in his methods.

Patricia had liked the idea of being wife to a successful rancher.

He'd sent her away three times before she'd finally understood that he wasn't interested in rekindling their romance.

That had been three years ago.

Three years of peace, and he didn't plan to ruin the streak.

But Sunday had made some big plans in front of her children. They'd be awfully disappointed if she didn't follow through.

CHAPTER FIVE

Her chest hurt.

Her pulse raced.

Her muscles felt weak.

Maybe she was having a heart attack.

Or maybe she was having a panic attack because of the lie she'd just told. To. Her. Children.

Plans for the day?

She had none. Aside from chair sitting and wall staring.

She and Flynn hadn't ever discussed anything regarding a fall festival or horses.

Horses!

She'd looked Heavenly in the eye and mentioned a horse, the words flowing off her tongue as if they'd been there for years waiting to be said. She knew Heavenly dreamed of riding. She knew she longed to own a horse. Not a pony. A real horse. The kind a teen could saddle and ride all day if she wanted.

Sunday had written about it in the journals.

That childish dream and how much she'd wished she could make it come true. But horses were expensive. Feed and medication and farriers cost money the family hadn't had. Now . . .

Maybe. There'd been an insurance payoff and fundraisers and silent auctions. People had been generous. Matt's brothers had been generous. Pleasant Valley Organic Farm was on firm financial footing. She and the kids didn't need to worry. She'd been told that by so many people, so many times, she couldn't forget it.

But there wasn't time for a horse.

There wasn't energy for teaching a teenager how to care for a large and intelligent animal.

But Sunday had opened her mouth and mentioned it as if it were going to happen.

"You're an idiot," she muttered, dropping into the easy chair and pulling the blanket off the floor and onto her lap.

It spilled over her knobby knees, covering the hole she'd torn in her sweatpants, the small splotch of blood still on her knee, the gnarly-looking scar that ran from her patella to mid-thigh.

"Staring at cream-colored plaster again?" Flynn asked as he stepped into the room. A cowboy hat shadowed his eyes and hid his expression.

Good. She didn't want to see censure. She felt bad enough as it was.

"I'm sorry," she said, before he could bring up the lie. "I don't know what got into me."

"You probably do. If you think about it long enough."

She looked up, realized he was digging through his suitcase. "I didn't want to slow them down."

"The kids?" he asked, straightening, a baseball cap in his hand.

“You heard what Heavenly said.”

“I heard a teenager who was annoyed because she didn’t want to be bothered, but I’m not her parent. Maybe that changed my perception.” He put the cap on her head, tucked hair under it and bent so that they were eye to eye. “Jeans are better for the kind of work we’re going to do. Long sleeves, too. You know the drill.”

“Drill?”

“If we’re going to spend time outside, it’s better to be covered. It looks to be a sunny day, and the sun is already high. I’ll grab canteens and fill them. You get dressed. You do have canteens, right?”

He was staring into her eyes, willing her to go along with whatever cockamamy plan he’d come up with.

“We do, but—”

“Where are they?”

“In the coat closet. There’s a box on the top shelf, but—”

“Any granola or jerky?”

“In the pantry, but—”

“Get changed. I’ll meet you out front in ten.”

“But,” she tried again, but his long legs had already carried him out of the room.

She thought about calling him back and asking him what the heck he had planned, but the hat was already on her head, and she had to change anyway. She couldn’t spend the day sitting in sweats and a tank top after she'd told the kids she was going to tour the farm.

Ten minutes, though?

It would take her that long to get up the stairs to her room!

She managed it in three, rushing as fast as she dared on legs that still didn't feel quite connected to her body. She'd used a walker for a while after she'd awoken. Then she'd limped with a cane. Now she was on her own, but still felt shaky and unsteady. A product of the brain injury, she'd been told. It was listed on the document she kept in the top dresser drawer. The one the doctor had written to keep her from panicking about lost memories and words, sluggish thoughts and hazy recall. She lost track of time and entire days passed with her doing nothing but staring at that darn cream-colored wall.

That scared her.

What scared her more was thinking that she was missing out on a million moments with her children.

So at night, when it was quiet, she'd sometimes panic about life and about how it had changed. She'd take out the list that her therapist had suggested and read over the common symptoms of traumatic brain injury. Just to remind herself that she was doing okay. That she wasn't failing. That she was trying her best.

She didn't have time to look at the list now.

The clock was ticking and she wanted to prove to herself that she could get dressed as quickly as any able-bodied person.

She pulled on a pair of jeans, buttoned it. It slid down her legs and puddled on the floor. The next pair did the same. And the next.

She opened the closet, pulled out the plastic bin of her mother's clothes. The top layer was a few things Sunday hadn't been able to part with. Beneath those were outfits from her mother's teenage years. Bell-bottom jeans. Tie-dyed shirts. A few maxi dresses made from synthetic fabrics.

"Sunday?!" Flynn called from the bottom of the stairs. "Is everything okay?"

She glanced at the bedside clock, but she had no idea how much time had passed. Either she hadn't looked at it when she'd walked in the room or she'd forgotten what time she'd read.

"I'm almost ready," she called as she grabbed the first pair of jeans she saw. Her mother had been a tiny woman. Always. Five-foot-two. A hundred pounds sopping wet. And that was after she'd had a child.

As a teen, she'd been like Heavenly. Skinny arms and legs, gangly body. Prior to the accident, Sunday had been a curvier version of her mother. She didn't expect the jeans to slide on, and she was shocked when they did. She buttoned them without a struggle, the bell-bottoms swishing as she grabbed a long-sleeved T-shirt from the dresser.

"Sunday?" Flynn knocked on the door as she pulled her arms through the sleeves.

"Coming," she replied breathlessly. She'd knocked the hat off in her hurry to change, and it was lying on the floor. She bent to retrieve it, straightened too quickly, fell into the bedpost and then the wall, her head meeting the old plaster with a hard thump that made her see stars.

The door flew open.

Flynn stepped into the room. Rushed in, really. Nearly flying to her side.

"Are you okay?" he asked, crouching beside her.

"I've told you at least a dozen times today that I'm fine," she replied, embarrassed that he'd felt the need to burst into the room. Embarrassed that she hadn't been able to manage the simple task of changing clothes quickly.

Just plain embarrassed, because everything was so darn difficult.

"You're going to have a bruise." He touched her forehead, and she winced away. Not because it hurt, but because she was tempted to let him prod at the bruise, offer ice, do all the things everyone always did when she lost her balance.

"I bruise easily. And I fall a lot. I'm fine." She stood, and his gaze dropped to her legs and the cuffs of the bell-bottoms.

"I guess the seventies are back?"

"I've heard they are."

"They're cute, Sunday. But not practical."

"They were my mother's and, currently, they're the only jeans I have that fit."

"How about Heavenly?"

"What about her?"

"She probably has jeans that'll work."

She laughed, the idea of squeezing into her itty-bitty daughter's wardrobe almost as amusing as the fact that Flynn thought she could. "You do realize she's tiny, right?"

"You are, too," he responded, walking into the hall and returning a few minutes later, a pair of dark blue jeans in hand. "I found these in her drawer. With a pile of things labeled 'too ugly to wear unless the gift giver is coming for dinner.' "

She laughed. "You're kidding."

"I'm afraid not. Everything is labeled: 'School appropriate.' 'Won't Make Sunday Blow a Gasket.' 'Sexy.' "

"Sexy?"

"That's what it says. I figure I will empty that section out after we do a survey of the land. I'll be in the hall. Everything else is ready."

He stepped out of the room and closed the door. She eyed the tiny pair of jeans, trying to figure out if he really thought she could fit into them.

"Do you need help?" he called.

"No!" she nearly yelled.

God no!

The last thing she wanted was one of Matt's brothers seeing her in her skivvies. She yanked off the bell-bottoms, slid into the jeans. They were snug but not uncomfortable. She didn't have time to think about how much weight she must have lost or how horrible she must look.

She grabbed the ball cap. Again. Shoved it on her head and nearly ran into the hall.

Flynn was leaning against the wall, a pair of work boots in his hand. "I grabbed these from the coat closet. They looked like your size."

"How, in the name of all that is holy, did you manage to go downstairs, find boots, and return in the time it took me to put on a pair of jeans?" She was panting, her brow beaded with sweat, her legs shaking. She managed to take the boots anyway, drop them on the floor, and shove her feet into them.

They were hers.

Just as he'd guessed.

"I had them in my hand when I knocked on your door. I heard you fall and dropped them. It took about half a second to pick them up. That's a pretty average response time, I think. Despite opinions to the contrary, I don't have superpowers."

"I guess I'm relieved. I can't keep up with average-bodied people. No way could I keep up with a superhero." She smiled, reaching to tie the boots.

“Let me.” He had them done before she could find the words to protest.

That was the problem with life right now. By the time her brain put all the pieces of information together and formed a coherent thought, opportunities had passed or the desire to do something was lost. Or she forgot what she’d been trying to say. Or the person waiting for her response filled the silence with words that muddled her thinking even more.

“I used to be fast,” she said, as Flynn straightened. “And I’m pretty sure Moisey thought I had superpowers.”

“I’m pretty sure she still does,” he responded, straightening the cap and tucking hair beneath it again. “All right. Let’s get this done.”

“You never did explain what we were doing,” she said as she followed him down the stairs.

“Exactly what we planned: We’re going to survey the land, find some good locations for tents and tables, decide if we should invite local vendors—”

“To the fall festival?”

“That is what you were planning, right? To have local vendors? Put an ad in a few regional newspapers. Let people know we’re here.”

“I hadn’t really been planning anything.”

“Now you are. So what do you think? Vendors?” They’d reached the foyer, and he lifted two canteens and a small canvas carryall from the floor.

"I . . ." She tried to formulate a response, tried to think of something intelligent to say. Something about money or finances or necessity. Something that wouldn't make her sound as stupid as she suddenly felt. All those beautiful words, the ones she'd known her entire life. The ones that had to do with farming, crops, profits, margins, planting, harvesting. Life as she'd known it when her parents were alive.

They were gone.

Lost with so many of her memories.

"It's not a test, Sunday," Flynn said as he opened the front door and ushered her outside. "You're not going to fail. Outside vendors? Yes or no?"

"Yes?"

"Then let's go see where we can set up tents. We could use the barn, but I think the kids were planning a petting zoo there."

"I didn't realize they'd been planning anything."

"I've heard them a couple of times. At the breakfast table on the weekends. They've been planning next year's festival this year. They are definitely your kids."

"Why do you say that?"

"Matt wasn't a planner. Not when he was a kid and"—he waved at the yard and the land beyond it—"certainly not as an adult, either."

"He planned plenty of things," she argued, compelled for some reason to defend the man who'd betrayed her.

"He dreamed plenty of things. You planned them." He walked across the gravel driveway and around the side of the house. The garage was there, double doors closed. Her heart jumped when Flynn opened them. She wasn't sure why. She knew the sporty Camaro wasn't there.

"I'm not sure how you came to that conclusion." She approached the garage the way she would have a rattlesnake. Cautiously.

"Observation." He disappeared into the yawning gray space beyond the doors and returned with the ATV Matt had purchased.

Because it was necessary.

All farmers had them. It helped with surveying the land and knowing what sections were ready for planting or harvesting.

She'd found that little snippet of Matt-fact in her journal, underlined twice with quotations around it. She wasn't sure why she'd done that. She guessed that she was frustrated by the purchase or by Matt's insistence that he needed something she knew was totally unnecessary.

Her dad had been a farmer his entire life, and he'd never owned an ATV. He'd used his old Chevy pickup, wearing trails through the dusty earth during the hottest part of the summer.

She remembered dust clouds on the horizon—a sure sign that her father was on his way back from the fields.

She also remembered agreeing to the ATV.

Although she couldn't recall how long it had taken for Matt to wear her down and get her to agree. She had no idea how many times she'd said no before she'd said yes. None? A thousand?

"This is a nice machine," Flynn said. "You ride it much?"

"I . . . don't think so."

"No worries. There's room for two, and I'll drive." He opened the cargo box at the back of the vehicle and dropped his cowboy hat and utility bag inside. "Do you have helmets?"

"Somewhere." She thought.

"Hold on." He walked back into the garage and returned carrying two helmets. He handed one to her and strapped the other on, the canteens hanging from his shoulder.

It took her a little longer to take off the ball cap and replace it with the helmet.

To his credit, Flynn didn't offer to help.

He just waited patiently while she made an hour-long project out of a one-minute job.

God, she hated this.

She did.

She hated how hard everything always was, how stupid and clumsy she often felt.

She hated seeing pity in the eyes of people who had once viewed her with admiration.

She met Flynn's eyes anyway, because she also hated being a coward. She hated being afraid.

She hated pretending that things were great

when her life was slowly imploding. "I'm done. Finally."

"It didn't take long."

"It took an eternity," she argued as he climbed onto the ATV.

"It only felt like that to you. Climb on. I'm curious to see the borders of your property. I've been out here a few dozen times, and I don't think I've ever seen all the land. It's two hundred acres, right?"

She missed the last part of what he'd said.

She was still thinking about the first part.

The part that went: *climb on*.

Because the only place to sit was right behind him, and she wasn't sure how she felt about that.

She knew she didn't feel comfortable. That was for sure.

Sure, he was Matt's brother, but she barely knew him.

"Ready?" he prodded, and she shook her head.

"I should probably stay here."

"Are you afraid?"

"No."

"Then why stay?"

"I just . . . probably should."

He eyed her for a moment, most of his face hidden by the helmet.

She could see his eyes, though. Blue as the midnight sky. Surrounded by thick black lashes. Fine lines fanning out from the corners.

He was smiling.

He must be.

"It's not really funny," she muttered, and his eyes crinkled even more.

"I don't recall saying it was."

"You're smiling."

"Just thinking you look like a kid in that getup. Climb on," he said again.

This time she did, refusing to think about what she was doing or how close they would be. He was Matt's brother, for God's sake. Not some random cute stranger who wanted to take her for a ride.

Cute?

Flynn wasn't cute.

Matt had been cute. Chestnut hair and gray-blue eyes and that impish smile that had made every girl in their high school giggle.

She remembered that. Remembered how proud she'd been to be the one Matt spent time with. He'd been an enigma. The rich kid from the mansion who'd dressed like he was poor. His mother had died when he was seven, and people had made allowances for him. Made excuses. Poor grades, missed assignments, skipped school. All those things were because his mother wasn't around.

At least, that's how Sunday remembered it.

She also remembered knowing the truth and being amused by the fact that Matt could so easily manipulate the adults in his life.

He'd probably been manipulating her. She could acknowledge that. Just like she could acknowledge that she'd made excuses for him, too. Years' worth of excuses.

"Ready?" Flynn started the motor, and she grabbed for the handholds on either side of the seat. The ATV had been built for two, but she couldn't recall if she'd ever been on it. She had no idea if Matt had been.

She only remembered that he'd wanted it, and he'd gotten it.

It hadn't helped him become a better farmer any more than buying a new computer had helped him keep better track of the business side of things.

There'd been other things, too. Other dreams, she guessed she could call them. They were hazy memories in the far reaches of her foggy mind. She didn't mind that she couldn't pull them out. She knew what she'd find if she could. One dream after another with no plan for achieving it, no goals for reaching it, no follow-through on attaining it.

A dreamer. Not a planner.

Flynn was right about that.

He took it easy and slow. Not something he normally liked to do. Sure, he was methodical and careful, but he enjoyed a good quick spin around his property. He preferred horseback to

ATVs, but he used both when he rounded up the livestock. He also used the old Chevy that had come with the ranch. Beat-up, dinged, rust spots speckling the faded green paint, the Chevy was the kind of vehicle his father would have laughed at if he'd been alive to see it.

Redneck vehicle for redneck people.

Unlike Flynn, he'd had no love for the outdoors and no desire to work with his hands. He'd been a computer programmer who'd made a fortune when the tech industry took off, but he'd been raised in Benevolence. On the wrong side of the tracks. So to speak. He'd told the story so many times, Flynn could still recite it:

My mother was a whore. My father was an alcoholic. I just happened to be born, and they didn't care much whether I lived or died. I guess I wanted to live, so I survived infancy. Made it to school, spent the next twelve years of my life being bullied by the stupid hillbilly hicks who lived in town. I couldn't wait to get out, and once I'd made my fortune, I couldn't wait to return.

Flynn had never been convinced that the story was true.

He'd done some asking around when he was a teen, talked to the local barber and a few other people who'd probably gone to school with his father. Most of them remembered him, but none had much to say. He'd been quiet, a little dirty, and had a nasty temper. They'd steered clear, but that hadn't meant they weren't impressed when he'd returned to Benevolence with a fortune in the bank and a beautiful wife on his arm.

If they'd known what had been going on in the huge mansion his father had purchased, they might not have been so easily enthralled, but, of course, that had been a secret the family kept.

Flynn suspected most people in town had known the truth.

He doubted teachers had missed the bruises on his arms and legs, the few that had been on his face. He figured the church had noticed how quiet the Bradshaws were when they attended service. There were no restless boys or loudly scribbling pens. There was just stiff, tense attention.

Sometimes, when Flynn allowed himself to delve deep into his own psyche, he wondered if he'd chosen ranching because he knew his father would disapprove. He wondered if he'd made that fateful trip out to Emmerson's farm out of spite rather than necessity. The kind of work Emmerson did had no value for a man like Rick, and that might have made Flynn value it more.

Then again, he had needed a job. He'd also needed to be away from the house and his father, so it was just as possible he'd taken the job because it was available.

That job had led to his interest in farming and farm equipment. Watching Emmerson take apart tractors and put them back together had sparked curiosity and interest that had never faded.

Even now, all these years later, Flynn loved taking apart broken equipment and making it right again. He loved the scent of loamy earth and wet leaves, the rumbling thunder of cattle racing across the landscape, the thick dust that hung in the air after they'd gone.

And yes. He loved riding fast horses, driving fast cars, and pushing ATVs to their limits.

But today he was going slow, meandering across the farm's rolling hills. Sunday perched behind him, her muscles stiff. She didn't lean into him. Not even when he bumped over a fallen log.

"Sorry about that," he shouted above the roar of the motor.

"It's okay," she shouted back.

"I thought we'd head up to the road and take the vehicle bridge across the other side of your property. You've got two hundred acres, right?" He'd seen the plat for the farm, but it had only included the east side of the river.

"On this side of the river. We've got another five hundred across it."

"Seven hundred acres?"

"Yes."

"That's a nice-sized spread for a small farm."

"It used to be a dairy farm. That was probably a hundred years ago. Back in the day when milk was delivered in glass jugs. After my great-great-grandfather retired from that, he let the land on that side go fallow. Crops weren't his thing. His wife maintained a garden, and that was pretty much it until my great-grandfather decided to plant alfalfa and sell it to local farmers."

"You know your family history."

"I've read about it every day since I was released from the hospital," she replied.

"Trying to make sure you don't forget?"

"Trying to remember why it was so important."

"It's important, because it's yours. Does there need to be another reason?"

"No," she said a little too quickly.

He wanted to ask a few more questions, dig a little deeper, but he'd reached the road and accelerated to keep from blocking traffic. The wind rushing past his helmet, the rumble of approaching vehicles, made communication impossible.

For now.

The bridge was a mile away. Two lanes and narrow. Barely enough room for one car let alone two. Most people didn't use it. Not because it wasn't safe. Because the only residence within five miles was Emmerson's old place, the clapboard farmhouse still visible through heavy summer foliage.

It had been white once upon a time. Now it looked gray. Either someone had painted it, or time hadn't been very kind.

"Do you know where your property marker is?"

he asked as the ATV bounced over a few dips in the dirt road.

"We're on it."

"What's that?"

"This road is the boundary line."

"You're sure?"

"Yes. Our property is to the right. Emmerson Riley's is to the left. Only, I think his son may own it now."

"He does. Or at least he did when I left town."

"I didn't realize you knew the Rileys."

"I worked for him a million years ago."

"Mr. Riley's son?"

"No. Emmerson. His son left town right around the time Emmerson got sick and slowed down. I guess he liked the idea of equestrian work, but didn't actually enjoy getting his hands dirty."

"I don't think I knew that."

"Probably not. You were young when I started working there. Probably too young to hear the gossip. Not that there was much of it. Anytime Emmerson got wind of someone talking about his family, he'd stand up at the end of church service and ask for prayer for the town's gossips. He always made sure to mention them by name."

"No!" she said with a quiet laugh.

"Yes. A man's got to fight fire with fire. If that doesn't work, he's got to fight it with the word of God. Emmerson said that all the time." Flynn stopped the ATV and climbed off. The land on

Sunday's side of the road was mostly clear, a few straggly pines jutting up haphazardly and several copses of trees grown where pasture had once been.

He could still envision it the way it had once been, though. Easy access to the river. Irrigation canals carved into the land by old farmers with weather-beaten faces and gnarled hands. Lush green fields that turned gold in the fall and winter. Plenty of food for a small dairy operation.

Prime land, too. With hundreds of riverfront feet.

Sunday's ancestors had chosen well.

"It's a beautiful piece of property," he said aloud.

"It is." She climbed off the ATV and took off her helmet. Her cheeks were pink again. This time, he thought it was from the heat.

He handed her a canteen. "Better stay hydrated. Clementine will have my head if you pass out."

"How would she find out?" She tried to unscrew the lid.

Failed.

Tried again.

It was painful to watch a grown woman wrestle with something a child could have managed, and he suddenly understood why so many people were so eager and willing to do so much for Sunday. She didn't ask. She didn't complain. She sat quietly in that damn easy chair. Probably because it was easier than struggling and failing in front of people she loved.

She finally managed to open it, and his muscles relaxed, his arms fell to his sides. He hadn't realized how tense he was, how ready to jump in and rescue her.

She met his eyes as she took a quick swallow of water. Bluebonnets at sunset and the purplish tracheostomy scar on her neck. She made a pretty picture standing in the middle of the overgrown field.

He probably shouldn't be noticing that.

Or the way she planted her feet deep in the dusty soil. She looked like she belonged there, sunlight streaming on her flyaway hair and skipping across her still-pink cheeks as she took another sip and recapped the canteen.

"You're staring," she said, pulling the canteen strap over her shoulder.

"Just thinking that you look like you belong here."

She laughed. "Well, that's good to know. Since I've been living here my whole life."

"And you've always felt like you belonged."

It wasn't a question, but she answered. "I have no idea. I can only remember some of my past. Not all of it."

"It seems to me, you've never felt like you should be anywhere else. This always seemed to be what you wanted. The land. The house. Your family. Those are my memories, though, so they may be skewed."

"By?"

"How happy you looked outside playing with the kids or feeding that old hog or planting the garden in the backyard."

"I'd forgotten about the garden."

"Not me. You made a lot of great meals with food from that garden."

She smiled, a hint of sadness in her eyes. "It's sad that you remember more about my life than I do."

"I suppose it is," he replied, not wanting to feed her platitudes or try to talk her out of the sorrow. He had plenty of memories he'd prefer to lose, but he thought her life had been mostly happy. Her family had been loving. Her parents had been good people. Her marriage to Matt . . .

He hoped it had been good. There'd certainly never been any sign that it wasn't.

Except for the neglected farm.

The overdrawn bank accounts.

The debt.

The obvious picture of a family that was struggling financially despite the fact that there was no mortgage to pay and plenty of food produced to feed a bunch of hungry kids.

He frowned, not much liking the direction of his thoughts.

Matt had been a good guy. A really good one.

Everyone in town said so. He'd yet to meet someone who hadn't liked and valued his brother.

"Were you happy with Matt?" he asked, the question sudden and unplanned. He didn't know why he'd asked, and the surprise on her face told him she didn't either.

"Of course I was," she responded quickly. "Matt was a wonderful person. I loved him. I still love him."

"Loving someone doesn't mean we're happy. It just means we know the real meaning of the word."

"I was happy," she said, crouching and lifting a clump of earth and letting it fall through her fingers. "Dry. We haven't had enough rain this year. If I ever planted over here, I'd have to irrigate."

She changed the subject, and he let her.

Because it wasn't his business.

Not really.

"Irrigation wouldn't be difficult or expensive. You have the manpower, and we can do it the old-fashioned way. Dig trenches from the river to bring the water into the fields. That area"—he pointed to a section of land that stretched nearly flat out from the river—"would be perfect."

"I can't ask your brothers to do another job for me. They've already done too much."

"My brothers are here to help. They'd be happy to run irrigation ditches. But it would also be a great job for the kids to help with."

"It would be more of a job for whoever had to supervise them," she replied, taking another handful of soil and letting it slide through her fingers.

"In other words, it would be easier to do without their help?" he asked, knowing he should close his mouth and butt out. He wasn't going to be raising the kids. He wasn't going to be the one to cheer them on at sports games or wipe tears off their faces when they'd had bad days.

He was going to be *that* uncle. The one who popped in every month or so, gave high fives, asked about school, and then went away again. The one who'd be there on graduation day but probably not for the prom.

It wasn't that he didn't want to be involved.

It was more that he had a life and a job that required a lot of time and attention. Plus, Porter and Sullivan had stepped in. Both seemed happy to relocate to Benevolence.

For Flynn, moving back wasn't an option.

"Everything is easier to do without kids involved, but that doesn't mean it's the best option. I like the idea of having them help with the project. I'm just not sure what we're planning to do with the land. Aside from the fall festival, that is. Speaking of which, we should probably get back to our survey." She straightened, and all the blood drained from her face.

She went from pink-cheeked to ghost white

and was falling before Flynn realized what was happening. He managed to grab her before she landed, lowering her onto the ground. He could see her pulse in the hollow of her throat, beating crazily against her skin.

He'd pushed her too hard, asked her to do things she probably shouldn't have.

Like leave the house. Ride on an ATV in ninety-degree weather.

Open her own canteen.

"You're an idiot, Flynn," he growled as he pulled out his cell phone.

"That's not a very nice thing to call yourself," Sunday replied sluggishly, her eyes still closed, her lips as pale as her skin. "And, if you're planning to call for an ambulance. Don't. I'm not going to the hospital."

"You need a doctor."

"I need to lie here for a while. That's it."

"You're in the middle of a field. Under the blazing sun. You lay there for more than a couple of minutes, and you'll roast."

"Bake." She opened her eyes. "It's a dry heat, Flynn."

That was enough to make him chuckle, but not enough for him to put the phone away. "We can discuss how many ways the sun can cook a person on our way to the hospital."

"I already said that I'm not going. There's no need."

"How about we let a professional decide."

"My blood pressure is low. If I stand too quickly, I get dizzy. That's it. No terrible disease. Nothing to do with the head injury. Just me trying to move more quickly than I should. Trust me. I know. Your brothers have shipped me off to the hospital a half dozen times for the issue." She was getting to her feet, and he took her arm, slowing her progress.

Really slowing it.

By the time she was fully upright, she was laughing, her cheeks pink again.

"Slowing down doesn't mean never getting there, Flynn," she said, smiling straight into his eyes.

And, of course, he smiled too, because she did make a pretty picture, standing there with the sun on her skin and a smile on her face.

"You're here. Upright and smiling. Mission accomplished. Slow or not," he replied, his hand still on her arm because he worried that she'd faint again. "A half dozen times is about five too many for my liking, by the way. I'm going to make you an appointment and have you get a thorough workup. Just in case."

"In case of what?"

"I want to make certain there's no underlying condition."

"Do you know how many blood tests, CAT scans, MRIs, and X-rays I've had?" she demanded, walking to the ATV and climbing on.

"A lot, but that doesn't mean you shouldn't get another test."

"In my book, it does. So how about we finish surveying the land? I haven't been out here in a while, and . . . it's nice to be outside."

That last part was enough to convince him.

Not the words. The way she said them.

It's nice to be outside.

As if she'd been locked up for too long, far away from the clean, sweet smell of summer and the neat, crisp feel of grass underfoot. "All right, but if you feel faint again—"

"I won't," she replied.

He didn't think she had any control over it. She sure couldn't promise the heat or the ride wouldn't make her woozy, but she was perched on the ATV, face turned up to the sun, hands held out as if she could touch the beauty of the day.

And no matter how much he told himself he should, he couldn't tell her they were going back to the house.

CHAPTER SIX

Unless it was raining, Sunday went outside every day.

It was part of her therapy. Physical and psychological.

Go outside. Get fresh air. Stretch your muscles. Take a walk. Feel the sun on your skin. Watch your children play. Imagine yourself stepping into your future free of fear and anxiety.

And on and on and on. So many great reasons to be outdoors.

But when she was, someone was always there. Hovering nearby. Issuing warnings. Telling her where the rocks and roots and hazards were.

She understood they were worried.

But she was worried too.

Terrified, really. Of another accident. Of getting hurt again. Of leaving her children the way Matt had.

But today . . .

Today she felt free.

Long blades of grass brushed her calves as Flynn maneuvered through what had once been pasture. He was being careful, taking his time, not gunning the motor like he might have if he'd been alone, but he wasn't going back to the house, and he wasn't insisting she go to the hospital.

He was letting her decide, and that was something she'd almost forgotten how to do. For months, people had been making decisions for her and for the kids. She'd been letting them because it was easier than trying to make her sluggish brain think through options and decide what was best.

Allowing others to do what she should was the path of least resistance.

But she knew it wasn't the best path or even a good one.

They bumped through a small ditch, and she lost her grip on the handholds. Somehow, she found Flynn's waist, clutched it as they descended to the riverbank. He was solid. Muscular. Strong. A guy who worked outside, who worked with his hands, who knew how to get things done. She tried to remember what that was like. How it had felt to wake up in the morning knowing how to tackle the day.

All she could remember was being tired. In those last few months before the accident, every day had seemed a chore. She didn't remember that. She'd read it in the journals, but the feeling was there, lodged in her heart. A feeling of inevitability, of lack of control, of pending and unwanted change.

Flynn stopped near a dry rainwater basin, the front tires of the SUV sitting on cracked red clay. In the rainy season, the shallow ditch formed a small pond that had once been used to water the dairy's cows. She remembered the pictures that had once hung on the walls of the barn: black-and-white photos of the farm the way it used to be. Matt had taken them down when he'd begun renovating. He'd never finished the job, and she had no idea what he'd done with the photos.

Or what she'd done.

She might have packed them away somewhere, put them in a safe spot to be rehung once the rotting joists were replaced.

Flynn climbed off the ATV, offering a hand so that she could do the same. He removed her helmet, probably because he was afraid she'd get overheated and faint again. Then he removed his.

His hair was mussed, his eyes glowing deep denim in his tan face. Sunlight dappled his long-sleeved cotton shirt and splashed across the razor-like edge of his cheekbones.

He led her across the clay and up a small hill to what must once have been a grazing field. She could see remnants of a fence in the distance. Just a few posts poking through the grass.

"We can fence twenty or thirty acres for the horses out here. Set up another pasture if you want to keep cattle."

"I don't even know if I want to keep horses," she admitted.

"You can't go back on a promise, Sunday."

"I didn't promise," she reminded him.

"You may not have said the words, but I'm

pretty sure Heavenly heard them. That's how teenagers work, right? Selective hearing? They hear what they want and don't hear what they don't want?"

"For someone who doesn't have kids, you seem to know a lot about them," she said, and he chuckled.

"I might have left home as soon as I turned eighteen, but I didn't abandon my brothers. We talked at least once a week. Sometimes more. Depending on how much trouble they were getting into. If I thought things were getting really bad, I'd offer to send them a ticket to come stay with me."

"I wasn't implying that you weren't a good older brother, Flynn. I hope you know that," she said hurriedly.

She hated hurting people.

She hated upsetting them.

She liked peace, calm, good relationships.

"I know, but it's not something I haven't thought about over the years. Leaving my brothers behind was one of the toughest things I've ever done, but my mother made me promise that I'd leave when I turned eighteen. My father and I didn't get along. I think she was afraid he'd kill me. Or I'd kill him," he said wryly. "I had a temper when I was a kid, and my mother's biggest fear seemed to be that I'd turn out like my dad."

"She said that to you?" she asked.

"No. She told me I was going to be a strong, compassionate father and husband. That I'd accomplish my dreams because I worked hard and I was determined."

"That sounds more like the woman everyone has told me about. I met her once, you know," she said, the memory faded and foggy. "Matt brought me to the house after school one day, and she was there. Making something in the kitchen." She could see her standing at a floured counter, her hands pressed into dough, blue-black bruises smudging her pale forearms.

Her face was hidden from Sunday's memories, her smile, her voice. All of it wiped out by the accident or by time.

But the bruises remained.

The pale skin.

The hands shoved deep into dough.

"You must have been young."

"Six or seven. I have no idea how I managed to leave the school and walk home with my best buddy, but I did. I'm sure my parents panicked and the school panicked and people were out searching for me before I even made it to your place. I can't remember any of that, but I remember your mother standing in the kitchen, kneading dough."

"She did that when she was thinking. Baked bread. She also sketched, painted, and journaled. My brothers and I found some of her stuff after our father passed away. She'd kept a notebook with stories about us. Mostly sweet little things about flowers we'd brought her or games we'd played. She also wrote about my temper and Matt's propensity to daydream and Sullivan's overactive imagination and Porter's aggressive tendencies. She was so worried we'd be like my father. Especially me."

"Just because she wrote those things," she said carefully, because this was his story, and she didn't want to try to change it. She didn't want to tell him he was wrong, or that he'd misread or misunderstood his mother's concern. "Didn't mean she believed they'd happen. I write lots of things that I worry about, but that I don't really think are going to come about."

"Like?"

"Heavenly smoking in the courtyard at school. The twins robbing a bank before they turn ten. Moisey staging a coup so that she can become President Princess Supreme of the United States."

He laughed. Just like she hoped he would. "Nothing about Oya or Twila?"

"Oya is too young for me to worry much, and my worries about Twila are more realistic."

"Yeah?" He took her arm, urging her toward the chapel.

"I wrote a lot about her book habit."

"Book habit?"

"The fact that she'd rather read than play

outside or talk or go to activities with friends. She's my quiet one. The child who is least likely to tell me what she thinks or feels. That seems to have been my biggest concern right before the accident." That and Matt. His long absences from the farm. His trips to Seattle and Portland to sell organic product to vendors.

Only there'd never been an increase of cash-flow, never any large deposits into their bank accounts. Certainly not enough to warrant traveling such far distances.

She'd reread those journal entries dozens of times. To put their last dinner and the accident into context.

"Not the farm?" he asked.

The question surprised her, and she wasn't sure why.

By the night of the accident, the farm had been heading toward bankruptcy. Matt had taken out a mortgage on the property without her knowledge, signing forms without her consent. There'd been back property taxes that she hadn't known about. Bills for farm equipment that she hadn't seen used.

God. It had been a mess.

"I was worried about the farm, too," she admitted, feeling as if she were somehow betraying a trust, speaking poorly of the dead. Speaking poorly of Matt. Of her husband.

And she'd never want to do that.

Not when he was alive, and certainly not now that he was dead.

"Matt wasn't a great farm manager," he said, poking at the sore spot, the secret place, the ugly truth that she'd kept from everyone, because she'd loved her husband. She'd wanted the world to keep seeing him the way she once had.

"He tried."

"Without expending a whole lot of effort, maybe."

"Is there a point to this conversation, Flynn? Aside from making me feel like a failure?"

"Why would you feel like a failure because my brother wasn't good at the job you entrusted to him?"

"Because . . ." *I chose him* was on the tip of her tongue, but that didn't sound right. It didn't feel right. She'd loved Matt. Despite his flaws. Despite his betrayals. Despite it all, she'd loved him. "My parents trusted me to take care of the property. It's been in my family for a long time, and I almost allowed it to be lost."

"You wouldn't have allowed it. Unless I miss my guess, you had something up your sleeve. Some way of saving the place."

She didn't think so.

If she had, she hadn't written it in any of her journals. She hadn't shared it with any of her friends.

It seemed to her, she'd been so caught up in the

drama that enveloped her life, that she'd put the farm on the back burner, ignoring obvious signs of neglect and mismanagement.

She could forgive herself for a lot of things, but that one was one she struggled with.

"Maybe." They'd reached the chapel, and her legs were a little bit wobbly, so she sat, back against façade, face turned up to the sun.

It felt good and right and more comfortable than anything had in a long time.

Flynn crouched in front of her, studied her face. "You're pale again."

"I'm fine," she said, because she didn't want to go back to the house and the easy chair, the cream-colored wall and soft creak of the floor.

"You're pale," he repeated. "I'll get the ATV. Wait here."

She let him go, because she was tired, and because the sun felt good on her skin, the warmth of the chapel perfect against her back.

She watched as he disappeared from view, then closed her eyes, breathing in late summer and dusty earth, peace and contentment.

"It's a good place to be," she whispered to the blue sky and the rustling grass and to God.

He was there, in the hot summer breeze and the sigh of air moving through the windows of the chapel.

Warm breath fanned against her cheek, and a velvety tongue swept over her ear. Startled, she opened her eyes, ready to bolt away from whatever it was that was taste-testing her.

The puppy was there. Deep red curls dry, tongue lolling, what could only be a smile on his face.

"What are you doing here?" she asked, and he nudged her cheek with his nose, licked her ear again.

"Moisey would say you found me, because our souls are connected," she explained, and the puppy's tail thumped.

Which made her smile.

"You're going to be trouble, aren't you, Rembrandt?" she asked, and his tail thumped with more vigor.

"It's okay. I have six other troublemakers at home. One more won't make any difference."

He huffed happily, plopping onto his belly, his chin on her leg.

She petted his soft head, closed her eyes, and let the moment seep into her memories. Maybe, this would be one she could hold on to.

Flynn managed to get Sunday and the puppy back to the house in one piece. No falls off the ATV. No fainting spells. Nothing but a wiggly, squirmy critter licking the back of his neck as he tried to drive.

A beat-up Chevy truck was parked near the garage. Sullivan and his wife, Rumer, arriving for another day of work. They'd been busting their butts for months, working like the land was their legacy, the house their home. Even now, when they were living in town, they worked the farm like it mattered.

Things would change in the fall when Sullivan returned to his job as an art history professor in Portland. He planned to teach online classes and commute to the college twice a month to meet with students.

Maybe it would work. Maybe he'd decide that Portland was where he really wanted to be.

And maybe he already knew it wasn't.

Rumer had been offered a job at Benevolence Elementary School, long-term subbing in the fifth-grade class while the regular teacher was out on maternity leave. They were talking about moving out of the mansion Flynn and his brothers had grown up in and moving into their own place. A cute little place in town.

How many times had he heard Rumer say that?

And yet, he still couldn't believe that his brother would be content with what Benevolence had to offer. Small-town shopping. Small-town culture. Small-town gossip. Small-town life.

He pulled into the garage, turned off the engine, and took the puppy from Sunday's arms. "We have time to bring him to the shelter, if you don't want the kids to have a dog."

"I hope you're not serious," she said, fumbling

with the strap of the helmet, but finally managing to pull it off. "Rembrandt found me twice. According to Moisey, we're soul-connected. I'll need to go into town to get a few things. I can call my friend Beatrice and ask her to bring me."

He almost told her he'd take her.

Almost.

Because she looked excited, her eyes glowing, her muscles relaxed. All the tension that had been so much a part of her since the accident seemed to have slipped away, and he wanted to make sure it didn't come back. He didn't want people to ask her the wrong questions or demand too much of her. He didn't want her to get confused about her reason for being at the store. He didn't want her to come back without the things she needed and then beat herself up over it.

He didn't want her to be sorry that she'd tried to do something on her own.

But she wanted to call a friend. She was an adult. Fully capable of making decisions.

So he nodded. "You have her number?"

"Yes."

"And you have mine just in case—"

"Don't," she said, some of the pleasure leaving her face.

"What?"

"This has been the nicest morning I've had in a long time. Don't ruin it by asking me a million questions before I go out with a friend."

"Okay," he said, and her smile returned, warm and sweet and open. It was the kind of smile that invited people in, that begged friends to come close, that spoke affection and inclusion without words.

She held nothing back from the people she loved.

She kept no piece of her heart.

That's what he'd thought the very first time he'd seen her—dressed for her wedding and hugging both her parents.

"Thanks, Flynn." She levered up on her toes, swaying and off balance but somehow managing to plant a kiss on his cheek.

He'd seen her do the same to other people. Dozens of times over the years, she'd planted a kiss on a cheek, put an arm around a shoulder. She'd offered words of encouragement as she'd patted backs or squeezed hands or offered her love in dozens of different ways.

And he'd watched. Astounded and a little uncomfortable with the display. Worried because it made her vulnerable. It opened her up to hurt and disappointment. She was his brother's wife, and he'd wanted her protected from people who might take advantage of her kindness.

He hadn't realized his brother was one of the people doing that.

At least that's what he'd been telling himself since he'd seen the state of the accounting books, walked out into the fields that he'd never bothered with during his visits every year and seen the fallow, weed-choked land. It was what he'd told himself as he'd signed off on the insurance claim for the expensive car his brother had been driving the night of the accident. As he'd paid off and closed out the credit card accounts that had fed his brother's trips to Portland and Seattle.

While Sunday and the kids stayed home, puttering around town in a fifteen-year-old van, his brother had taken business trips and bought expensive toys. A car. A hunting rifle that Flynn knew for sure he'd never used. Nice clothes and shoes. Equipment for the farm that was eventually sold for pennies on the dollar.

By the time Matt died, all that was left in the barn was old, outdated equipment and rusted tools.

And in the ten years she'd been married to him, Sunday had never said a bad word to anyone about Matt.

If she had, Flynn would have heard about it. Not at the funeral, but later. Maybe at the hospital when friends and church family were standing vigil outside the ICU room, praying for her recovery. Or later, when she'd been in rehab, fighting to come to full consciousness, fighting to come back from whatever place the accident had thrust her. There'd been meals brought to the house, prayer meetings at the church, fundraisers and unexpected donations of time and farm equipment. Dozens of helping hands had brought Sunday's home back to life, but not one of the people who'd helped or visited or prayed had said anything about Sunday and Matt's struggles.

If anything, people acted surprised by the farm's disrepair, by the lack of functional farming equipment, by the financial need the Bradshaws had.

Flynn suspected they only knew the good side of Matt. The happy, charming person who'd do anything for anyone. Like their mother, he had charisma. Unlike her, he didn't feel things all that deeply. He had good relationships because it was easy for him. He knew how to be part of a group, how to lend a hand, how to be there for people who needed it, but Flynn didn't think he knew how to sacrifice.

Not like their mother had.

Not like Sunday had.

Love was a funny and fickle thing.

It made people blind and deaf and dumb.

Flynn had loved his brother, and he'd allowed himself to see those good qualities and ignore the bad ones. He'd believed the smiling, happy faces that greeted him when he'd arrived on Christmas Eve or late on a summer evening.

He'd allowed himself to forget the truth of the life he and his brothers had lived. One where a façade of respectability hid a hellhole of abuse.

Not that he believed Matt was abusive.

God! He hoped his brother hadn't been that much of a bastard.

Sunday had already stepped out of the garage and was moving toward the house, her phone in hand.

"Sunday?!" he called, planning to ask if she needed help finding her friend's number. He sure as heck didn't plan to ask if she'd ever been abused by his brother. If she'd ever been hit or pushed, yelled at or demeaned.

She stopped, swinging around to face him, her hair flying in silky waves, her narrow frame silhouetted by sunlight. For a split second, he was back in time, watching his mother walk through the backyard, her shoulders bowed from illness and from too many years of abuse. She'd been frail and emaciated, just months away from death.

He hadn't known that then, he'd only known that she'd looked beaten down and defeated, and she hadn't always been that way. There'd been a time when she'd laughed. When she'd danced through the kitchen, giggling with Flynn and his brothers.

That joy had been stolen from her, and he'd vowed to never let that happen to another human being. Not if he had the power to prevent it.

"Was Matt good to you?" The question slipped out, hung in the air for a few seconds too long.

Finally, Sunday answered, her tone careful, her words measured. "Of course he was good to me."

"Don't lie, okay? You're not good at it." He sounded angry, and maybe he was. He wanted the truth. Not a pretty lie that would make him feel better.

"I'm not lying," she said. "Matt was good to me. He was good to our kids."

"Then why did he have the fancy sports car?"

"That was our car."

"Only his name was on the loan."

She sighed. "What does it matter, Flynn? He's gone."

"It matters to me."

"Then hear what I'm saying. He was good to me. He bought me . . ." She scowled, and he knew she was struggling, reaching for words she should know. He'd seen it happen before, when she was stressed or tired or overwhelmed.

"It's okay. You don't have to answer," he said, because he felt like a bastard for upsetting her when she'd been so happy.

"Flowers." She finally managed to get the word out. "He bought me flowers almost every week. And my favorite fudge from that place in town."

"Chocolate Haven?" It was the only place in Benevolence that sold fudge, and it sold the stuff in a big way. People came from all over the region to purchase Lamont family fudge.

"Yes. But it wasn't chocolate fudge."

"No. It wouldn't be. You prefer peanut butter. Which is something I've always thought was strange." He hoped to distract her. Maybe make her smile.

But she was upset, and there was no shaking her from that. "He brought me fudge once a month and flowers once a week. He encouraged me to buy things for myself and the kids. It wasn't like he was out spending money and telling me not to. He wanted me to have nice shoes and clothes and . . . stuff. I wrote about it in my journal. I'll show you, if you don't believe me."

"Sunday, you don't have to explain, and you sure as heck don't have to show me your journals," he tried again.

"You shouldn't have asked, if you didn't want an answer. Matt was good to me. He just wasn't good with money. Or with work. Or with being . . ." She pressed her lips together, and he knew she wasn't struggling for the words. She'd simply decided not to speak them.

"What?" he prodded.

"I need to call Bett . . . Bes . . ."

"Beatrice?" he offered.

"Yes." She scowled, her eyes filled with tears.

Dear God! He'd made her cry.

"Sunday, I'm sorry." He touched her shoulder, but she flinched away. "I shouldn't have brought it up."

"Then why did you?"

"Because I wasn't here when I should have been. I wasn't kicking my brother in the butt, getting him to do the things he should have."

"It wasn't your job to do those things. We were adults. Living our lives. Just like you were."

"You were babies when you married."

"We were eighteen."

"Kids."

"We loved each other, and we were ready."

"*You* were ready," he corrected. Gently. Because he didn't want the tears to spill from her eyes and down her face.

Not because he wasn't good at dealing with tears. Not because he didn't want to deal with them. Because he knew she hated crying. He knew she'd be embarrassed, and he didn't want to make things worse than he already had.

"You're probably right, Flynn. I was ready. He wasn't. But what does that matter now?"

"You could have used a little help. A lot of help, and all I gave you was two visits a year and some presents for the kids."

"Yeah. Well, I could have asked for more, if I'd wanted it. I could have asked any one of you to talk to your brother or help out on the farm or help us financially, and you would have. But I didn't, because Matt and I somehow always made it work."

He thought about Twila's adoption and the money he'd given his brother. They hadn't made it work. Not the way she'd thought. Matt had borrowed from him. Probably borrowed from Sullivan and Porter. He'd used credit cards and taken out a loan against the farm. Used part of that money to buy a car.

They hadn't been making it work, and he was certain she knew it.

But he'd already brought tears to her eyes, and he wasn't going to do worse. "If I'd known you needed me, I would have been here."

"How could you know you were needed, if I never let on that we were struggling? What you and your brothers found when you arrived after the accident? It was as much my fault as it was Matt's. I could have talked to him about our finances. I could have asked him to meet with a financial planner or an accountant. I could have suggested reading material or classes. I could have done a lot of things that I didn't do, because I wanted Matt to be happy. If I could do it over again, I'd handle things differently. But I can't. So I'm here. Stuck with the knowledge that my marriage wasn't what it should have been, because Matt and I weren't what *we* should have been."

"Don't blame yourself for my brother's failures. You were here. You were working. You were in the thick of things while he was off doing God knows what in Seattle and Portland."

She straightened her shoulders and raised her

chin, and they were looking right into each other's eyes.

And he didn't see what he'd expected—tears, remorse, sorrow, fragility.

He saw strength.

"Aside from me, you're the only person who has ever questioned those *business* trips," she said, and then she turned, a little jaggedly, a little off balance, and walked away.

CHAPTER SEVEN

It wasn't easy to avoid a person who was sleeping in your living room, but for the past two weeks, Sunday had been making every conceivable effort to do it.

Rather than spending sleepless nights in the kitchen or living room, she spent them in bed, staring at the ceiling, counting the quiet click of the grandmother clock and listening to Rembrandt snore.

Despite Moisey's obvious love for the puppy, he seemed to have chosen Sunday as his person. Which might have been nice.

If Flynn hadn't been sleeping in the living room.

And if she hadn't been avoiding him.

Like the plague.

Two weeks, and she'd only seen Flynn in passing. A quick hello as they walked past each other in the hallway. A nod of the head when she saw him outside. From what Rosie said, he'd been spending most of his time on the far side of the river with his brothers, building a fence to enclose the back pasture.

Not just the brothers.

Several people from town were helping.

Sunday couldn't remember who. Despite the

fact that she'd been told a dozen or more times, the names kept slipping through her mind and disappearing into the fog of brain injury.

"I hate it," she said, and Rembrandt stirred, rising from his puppy bed and jumping onto hers.

He wasn't supposed to sleep there.

As a matter of fact, he had a crate filled with soft bedding. He'd been locked in there the first few nights. By the third night (or had it been the fourth?), he'd figured things out and would scratch at the bedroom door when he needed to go out.

Now he was supposed to sleep on the bed Moisey had made for him.

Or had Twila made it?

She hated not remembering things that had happened eons ago, but she hated losing new memories even more. Names and dates and places slipped in and out of her mind, a confusing jumble of information that took an extraordinary effort to organize.

Many days she felt too tired to try.

As a matter of fact, if it weren't for the kids, she wouldn't try. She'd watch mindless television or play mindless games on her phone. Maybe she'd sit on the porch and stare at the world as morning turned to afternoon and then to evening.

She wouldn't make lists, that was for sure.

Of dates and events and names and activities. She wouldn't write details of the stories Moisey told or the books Twila explained. She wouldn't scribble down the titles of songs Heavenly sang or snap photos of her shoe and clothes sizes.

She wouldn't count the heart-shaped rocks Maddox had continued to bring her. Seven to date.

She wouldn't remind herself every morning that Milo had been chosen for swim team or that Moisey had been invited to a special dance camp.

If it weren't for the kids, she'd stop struggling so hard. She'd accept her limitations more gracefully and with less dismay.

Because it wouldn't matter if she forgot things.

It wouldn't matter if entire weeks went by without her saying a word or putting together a coherent phrase.

There'd be no expectations and no one to care if she failed.

There were days when that sounded terrible.

There were other days when she thought it wouldn't be so bad. When the kids were grown and off living their own lives, and she was left alone. She didn't think she'd cry for what she missed, but she hoped she'd remember enough to know what it was.

She sniffed, and Rembrandt licked her face, his tail thumping rhythmically. He still had puppy breath and velvety fur, but he had a good nose and a keen desire to work. Yesterday, the kids had played hide-and-seek in the yard, and they'd included the puppy. He'd found each of them easily, nose to the ground and tail high, prancing along happily.

Jolly . . .

No. Jaunty.

That was the word of the day. Twila had written it on Sunday's palm, tracing each letter three times with her finger when she was done, because a therapist had told her that tactile involvement helped memories form.

"She's a good girl, isn't she, Rembrandt? Smart, too."

Thump, thump, thump went his tail in response.

"And you're smart. You're going to make a great . . ."

What?

The kids had told her something about Flynn training Rembrandt for a job. Not hunting. It wouldn't be that.

She closed her eyes, trying to picture the conversation, the faces of her children when they'd been speaking to her.

She saw nothing but black laced with squiggly lines. No faces. No kids. No words floating toward her.

"Dear Lord, I hate this so much," she muttered, frustrated and not sure why. She dealt with it every day. She'd continue to deal with it for the rest of her life.

She knew the drill.

If she wanted to remember, she needed to go

through the notes she'd taken, read every page until she found what she was looking for.

She switched on the light, pulled out the notebook she kept in her nightstand. There was another one in the living room, tucked in a coffee table drawer. A third one was in the kitchen drawer closest to the back door. There was one in the glove compartment of the van. One in her purse. She liked to have one available wherever she went, because if she didn't write things down, she forgot. She'd disappointed her kids one too many times. Forgotten shopping trips. Forgotten church events. Forgotten playdates.

Thank God for Rosie. She kept on top of the schedule, made sure the kids didn't miss out.

Without her . . .

There would be a lot of hurt feelings and tears. Sunday's and the kids.

She opened the notebook to the last page, skimming paragraph after paragraph, trying to find the correct information, because not knowing was bugging the heck out of her. She'd been the regional spelling bee champ three years in a row, for God's sake. She'd memorized the first seventy digits of pi during her senior year of high school. She'd recited the Gettysburg Address and "I Have a Dream," and at least a dozen other speeches whose titles she could no longer remember.

She'd had a great memory.

One that had served her well.

She wished she hadn't taken that for granted.

She wished she'd known how wonderful and miraculous it was to be able to store facts and then retrieve them, how complicated the process of recall really was, and how easily it could all change. How quickly a person could go from remembering to forgetting.

She flipped through a few more pages, but the information she was looking for didn't jump out at her. Not surprising. Her writing, since the accident, was atrocious, the letters shaky and misshapen. She'd regained much of her fine motor control, but not all of it, and it showed. Skimming through nearly illegible writing wasn't going to work. She'd have to read carefully, pick through the letters, and try to make sense of them.

But not tonight.

She tossed the notebook on the floor, wincing as it bounced and then skittered across the wood. It was past midnight. The house had been quiet for a while, the kids tucked into bed, Rosie sleeping.

And Flynn . . .

Flynn who was becoming a problem, because he saw too much and asked too many questions. She climbed out of bed and grabbed the notebook, knowing exactly where she could find the next bit of information she wanted. The page was dog-eared, the words underlined.

You were in the thick of things while he was off

doing God knows what in Portland and Seattle.

She'd silently chanted those words all the way from the garage into the house and up the stairs to her room. She'd written them down, because she hadn't wanted to forget. Flynn knew the truth. Or suspected it.

At least, he seemed to.

She hadn't asked.

She'd been too surprised. As far as she remembered—which, she'd admit, wasn't always very far—no one had ever questioned Matt's business trips. Even she hadn't until those last few months.

She walked to the end of the bed, Rembrandt beside her, the old floor creaking, the house settling, the night still and silent around them.

An old quilt lay across the top of the hope chest, and she tossed it on the floor. A hundred years ago, her great-great-grandfather had made the chest for his daughter, hand carving a dove, a heart, and a cross on the top and a wreath of flowers on the front. She ran her hand over the satiny wood, imagining the hours he'd spent, the dedication it had taken.

She could remember her mother telling her the story, could almost see her hand tracing the carved heart, the dove, the cross.

She opened the lid, lifted out stacks of folded blankets and quilts, and pulled out a large leather-bound journal. A date had been written across the front. Calligraphy-style. Or her version of it—

swirly open letters that seemed to skip across the leather.

"Better days, huh, Rembrandt? When I could control a calligraphy pen well enough to make a go at fancy writing."

He was too busy peering into the chest to pay attention to what she was saying.

"What? Not interesting enough for you? Come on. Let's close the lid." She patted the floor, but he was having none of it. Like any intelligent puppy, he was curious. Currently, his curiosity was focused on the chest and the stacks of journals inside it.

"Okay, buddy. Really. You need to move." She set the journal she planned to read on the bed, then lifted the puppy. He wasn't light, and she nearly dropped him before she managed to set him down a few feet away.

She grabbed the stack of blankets, was lowering them into the hope chest, when Rembrandt jumped on the bed and grabbed the journal. His tail wagged a high fluffy salute of pure joy.

Game time.

She knew this one. He loved grabbing unattended pens and books and pencils and racing through the house with them while the kids gave chase.

Fortunately, her door was closed.

There was no escape, and she figured she'd be able to snatch the journal back before he tore it to pieces like he had two of Twila's library books.

Three?

Twila had told her.

Or maybe she'd just heard her telling someone else.

"Focus!" she muttered, because Rembrandt was backing away, puppy body vibrating with excitement. Remembering how many of Twila's books he'd eaten wasn't nearly as important as getting the journal back.

"Drop it!" she commanded.

He smiled. She was dang sure of it. His dark eyes gleamed with happiness. His tail thumped the mattress and the cotton sheets.

"This is not the time for games, pup." She eased closer, and he ran, leaping off the bed, scrambling across the floor, paws clawing hardwood as he tried to get purchase.

She followed, grabbing for his furry nape and missing. Of course. Because he was young and fast, and she was old and damaged. At least, she felt old. Nearly thirty should be the prime of a life. The coming decade should be the one where she found her groove, felt the most beautiful, the most vibrant, the most alive. Beatrice had talked about it when they went to buy puppy supplies. About how exciting it was that they'd both be turning thirty. And something about a party or a celebration.

She didn't remember.

She hadn't written it down.

She didn't want a party or celebration.

She wanted life back the way it had been.

"This is not the time," she reminded herself, dropping to the floor as Rembrandt dashed beneath the bed.

She tried again to grab him. God knew, she did. But her sluggish brain fired commands that her body didn't seem to recognize. The dog was under the bed, tearing at the pages, and she was lying prone, arms stretched uselessly in front of her.

She lifted the dust ruffle, peered under the bed.

And there he was, the corner of the journal between his puppy teeth, chewing happily.

"Rembrandt, let's be reasonable about this."

His tail thumped, stirring up a cloud of dust.

"Darn it, Rembrandt! That's not a toy."

He glanced her way, thumped his tail, and kept chewing.

"Rembrandt!" she hissed, reaching under the bed, her fingers grazing the edge of the journal.

He scooted away, the leather still between his teeth, tail thumping wildly in joy at the fun new game they were playing.

Only it wasn't a game.

She needed that journal. She'd made entries up until the night before the accident.

She shimmied under the bed. Head. Shoulders.

A page tore. Rembrandt's tail swished as he moved to the far wall. She'd have to move the entire bed to reach him.

"Why in God's name did anyone think a bed this size was a good idea?" she muttered, trying to shove her body closer to the dog. Her shoulders were pinned between the floor and the box spring. She needed a Moisey-sized human to get farther under the four-poster bed.

"Dog, really," she said. "I don't like this game."

He grinned, his tongue lolling out, the journal under his front paws. At least he'd stopped chewing on the cover and ripping out pages.

Someone knocked on the door, but she was afraid to take her eyes off Rembrandt.

She needed that journal.

"Come in," she called, expecting Rosie or one of the children to walk in and give her a hand.

Boots tapped the floor, and she knew—knew!—that Flynn was there.

The guy who'd hinted at a truth she never planned to share.

The man she'd been avoiding for two weeks.

Was. In. Her. Room.

She tried to scramble out from under the bed, but she moved too quickly, raising her head before it cleared the frame, slamming it so hard she saw stars.

She lay stunned, face to the dust-coated floor, palms pressed to the floor.

"You okay?" Flynn asked, dropping down beside her. She turned her head, realized they were now eye to eye.

He'd shaved recently, and there was just a hint of stubble on his face.

"The dog has my journal, but it's nothing I can't handle."

"Okay," he replied, looking into her eyes, studying her face, asking silent questions she had no intention of answering. Not even if he spoke them out loud.

"Really. I can manage. He just wants to play."

"It's not a game if someone gets hurt." He touched her shoulder, and she realized she'd scraped it on the box spring or frame. She also realized she was wearing a Moisey-sized tank—small and tight, clinging to her skinny frame and showing off the deep scar between her breasts, the one on her shoulder. The many small white scars that crisscrossed her arms.

She sat up, grabbing the old quilt and tossing it around her shoulders, pulling it tight around her chest.

"I've seen the scars," he commented. "On many occasions."

"Not since I've been out of the hospital," she replied. As if that mattered. As if that made her actions any less ridiculous. He was Matt's brother, for goodness' sake! Not some random guy she'd met in a bar.

She almost laughed at the thought.

She'd never been to a bar.

She'd never been to a club.

She'd been the good kid doing good things making good decisions.

But karma wasn't all it was cracked up to be, and sometimes God sat on His throne, watching while okay people had crappy, horrible things happen to them.

Because that allowed for learning and growth and all kinds of wonderful things to come.

How many times had she been told that since the accident?

So many, she didn't have to open a journal to be reminded. She didn't have to grab a notebook and thumb through the pages to remember.

She knew the platitudes.

What she wanted was the truth. Some mystical, mysterious balance of the scales that proved that bad things happened to good people, but that, in the end, it all worked out. Because goodness mattered, kindness mattered, love mattered, and throwing those things out into the world really did bring them back to you.

"I've seen them after that, Sunday," he said gently. "You wore a sleeveless dress to church last week, remember?"

"No." She spit the word out, and she tasted the bitterness on her tongue, felt it in her soul.

She hated that as much as she hated her muddled thoughts and missing memories.

"Heavenly bought it for you when she went out to shop for her choir dress. Rumer helped her pick it. They put it in a gift bag the color of your eyes. Moisey said it was blue. Heavenly said it wasn't. And I—"

"Said it was the color of bluebonnets at sunset," she said, the memory suddenly back. She'd been sitting in the easy chair, holding a dress she felt too old to wear—an ivory sundress with tiny blue flowers on the hem and bodice. The girls had been bickering about the color of the gift bag. She hadn't been listening, she didn't think. Not until Flynn spoke.

He'd been standing in the doorway, dusty cowboy boots and jeans, sweat rolling down his temples. It had been hot that day. Wretchedly so.

"You remember." He stood, pulled her to her feet, his palm calloused, his skin warm. When the quilt dropped to the floor, she let it stay there.

Because he was right. He'd seen her scars. He knew their cause, and there was no sense hiding them.

"Some of it." She turned her attention to the bed, because she couldn't look in his eyes and face. She didn't want to think about that moment in the living room, the way he'd stood in the doorway, and he'd seemed to fit in a way Matt never had. His clothes. His hair. The sweat sliding down his face. The dust and rough hands and gritty, parched voice.

God!

What the heck was wrong with her!

Of course, Matt had fit! This had been his house. His home. Their home.

"Rembrandt," she called a little too sharply. "Come out of there."

"Want me to try?" Flynn asked. He'd taken a step away, was staring at the photos displayed on the dresser. So many photos of family. The kids. Matt. Her parents.

"Sure."

"Front!" he commanded, and the puppy appeared.

He trotted to Flynn, sat in front of him. Maybe six inches from his feet.

Smiling. Darn the little beast.

"How did you do that?" she asked.

"We've been working basic obedience. He's smart, and he likes to work. Down," he said, and Rembrandt dropped to his belly. "Stay."

Flynn stepped to the foot of the bed, lifted the heavy wood frame just enough to pull it away from the wall, then reached in and scooped up the journal and a few torn pages. "Here you are."

She took them, placed the pages inside the journal while he moved the bed back into place. He was still wearing work clothes—a faded denim shirt, rolled up at the sleeves. Dark jeans and cowboy boots. No hat, but she could see where it had been sitting, his hair matted down from it.

"Did you just get back from the fields?" she asked, and he shook his head.

"I made a trip to Palouse today. There's a guy there retiring a couple of broodmares. Good stock and gentle. Both are five. He's also got one of their fillies for sale. She's a firecracker, and needs a firm hand, but I think, eventually, Heavenly will be able to handle her."

"Heavenly went?" she said, suddenly sad for what she'd missed out on while she was hiding from him.

"No. I didn't want to get her excited and then disappoint her."

"So did you bring them home?"

He raised a dark eyebrow, shook his head. "It's your decision to make. I'd have brought you with me, but you've been . . . occupied."

"That's a nice way of pointing out that I've been spending a lot of time in my room."

"I think the word you're looking for is *hiding,*" he replied, taking the journal from her hands and eyeing the gnawed edges. "It's not a complete loss. I can have someone rebind it, put on a whole new cover."

"It's not the cover that matters. It's what's inside it." She touched the edge of a torn page, her fingers brushing his. A quick, light touch that she hadn't intended, but her heart thumped crazily at the contact, and she pulled her hand away.

"You find your memories inside, right?" He lifted the hope chest lid and set the journal on top of the quilts. She didn't ask how he knew it belonged there. She assumed he and his brothers had gone through the room, looking for important documents. Life insurance. Bank account information.

"Yes."

"Maybe it's time to start looking somewhere else."

"I keep notebooks."

"And you're so busy filling those up, you're letting the moments slip through your fingers."

"What's that supposed to mean?"

"It's just an observation. Emmerson used to say that a smart man knows the trees from the forest. Make sure you don't miss out on one for the sake of the other. That's all I'm saying." He smiled to take any sting out of the words, but they had stung, because he was right.

She spent a lot of time collecting memories, because she was so darn afraid to lose them.

But she couldn't remember if she'd spoken to Heavenly that morning, if she'd asked about the state choir event that was looming.

An audition, maybe. Or a competition.

And that was why she didn't ask, because she was afraid to get it wrong, to make her children think she didn't care enough, or pay attention enough to remember.

"I've upset you," he said, nudging her chin up with a finger, forcing her to look into his eyes.

"Sometimes, the truth hurts. I'd still rather have that than a bunch of pretty lies."

"In that case, we should get along just fine."

"We do get along. Don't we?"

"We haven't been running in the same circles these past few days, but . . ." He stopped, as if he'd thought better of what he planned to say, and shook his head.

"What?" she prodded, because, of course, now she really wanted to know.

"Nothing we need to worry about right now."

"But we're going to have to worry about it later?"

"Not worry. Just . . . make some adjustments."

"What kind of adjustments?"

"Sunday, now isn't the time. And it's not my information to share. I shouldn't have brought it up."

"But you did," she pointed out, taking a step closer. She had to crane her neck to look into his eyes, but she did it. "What's going on?"

"You know Clementine and Porter are getting married in the fall?"

"Yes."

"They're planning an early October wedding. Right as the pumpkins are ripening and the cornfields are golden-yellow. Outdoors. At sunset. When the air is just beginning to chill, and the sky has a blue velvet sheen."

"You have a way with words, Flynn," she

murmured, caught up in the story he was weaving, the picture he was painting. Thinking that he was all the qualities of his brothers rolled into one person. Porter's toughness. Sullivan's artistry. Matt's flare for words.

"I'm Porter's best man."

"That's wonderful."

"And you're Clementine's."

"Her what?"

"Whatever the female version of a best man is," he replied, and she felt her heart sink, her stomach drop, her entire being shout *no!*

"I can't do that."

"Of course you can."

"It's impossible. There's no way," she said, panicked, frantic, because she most certainly could not. She could barely remember what day it was. She couldn't remember to eat breakfast if someone didn't remind her. God help her! She'd forget her name if she hadn't been hearing it her entire life.

There was no way . . .

No way. Ever.

That she could help Clementine with her wedding.

"Landing on the moon was impossible. Until it was done. Wireless technology? Impossible until someone figured it out," he responded, cupping her shoulders, seemingly trying to will his calm into her. "The nuclear bomb? Impossible. Electric lights? Impossible. But here we are. Standing under a light bulb in a world that has been shaped by the threat of nuclear war."

"What's your point, Flynn?" she asked, her heart thudding painfully, her entire body cold with the thought of failing Clementine.

"That nothing is impossible once it's done." He turned her around, and she was facing the bed and the entire wall of folksy quotes that she'd hung. Painted on old boards. Written in calligraphy or print or fat happy letters.

"Look," he said, one hand on her shoulder, the other pointing to a long green board, ivory letters strutting across its surface. *Nothing is impossible. The very word says I'm possible.*

"That is the stupidest, corniest thing I've ever had the misfortunate of reading," she said, but she was laughing.

"You're the one who hung it on the wall," he pointed out. She could feel the words rumbling through his chest, and she realized she was leaning into him, her back pressed to soft denim.

"How do you know Matt didn't?" she asked, suddenly very conscious of the hand still on her shoulder. The long fingers splayed against her collarbone. The way his breath ruffled her hair and made goose bumps rise on her arms.

"It looks like a job that took a while. He didn't stick to tasks for very long."

True.

So true, all her amusement fell away.

"Sunday?" someone said, and she jumped away from Flynn's hand, swinging toward the door so quickly, she fell sideways.

Flynn caught her, his arm hooked around her waist, his gaze on the doorway

On Heavenly.

She was standing on the threshold, hair brushed away from her face, skin clean of makeup, a long nightgown trailing the floor.

She looked young and soft. Sweet in a way she never was during the day.

"What's going on?" she demanded, stepping into the room, her gaze shifting from Sunday to Flynn and back again.

"Rembrandt," Sunday said quickly. "He stole one of my journals. Flynn came to help."

"Where's the journal?" Heavenly asked suspiciously, her gaze on Flynn again, her eyes blazing.

"In the hope chest." Sunday planned to open it, remove the journal, and prove her story, but Flynn still had his arm around her waist, and when she tried to move, he tugged her back.

"I don't think you need to prove yourself to your thirteen-year-old daughter," he said, and Heavenly scowled.

"She's not the one I want proof from. You're the one who isn't where he belongs."

"Heavenly! Watch your tone when you're speaking to your uncle," Sunday chided.

"He'd speak to my boyfriend in the same tone, if he found him in my room in the middle of the night."

"You have a boyfriend?" she and Flynn said in unison.

Heavenly's scowl deepened. "No. But I would if Sullivan hadn't been such a butt about it and gone over to Andrew's house and told his parents that we had a thing going."

"When did this happen?" Sunday asked.

"While you were in the hospital."

"You were twelve!"

"Now I'm thirteen."

"And you're still too young for a boyfriend," Sunday said, panicking again. This time for good reason.

Thirteen was young. It was hormones. It was poor decisions made in the heat of the moment.

Thirteen was not a good age to be dating.

"I agree," Flynn chimed in, apparently immune to the death-ray glare Heavenly was shooting in his direction. "But you're not too young for a horse. As a matter of fact, thirteen is the perfect age to take on the responsibility."

Heavenly's mouth dropped open.

Sunday's did too.

She closed it quickly, because that was what the fenced pasture was for. The one Flynn and the kids had been working on for two weeks. It's what Flynn's trip to Palouse had been about. It was the thing she could have stopped if she'd wanted to. She hadn't. She'd let the plans move forward. She'd let the fence be built while she hid in her room because she hadn't wanted to be asked the question again.

The one about Matt and his business trips.

She'd been missing out for the sake of a man who wasn't around to appreciate it.

And now horses were in the plans, and there wasn't a thing she could do about it without looking like an ogre.

Plus, if a horse could replace a boyfriend in Heavenly's world, who was Sunday to say it shouldn't happen?

"You look surprised, Heavenly," Flynn said, speaking into the sudden silence.

"Sunday said horses would have to wait until the end of the school year."

"I did?" Sunday asked, her muscles tense, her narrow waist taut beneath his hand. He let his arm drop, stepping away, because having his arm around her had felt a little too good and a little too right.

"Yes. We were talking about the county junior choir, and how if I got in, I wouldn't have time for things like horses."

Sunday frowned. "If that's what I said . . ."

"You didn't say it. Exactly. You said that you didn't want my grades to fall because I was traveling forty minutes twice a week to go to choir rehearsal, and then you said that probably that was all I should do this year. No other extra activities like sports or horse riding."

"It seems like reasonable advice," Flynn said, but Sunday shook her head.

"Not really. Heavenly is a straight A student. She doesn't need to be reminded to keep her grades up. I'm sorry, honey, if I upset you." She reached for the teen, offering one of the bear hugs that Flynn had observed so many times before the accident.

The kind that enveloped the whole person. The kind that involved arms and hearts and souls.

"I wasn't upset. I just figured we'd have to wait." Heavenly allowed herself to be hugged for a few more seconds than Flynn would have predicted, and then stepped away, sliding her hands over Sunday's flyaway hair like she was the mother and Sunday the child. "You've got crazy hair again."

"That happens a lot since the accident," Sunday said with a quiet chuckle. "And it'll happen more if I manage to get myself up on one of the horses."

"You're serious? About the horses?"

"Sure. Horses are a big part of growing up on a farm. At least, they were when I was a kid. We couldn't have them after your grandparents died. They're expensive and do require a lot of attention and work." Sunday smiled, but there was a brittle edge to her voice, an unspoken thought that didn't make her happy.

"So you're really, really serious. We're going to get a horse?" Heavenly repeated, not even a hint of enthusiasm in her tone.

Flynn could see it in her eyes, though. Flickering in the depth of her gaze. Pulsing there in an insistent beat that would have burst out of a kid like Moisey.

Heavenly had more control.

Maybe too much control.

Her emotions in check, her I-don't-care persona fully and rigidly in place. Unless she was chasing her siblings around, yelling at them for whatever crime they'd committed against her. Then there seemed to be no control. Just rage and an overwhelming desire for retribution.

"That's what I'm saying," Sunday confirmed, meeting Flynn's eyes. "Your uncle went to . . ." She frowned, her brows knit together, her frustration obvious. She didn't wait for him to fill in the blank, though. "He went and looked at some mares today."

"Were they great? Were they?" Heavenly asked, enthusiasm and excitement finally breaking free of her iron control. She was bouncing on the balls of her feet, nearly bursting with energy. "What color? Brown? I don't mind plain old brown mares. They're lovely. Or black? Black horses are cool."

"One is gray with a white star on her head. One is rust."

"Red? One of them is red?" Heavenly nearly squealed, grabbing Sunday's arm. "Did you hear that, Mom? Did you?"

The fact that she'd been called *Mom* by a girl who continually insisted on calling her by her first name wasn't lost on Sunday. She swallowed hard, and Flynn thought she might be forcing back tears. "They sound wonderful. They really do, sweetheart."

"Were they, Uncle Flynn? I mean, it's not just about the way they look. I know that." She was trying to rein in her enthusiasm, but wasn't having much success. Her entire body was moving, bouncing, filled with energy and excitement.

"I thought so, but I want you and your mom to meet them before any final decisions can be made."

"Now?" Heavenly lifted the hem of her nightgown and let it fall. "I just need a sec to get changed. I won't even put on makeup. I'll be quick. Don't leave without me."

She darted for the door, and he caught her arm, pulling her up short.

She stiffened.

That was Heavenly, guarded, careful. Always needing personal space. Especially from the men in her life.

He knew that. Had known it from the first day they'd met. She'd been tense around Sunday, but she'd been nearly catatonic with Matt and Flynn. Silent. Still. Not willing to answer questions, to eat, to relax.

He'd kept his distance then, and he kept it now. Releasing her arm and stepping back. "It's after midnight, Heavenly. We can't go look at horses."

"Oh. Right. I forgot. Tomorrow, then?"

He met Sunday's eyes, and she nodded.

"Sure. I'll call the guy who owns them first thing in the morning and see if he has the time."

"What if he's already given them to someone? What if they're already gone?" Heavenly asked, and Sunday hugged her again.

"Then your uncle will help us find other horses. Now, go on to bed. You're going to have a long day tomorrow if you go with your uncle."

"Right. Like I'll be able to sleep!" Heavenly grumbled, but she hurried off, the bounce still in her steps.

"I really appreciate this, Flynn," Sunday said, turning to face him. Those scars she'd tried to hide, dark pink and purple. The trach scar in the hollow of her throat. The one that slid from the top of her sternum down her abdomen. She'd had a lot of internal bleeding.

So much, she'd coded twice before the ambulance arrived at the hospital.

But she was standing there now. On her own two feet. Maybe not completely whole, but not completely broken, either.

“Appreciate what? Me finding a couple of mares your family might enjoy?”

“You taking the time to bring Heavenly to look at them. I don’t remember ever seeing her this excited. Not that I have a lot of memories of her.” She smiled, but there was a hint of regret in her eyes.

“I’m taking Heavenly and you to look at the horses,” he corrected.

Her smile fell away.

“I can’t go to Portland.”

“Palouse,” he corrected.

“Same difference,” she argued.

“How? We’re talking an hour-long trip compared to a five-and-a-half-hour one.”

“It’ll still take a half day. I can’t be away from the kids for that long.” She tossed the words out and then crouched to pet the dog. Maybe hoping Flynn would buy her excuse and leave her alone.

Wasn’t going to happen.

“You were away from them for months, Sunday. They all survived.”

“And look how much I missed out on. Heavenly had a boyfriend,” she whispered, finally meeting his eyes. “Do you realize what a disaster that could have been?”

“If it’s Heavenly you’re worried about, you’ll

be spending half a day with her. Plenty of time to hash out all the rules of engagement when it comes to relationships with boys."

"Flynn," she began, but he was tired. He'd spent the last couple of days working with a group of townspeople to fence the back pasture and build a corral. The sun had been blazing hot, the days dry, and he'd returned every night, bone-tired and parched.

He loved getting things done, but he was working full-out during the heat of late summer, and he felt it. In his arms, his shoulders, his back. He'd had a headache for three days running. A thirst that no amount of water seemed to be able to quench. But there was still work to do. The barn needed an overhaul. The fields needed to be plowed and planted with field grass and alfalfa. He and the kids had cut irrigation ditches into the sunbaked earth, but he wanted to dig a well, too. Put in a livestock watering system that would catch rain and feed it into a trough.

He had six months of work to do before he returned to the ranch. And less than two months to do it. The wedding was in October. He planned to return to Texas the first week of November. Time was ticking away, and he didn't plan to waste it explaining a simple concept to a very intelligent woman.

He also didn't want to waste valuable minutes listening to Sunday's excuses. He didn't want to discuss things, reason them through, try to convince her of anything.

If she didn't understand that her daughter needed her, Flynn wasn't going to spend time and energy explaining it.

But, of course, she did understand.

And that pissed him off.

Royally.

"You don't want to come, don't come. But don't make up a bunch of excuses, okay? Just be honest. Say you don't feel like it, or you're too worn out, or you don't care enough," he said.

"Of course I care enough!" she countered.

"Tell you what. Let's withhold judgment on that for a few years? We'll see what Heavenly has to say when she tells her kids the story of getting her first horse."

"What's that supposed to mean?" she demanded, getting to her feet. Too quickly.

The color drained from her face, and he almost grabbed her arm, held her up, because he was afraid she was going to pass out again.

But she held on to the wall, shooting him a look that was meant to freeze him in place.

He'd have ignored it, but he'd never made a habit of overshooting boundaries and forcing himself into situations where he wasn't wanted or needed. Plus, she was still on her feet, still shooting daggers in his direction.

"It's not what we tell ourselves or other people

that is important," he said, because she'd asked a question, and he wanted to give her an answer. "It's what our kids say after they've left our home. It's what they say after we're gone. It's the stories they pass down to their kids and to their grandkids that tell the truth about a matter."

"Is that another Emmersonism?" she asked, the irritation seeping from her face and from her eyes. She knew what he was saying, but she'd known before he'd explained.

"It's a Flynnism. Learned from watching my father and listening to him. Funny. No matter what he said to other people about his great and awesome parenting abilities? It didn't change what my brothers and I said to one another, and it didn't change what we told other people when we left the home. It didn't change the truth, Sunday. It never could."

"Flynn, I'm sorry. I—"

"I need to get some sleep. It's been a long couple of weeks, and tomorrow is going to be another long day." He cut her off. "Good night."

That was it.

He was done.

Out of there, because he wasn't going to say more.

He sure as heck wasn't going to pile guilt on the head of a woman who already had too much of it.

He strode to the door, walked into the hall, gave

Rembrandt the command to break from stay, and shut the door.

Quietly.

Gently.

Because he wasn't his father.

And he never would be.

CHAPTER EIGHT

She set the alarm for five a.m. She was awake at four. Digging through her dresser drawers, trying to remember what she used to wear when she rode the old stallion her father had owned.

She settled on jeans, a lightweight button-down shirt that had probably belonged to Matt, and dusty cowboy boots she dug from a box of old shoes that her mother had kept in the closet. Apparently, Sunday hadn't been able to part with them.

Every pair of shoes had held a memory.

Once.

Now they were just shoes. Old and dusty. Worn from years of walking and running and jogging and dancing. She'd throw them out. Eventually.

For now, though, she closed the box, shoved it back into the closet, and walked back across the room, the cowboy boots a little snug but not uncomfortable.

They must have been hers.

Long ago.

When her parents had been alive.

She could see herself in the mirror, ghostly pale and moving with jerky, disjointed steps that had made her cringe when she'd seen herself in a video Twila had uploaded for a project she was working on.

Something to do with the wedding, she'd said

as she'd leaned over her keyboard and clicked the mouse.

Twila hadn't explained what she was creating or how it was connected to the wedding. Sunday didn't even think she'd said whose wedding she was creating it for. She'd assumed it was for Clementine and Porter's, but she hadn't asked.

That seemed to be her pattern lately.

Being there just enough to say she was.

But not enough to matter.

She hadn't written down the words Flynn had spoken before he'd left her room. She hadn't really wanted to remember them. But like Matt's betrayal, she hadn't been able to forget.

She couldn't quote him word for word, but the gist of what he'd been saying was lodged in her heart and in her brain, beating an endless rhythm that she couldn't ignore. No matter how much she wanted to.

She lifted the calendar from her dresser. She thought Twila had bought it for her, but she didn't know. What she knew was that important events were written in boldly colored ink. Pink. Red. Blue. Orange. Yellow. Green. Purple. A key had been drawn in at the bottom of each page, neatly explaining the color system. Pink for Moisey's events. Red for Heavenly's. Purple for Twila.

The calendar had been there for at least two months.

She couldn't remember the day it had arrived.

She couldn't remember who had brought it.

But she'd known it was there.

God! How could she not? It was positioned dead-center in the middle of the dresser, next to the only complete family photo she had. Taken at church, she thought. Probably after Heavenly's adoption was finalized. All the kids were in it. Oya just a tiny baby in Sunday's arms. Matt standing close, his arm circling Sunday's waist, his gaze on the photographer, his smile broad.

Sunday was looking at Heavenly. Smiling as if every dream she'd ever had were coming true.

She'd known, even then, that Matt was cheating. She'd written about it in the journals long before the adoption paperwork was final.

She'd hidden her heartache well.

Either that, or she hadn't felt it.

Maybe she'd grown tired of investing in someone who wasn't always invested in her.

She didn't know, because she couldn't remember.

All she could do was read journal entries and try to piece together the life she'd been living.

She touched the photo, and then the calendar, running her finger over the top page. Every month, someone removed it to reveal the one below.

Not Sunday.

She hadn't touched it since it had been placed there.

She'd barely looked at it, because she hadn't

been expected to attend meetings or go to ball games or take the kids on playdates. Since the accident, there'd always been someone to do that for her. Someone to step into her role and make certain the kids had what they needed.

Only, maybe, what they needed was her.

She turned the page of the calendar, looking ahead to the beginning of the school year, counting the days. Just fifteen before the routine began again. Waking early. Going to bed early. Homework and sports and projects.

Rosie had helped them at the end of the last school year.

And Rumer. Sullivan. Porter.

There'd been a lot of trouble. She'd heard about it from friends and from the kids. Her brothers-in-law hadn't mentioned it. They'd dealt with the twins' antics, Heavenly's attitudes. Moisey's daydreams and drama. They'd taken Twila to the library and all the kids clothes shopping and taught Oya how to walk.

They hadn't complained about the work.

They hadn't mentioned how difficult it was.

They hadn't told her how ill-equipped they were—three childless bachelors suddenly parents to six kids.

They'd done what they had to, and now it was her turn.

To step up. To step in. To make her kids' story one she would be happy to hear in years to come.

But, dear God, she was so scared!

Somehow in the months she'd spent in the hospital and rehab, she'd forgotten how to be a mother. She'd forgotten how to be there the way a parent should. She'd forgotten how to go with the flow and enjoy the ride and be part of something that wasn't just about her and her recovery.

She'd become someone she didn't know and didn't much like and felt helpless to change.

She flicked off the light, tired of looking at the calendar and at herself—that ghostlike reflection in the mirror. That shade of who she'd been.

"You want to know the truth, Matt?" she whispered, sitting on the edge of the bed.

Rembrandt jumped up beside her, curling into a ball with his nose tucked near her thigh.

"I blame you for this," she said.

The words hung there, ineffectual and impotent, incapable of changing anything.

A tear slipped down her cheek, and she brushed it away, as surprised by it as she was by the fact that she was sitting in bed before dawn, talking to a husband who'd have left her if he could have done so without hurting the kids.

She didn't think he'd ever said that.

But she wasn't sure.

She didn't remember ever having an argument with Matt. She didn't remember fighting with him. They'd had an easy, calm relationship that Sunday had been told was the envy of others.

She would rather have fought than been lied to.

All the flowers and the candy and the sweet words? They meant nothing, because she knew he'd been giving the same to other women.

He'd been good to her, sure. But he'd been good to them, too.

That was a truth she couldn't forget. No matter how much she wanted to.

It was also one she couldn't change, so she needed to stop torturing herself with it, pulling it out when the house was quiet and studying it as if it could explain everything that had happened in her life.

This was where she was: a young widow with six kids, a stitched-together body, and a hole-filled mind.

"I blame you for it, Matt. I want you to know that. You did this to me and to us. With your fancy car and fancy stuff and all your big dreams that you pretended didn't matter. They must have mattered. If they hadn't, you wouldn't have been wining and dining other women while I ate boxed mac and cheese with the kids. Really, when all is said and done, you were a lying, cheating bastard who cared more about what he wanted than what he had."

Saying it didn't make her feel better.

It didn't make her feel worse.

It just was . . .

Something she'd thought too many times

for too many months. Something she'd had to breathe into the air and release into the cosmos.

The truth didn't change from lack of speaking it.

If her marriage had taught her nothing else, it had taught her that.

"But I did love you," she whispered. "I did, and maybe we could have made it work. If we'd both wanted it enough."

A floorboard creaked outside the door, and she tensed, waiting for one of the children to knock. Instead, she heard the soft clatter of something skittering across the floor.

Whatever it was, Rembrandt didn't seem perturbed. He snored softly as she crossed the room and yanked open the door.

She expected to see one of the twins scurrying away. Perhaps running from some prank he was trying to play.

The hall nightlight gleamed soft yellow, illuminating closed doors and the silent corridor. She stepped across the threshold, her toe kicking something. A small rock. Shaped like a heart. Black and glossy. Onyx maybe.

She had no idea where Maddox would have found a stone like this one, but she tucked it in her pocket and walked to his room, knocking softly before she opened the door. The boys shared bunkbeds. Maddox on the top, Milo on the bottom.

Tonight, they were both on the floor, lying inside a fort they'd constructed out of sheets and chairs. She knew they were asleep the way a mother always knows, and she retreated, closing the door quietly behind her.

She checked the other rooms, making sure no one was up and wandering the house. Or worse, outside finding trouble.

Moisey had fallen asleep sitting up, a tiara on her head. Twila had a book beside her bed and one near her pillow.

Oya lay with her butt to the air, her thumb in her mouth, and Sunday resisted the urge to lift her out of the crib, hold her close, try to memorize the way it felt to hold a baby in her arms.

She didn't open Heavenly's door.

She knew the teenager was probably awake, texting someone or watching a movie on her phone. Or maybe, like Sunday, she'd scoured her closet for appropriate horse-riding clothes and was sitting on her bed, waiting impatiently for the sun to rise.

One way or another, she wasn't walking around in the hall, dropping heart-shaped stones.

A cold nose nudged her hand, and she jumped a foot, her heart skipping crazily as she looked down into Rembrandt's furry face.

"You scared me," she whispered, not sure why she was so jumpy.

Certainly not because of the rock.

What had Moisey called her brother's heart-shaped finds?

Hugs from God?

Kisses from God?

Neither sounded right, so Sunday grabbed Rembrandt's leash and led him down the back stairs and into the kitchen. She took the notebook from the drawer, moving as quietly as she could, because Flynn was in the living room.

When she stepped onto the back porch, the security light came on, and she thumbed through her notebook as she walked down the stairs.

There! She found the entry, the words she was looking for circled several times.

Kisses from heaven.

As if Matt might blow a kiss down to earth and that kiss may land in pebble form: heart-shaped and beautiful.

If only life could be so sweet and simple.

She let Rembrandt lead her to the edge of the yard, through the flowerbeds and around the house. He took sniffing seriously, and she let him explore, her mind filled with Moisey's words, the small rock pressing against her thigh as she walked, reminding her that it was there.

The morning was chilly, the air crisp and cold. Fall would be there soon.

School.

How many days away?

She closed her eyes, trying to see the calendar.

She couldn't, but she managed to remember the days. Fifteen.

And the kids would be up at dawn, bickering over boxes of cereal and bottles of chocolate milk. Saturdays had been for pancakes, eggs, and bacon or sausage.

Funny how she suddenly remembered that, and remembering made her want to do what she'd done so many times before—whip up a batch of pancakes, scramble some eggs, fry some bacon.

The kids would enjoy that.

Even on a non-weekend day.

But, of course, she hadn't cooked anything since the accident. She couldn't remember recipes, and multitasking was nearly impossible, so she stayed away from the kitchen and let Rosie handle things there.

It was easier that way.

But maybe not better.

And maybe the kids would rather her try and fail than not try at all.

"Okay, Rembrandt," she said. "That's what we're going to do. We're going to make a nice breakfast, so the kids have full bellies for whatever today brings."

The puppy seemed excited about it.

He dashed up the porch stairs and rushed back inside.

Sunday wasn't nearly as excited.

The kitchen felt foreign, the refrigerator like

a stranger's when she opened it to grab eggs.

And milk.

She needed milk.

And bacon.

Was there any?

She managed to find a package in the meat drawer, and she set it on the counter.

She also needed something.

Flour? And sugar? She needed those for pancakes.

She thought.

She searched the pantry until she found both, doing her best to stay quiet. She didn't want company while she attempted to cook her first meal post-accident.

She just wanted to be left alone.

To focus and concentrate.

Rembrandt tried to nab the bacon, and she caught him by the collar.

"I think you should sleep with Moisey for a while," she said. "She'll like that."

She hefted him into her arms and managed to carry him upstairs. Moisey didn't seem to notice when she set Rembrandt on her bed, and the puppy seemed happy enough to snuggle in close to one of his best friends.

She left them there, closing the door and returning to the kitchen to make pancakes.

Eggs?

She saw them on the counter. Saw the milk.

The bacon. Realized she needed pans. A couple of them.

She opened cupboards until she found them.

She set them on the stove, her heart beating a little too fast and a little too hard.

She was scared, for crying out loud!

Afraid to turn on the gas burners.

Something she knew she'd done hundreds of times before.

Probably thousands.

"You can do this," she told herself, turning the knob and watching as blue flames shot out.

"Okay. That was easy. Now . . ."

What?

Bacon first?

Pancakes?

Eggs?

Why was this so hard?

That's what she wanted to know. It was all she wanted to know.

That and what to do first. Mix the pancakes or the eggs or cook the bacon.

She had to do something. Flames were leaping out from under the cast-iron pan, lapping at the handle.

She turned down the heat, grabbed the bacon, and cut open the package, laying slabs of bacon across the hot pan and listening as they sizzled.

Then she grabbed the eggs and cracked them into a mixing bowl, her hands shaking as if she were performing a piano sonata in front of an audience without ever taking a lesson.

"You have done this before," she reminded herself as she dug through a drawer and looked for a whisk.

The bacon was sizzling. Maybe burning. She abandoned the drawer and the search, raced to the pan, was relieved that the bacon wasn't scorched.

She had nothing to turn it with though.

She ran to the drawer again, grabbing a fork and using it to flip the bacon.

Now what?

She whirled around, went back to the eggs and used the fork to scramble them.

She could do this.

She could.

She hoped.

She was wearing cowboy boots, threadbare jeans, and an oversize button-up shirt secured at the waist with hair ties. The ends of it jutted out at her side, jumping and bouncing as she worked. A sliver of creamy flesh was visible above the waistband of her jeans, and he could see her shoulder blades jutting against her shirt as she measured flour and sugar and poured them into a dark red bowl.

Her hands were shaking.

He could see that, too, but he couldn't see her face.

She had her back to the doorway, her attention

fixed on a piece of paper lying next to the bowl.

A recipe?

She reached for a bottle of vanilla, struggled with the lid, and finally managed to open it enough to pour some into a teaspoon measure.

She poured over the bowl.

And her hands were shaking.

So, of course, more than a teaspoon of vanilla sloshed into the bowl.

"Darn it," she growled, using a fork to beat the mixture into submission.

"This is going to taste terrible," she continued as she carefully measured out oil and poured it into the bowl.

"I don't know about that," he responded, finally deciding to step in. Not because she needed help with whatever she was making but because there was bacon on the stove, and he could smell it burning.

She swung around, the fork in her hand, batter flying across the room and splattering his T-shirt.

"Oh my gosh, Flynn! I'm sorry!" She grabbed a rag and rushed toward him, rubbing at the spots, her head bent so close to his chest, he could feel the silky strands of hair brushing his neck.

Something shifted in the region of his heart.

That's the only way he could describe the feeling, the way he was thinking about burning bacon one minute and tucking strands of hair behind her ears in the next.

His fingers lingering against velvety skin, as he scanned her face, thought about how different she was from the young woman he'd met at his brother's wedding.

Her wedding.

Their wedding.

That would be a very, very good thing to keep in mind.

He took the rag from her hand and stepped away.

"The bacon's burning," he said, to distract himself as much as to warn her.

"Dang it!" She rushed to the pan, tried to lift crispy bacon with a spoon she grabbed from the draining rack.

The bacon slid off the spoon, splattering grease across the counter and her hand.

She jumped back, her elbow knocking the bowl and nearly upending it.

"This is a disaster," she muttered as she found a fork and tried to remove the bacon again.

He reached around her, turning off the burner before something caught fire.

Like her.

"I should have done that ten minutes ago," she said, sighing as she scooped up shriveled bacon and put it on a plate.

"I'm more worried about your hand than I am about the bacon. Did you burn it?"

She ignored the question, removing the

remainder of the bacon, and setting the frying pan in the sink.

"Sunday?" he prodded. "Your hand?"

"It's fine." There was a hoarseness to her voice that might have been the beginning of tears, but he told himself she was tired or overwhelmed or frustrated, because any of those things would be easier to deal with.

"Let me see." He turned her gently, and he thought again about how much she'd changed from the girl she'd been.

Her hair had darkened from honey to caramel, her freckles spreading from a few dots on her face to dozens on her cheeks and brow. She'd been pretty before, now she was beautiful.

But there was more to it than that.

There was an indefinable quality that spoke of experience and disappointment and pain and triumph.

"I said, it's fine," she repeated, and this time there was no mistaking the tears in her voice.

Or the ones on her face, trailing down her pale cheeks and splashing the front of her shirt.

"What's wrong?" he asked, wiping them away, his hands lingering on her cheeks, holding her still so that he could look into her face.

He wanted the truth.

Not some lie she made up to make them both feel better.

"That," she pointed at the bacon. "That." She

pointed at whatever was in the bowl. "And that."

She pointed at a pile of egg shells.

"All I wanted to do was make them breakfast, and I couldn't even manage that."

"It looks to me like you've got a good start."

"Burned bacon?" she asked, sniffing back more tears and running water into the pan.

"I have it on good authority, that's the best kind."

"From who?"

"The twins. Milo especially loves extra crispy bacon."

"I hope he also loves lumpy pancakes and shells in his scrambled eggs, because that's pretty much what I'm going to be serving."

"Pancakes, huh?" He glanced in the bowl and then at the recipe card.

"It used to be I didn't have to follow a recipe. Everything I needed to know was here." She tapped her head, her finger just missing the edge of the scar that peeked out from the hair near her temple.

"Is that the real reason you're crying? Because you've lost so much?"

"Maybe. Or maybe I'm just tired of everything being so difficult."

"I get that."

"I doubt it. From what I've seen, nothing is ever difficult for you."

"Obviously, you haven't seen much. The day I

started working for Emmerson? It was the worst day of my life."

"Yeah?"

"Yeah." He opened a drawer and pulled out two frilly aprons. He tied one around his waist and the other around hers. It nearly wrapped around her twice, and he made a note to make sure she was eating. Every time he saw her, she seemed smaller. "I was twelve, and I thought I knew a lot."

"Most twelve-year-olds do."

"Maybe, but I think I cornered the market on bigheaded pride. School was easy. I never studied, but I always got As. I thought I understood a heck of a lot more than I did, so I was mouthy and rude, brash and full of myself." He dumped the lumpy batter into the sink and handed her the bowl. "How about you start this again, and I'll tackle the eggs? We can put the bacon in the warmer."

"Warmer?" For a second, she looked confused, and then she glanced at the 1920s stove with its old-fashioned knobs and huge gas burners.

"Right." She opened a small cupboard attached to the stove and put the bacon inside.

"Right?" she asked as if she needed reassurance.

"Right," he agreed, lifting a second bowl, this one filled with eggs, bits of shell bobbing on the surface.

"The thing about Emmerson?" he continued the story. Mostly to distract her. "He didn't like snotty, loudmouthed kids, but he needed help, and I was there. So after I told him I was absolutely prepared to take over his equestrian operation . . ."

"You didn't."

"I did. I had a prepared speech that sang my praises and let him know just how good an employee he was going to get when he hired me."

"When?"

"Like I said, I was cocky with confidence. I finished my speech, and he offered me the job. But instead of going out to the stables and telling me what he wanted done, he said that since I was ready to take over the operation, I could go ahead and do it. He handed me a shovel, put a cowboy hat on my head, and wished me luck."

"And?"

"There may have been tears," he admitted. "Mine and the horses'. I had no idea what they ate. I had no idea whether they were supposed to be in the barn or out of it. I had no idea they were so . . . big or smart or determined to have their way. In an hour, I'd managed to get kicked by an old mare, nipped by Emmerson's donkey, and knocked over by a filly. I was lying in a pile of horse manure, staring up at the sky, when Emmerson finally came out to rescue me."

"What did he say?"

"Boy, it took me seventy-five years to learn this business. Did you really think you could learn it in a day?"

She laughed, the sound light and easy, her movement slow and precise as she measured flour and sugar, added baking soda, and scooped in a handful of oats. "He sounds like a great guy."

"He was. He taught me everything I needed to know to open a cattle operation, and he taught me how to be a man. A real one. The kind that knows how to shoe a horse—"

"And pick shells out of eggs?"

He met her eyes, realized she had been watching him as he strained the eggs through a fine-meshed sieve. "This skill is one I learned myself. My wife wasn't the greatest cook, and sometimes I had to salvage the meal."

"You were married?!" She looked surprised. "I didn't know. Or I've forgotten."

"I was married a year before you and Matt tied the knot and divorced four years after. Patricia and I had different ideas about things, and eventually that put too much of a strain on our relationship."

"What kinds of things did you have different ideas about?" she asked, ladling thick batter on the griddle. It formed a perfect silver-dollar-sized pancake.

"She liked the city. I liked the country. She liked . . . stuff. Cars and purses and matched dishes. I liked crops and cattle and the hot sun on my face."

"Sounds like me and Matt," she said as she flipped the pancake.

"Does it?"

She must have realized what she'd said, because her cheeks went pink, and she shrugged. "A little. He liked things. I liked the farm."

"He wanted more, and you were content?"

"Something like that."

"That was Patricia's fatal flaw, too."

"What?" she asked, putting the perfect golden pancake onto a plate and pouring two more.

"Discontentment. She wanted more than what she thought I could give, so she went out and found what she thought she wanted. For a while, he seemed to make her happy." He wasn't sure why he said it. Maybe he was hoping she'd open up about her relationship with Matt, tell him the truth about the trips to Seattle and Portland, the fine dining and the flowers that had been sent to places other than their home.

He'd seen all those things in their bank records, and he'd kept quiet, because he hadn't wanted to hurt her or the kids by suggesting something that might, or might not, be true.

He'd assumed that Sunday had been in the dark, that she'd had no clue that Matt might be cheating.

Had been cheating.

Flynn knew the signs. Hell, he'd seen them in his marriage.

And ignored them.

For a while.

So he'd known what he was seeing when he'd looked at the bank account and credit card statements. He'd thought that Sunday hadn't realized the truth, because there'd never been a time when he'd visited that she'd hinted at unhappiness, acted hurt, or showed any indication that her marriage was anything but fulfilling.

But she had known.

She still knew.

He'd seen it in her face when he'd mentioned Matt's trips to Seattle and Portland. The fact that she'd gone through extraordinary effort to avoid him in the two weeks since then? Another nail in the coffin of proof.

Yeah. Matt had been cheating.

Sunday had known it.

Maybe they'd gone out to dinner for their anniversary hoping to mend fences and make things right. Maybe Matt had wanted to save his family and his marriage, and he'd thought a nice dinner would be the best way to do it.

Maybe he'd bought her flowers that weren't ordered from the same company he'd used for his side chick, and maybe he'd given her a gift that was worth more than money.

A promise of fidelity.

A sincere apology.

A vow to make things right.

And maybe Sunday had agreed to keep trying, keep working, keep being married. Because she'd loved him, or because she hadn't wanted the kids to have a broken home.

If so, Matt had been damn lucky.

Because if Flynn had been sitting at that table, he'd have told his brother exactly what he could do with his apologies. He'd have reminded him of just how many times their father had offered the same to their mother and to them.

Change required more than words.

It required hard work and soul-searching and sacrifice.

Matt hadn't had a chance to give that a try.

Or maybe he had.

Maybe this had been a pattern with him, and maybe Sunday had been as tired of it as Matt seemed to be of farm life.

Whatever the case, she was keeping her silence, pouring one pancake after another like she'd never forgotten how.

He wasn't going to ask, because Matt was gone. His mistakes were in the past, and Flynn was there to help Sunday find her way back from wherever the accident had taken her.

Nothing more.

That was another thing that would be good to keep in mind.

CHAPTER NINE

The horses were set to be delivered a week later.

Work on the pasture and fencing and barn had been in high gear since Sunday and Heavenly had been introduced to the beautiful mares. Now the fields were quiet, the river lapping against the shore. The sun, just rising above the mountains, drifted in hazy clouds that might bring rain later in the day. The moon hung low above the river, a white-gold orb against the purple sky.

Sunday could see both from her vantage point.

Perched on the top railing of the new fence, her feet planted on a lower railing, she inhaled the crisp scent of late summer and the musty aroma of freshly plowed earth.

"Do you think they'll be here soon?" Twila asked, hip pressed against Sunday's, arm wrapped firmly around her waist. She was afraid that Sunday would fall. So afraid, she'd tried to talk her out of sitting there.

Moisey had been more eager, climbing up beside Sunday and snuggling in close, bubbling up with excitement because she'd been allowed to leave the house before dawn, walk across the footbridge, and sit in the fading moonlight.

"You've asked that a million times, Twila," Moisey said. Like her sister, she had her arm around Sunday. Her grip was lighter, though, her legs swinging happily.

"I have not," Twila responded mildly. "I've asked five times. I've counted, because I don't want to be annoying."

"You aren't ever annoying," Moisey said, and Sunday smiled.

She'd forgotten how close the girls were, how often they defended each other. Despite the three-year age difference, they were friends.

"Heavenly thinks I am."

"Heavenly thinks everyone is annoying," Moisey said, her legs still swinging, her fingers tapping Sunday's side. "Doesn't she, Mom?"

"She's a teenager," Sunday replied. "That's par for the course."

"I bet it wasn't for you. I bet you were nice. I bet you never called people annoying," Moisey exclaimed, jumping off the fence and walking to the hay bale that sat beside it. The twins were there, playing with green army men while they waited for the horses to arrive.

Two mares. A filly. And a donkey.

A pony?

She knew that the owner of the two mares had offered the filly and something else for free after he'd met Heavenly. She could remember that. She remembered the way the gnarled ancient farmer had lit up when he'd seen Heavenly with his horses.

But she couldn't remember what he'd said.

Something about the filly being a good horse for Heavenly in the future and . . .

Another horse being retired and needing a home?

No matter how hard she tried, Sunday couldn't recall the conversation. She just knew she had four names written on her palm. She glanced at it. Just to remind herself.

Whisper.

Early.

Lively.

Chance.

"Those are funny names," Twila said, and Sunday dropped her hand, smiled at her second-oldest daughter.

"They are, aren't they?"

"Do you think Heavenly will want to change them?"

"It's not just Heavenly's decision, sweetheart."

"She's the one waiting at the end of the road with Uncle Flynn to show the trailer driver where to turn. She's the one who already met them."

"Does that upset you?" Sunday asked, trying to step into the role of mother, because she was tired of the role of invalid. She was tired of letting life pass by while she waited for her memory to improve, her movements to become more fluid, things to go back to what they'd been.

It was possible she'd never make breakfast the

way she had prior to the accident—with ease and efficiency, her brain only half-focused on the task, because her muscles knew exactly what to do.

But she *had* made dinner twice since the bacon fiasco, because the kids had been so pleased when they'd come into the kitchen and seen her at the stove. They'd been happy to eat burned bacon and less-than-fluffy pancakes and eggs that had had to be strained through a sieve.

She'd written about it in the journal. The one whose last entry had been the day before the accident. There were more entries in it now. Written in her messy writing, in whatever color pen she happened to find.

She hadn't bothered taping together the pages Rembrandt had torn. She'd simply decided to move on, writing details of her new life as best she could remember them.

And she'd remembered the moment the kids had walked into the kitchen.

She'd remembered their smiles.

She'd wanted to replay that moment a dozen times every day, just so that she could remember what it felt like to make them happy.

"Why would I be upset?" Twila asked.

"Because your sister got to do something that you didn't."

"It would be silly to be upset about that. Heavenly is the oldest."

"Yes, but—"

"And her going to see the horses is just a matter of fact. She wanted a horse. I did not."

"You don't like horses?"

"I never thought about horses."

"And now?"

"It might be fun to ride a horse. Lots of characters in the books I read do," Twila responded, her gaze on the distant mountains and the steel-gray clouds that were beginning to form.

"Do horses like rain?" she asked.

"I'm sure they do."

"Mom, really." Twila shifted, moving her hand from Sunday's waist to her shoulder, looking into her eyes, as serious and as focused as any adult. "Do they? Most animals find shelter when it storms. What will the horses do? They're fenced in."

"They can escape, if they really want to. They can jump fences pretty easily," Sunday assured her. "But if it's storming, they'll go into the barn. Your uncle has the pasture fenced in sections. There are gates that can be opened to allow the horses through. Some on this side of the river, and some on the other. We can open and close gates and bring them closer to home when we want them there."

"Uncle Flynn showed me the way it works," Twila said. "But how will they ever know to do it? This is a new place, and they might not know the way."

"Uncle Flynn will show them. Tonight, he'll bring them across the river and stable them. After that, they'll always know the way back home."

"That's a nice thought, but I'm not like Moisey. I don't believe in fairy tales. I believe in reality. Like the sun coming up, and the moon. Like the tide flowing in. Like the boys getting into trouble, and Heavenly complaining and you . . ."

"What? You can say it. Whatever it is."

"Making eggs with shells in them."

That surprised a laugh out of Sunday. "I'm sorry, honey. I'll try to do better. I know they're not as good as before the accident."

"They're better," Twila said. "Before the accident, there were a lot more shells."

"There were?"

"Sure. But it wasn't your fault. You were busy. Talking on the phone planning things for church or for school or for Dad. Or you were making lists or helping us with homework or trying to get the twins to clean up their messes. Or worrying about the bills. Or paying them. Or wiping down the counter or the table or washing the floor. Now you don't have as much to distract you."

"But . . . you and your siblings talk about my cooking all the time. You're always telling me how wonderful it was and how much you miss it."

"Because it is wonderful, and we do miss it."

"Shells and all?"

"No one cares if there are shells in the eggs. Not when you're the one making them. Look"—she pointed at lights moving toward them—"I bet that's the trailer."

The other kids had noticed too. They were on their feet, watching as the lights drew closer.

"Horses!" Moisey squealed, darting to the fence and climbing up beside Sunday again. "I can't believe the day has finally arrived. All my hopes and dreams are being fulfilled."

"Nah," Maddox said, climbing up beside her and slinging his arm around her neck. "This is Heavenly's dream. Your dreams are all about being a princess."

"Every princess needs a horse," Moisey huffed, but she was smiling.

"She has a point," Milo agreed, climbing onto the lowest rail, his arms dangling over the top of the fence. "A princess needs a horse. So does a hero. How many are coming, Mom?"

Sunday glanced at her palm. Quickly. Just to be certain. "Four, but no one will be riding them today. Probably not tomorrow, either, and definitely not when there isn't an adult around."

"Don't worry. We're not allowed on this side of the river by ourselves," Maddox said as if she didn't know the rule.

"She knows that, silly," Moisey said. "She made the rule."

"No. She didn't. Uncle Sullivan did, remember?

Right after we tried to catch Twila a goldfish for her birthday."

"There aren't goldfish in the river," Sunday said as the words sank in.

The boys. Trying to catch fish near the river.

"You weren't at the river alone, were you?" she asked.

"Yes, they were," Moisey answered. "But don't worry, they got in severe trouble for it. Uncle Sullivan and Rumer weren't happy at all. Look! They're here!" she squealed as the trailer pulled into view.

Flynn had borrowed his brother's truck, and it led the way, the paint gleaming in the early morning light.

Sunday knew Heavenly was in the front seat, Rembrandt beside her. And she knew Flynn was driving, his hands loose on the steering wheel.

She could picture him easily, the perpetual five-o'clock shadow, the tan skin. The dark hair, a little scruffy and a little too long. The fine lines at the corner of his eyes, the tiny white scars on his knuckles and hands from years of hard labor.

In her mind, he was as clear as the sun in the sky, the moon sinking below the horizon. As clear as the distant clouds and the mountains rising from the landscape.

It was Matt she had trouble remembering. The color of his hair and his eyes, the way his mouth curved when he smiled. Every night, she closed her eyes and tried to picture him the way he'd been. On their wedding day. Their first anniversary. On their trip to China to meet Twila or their trip to Haiti for Moisey. She tried to remember the way he'd looked at the courthouse when their adoption of the boys had been finalized. The look in his eyes when Oya had been placed in his arms minutes after she'd been born.

She'd written about all those things. She'd read about them dozens of times.

But Matt's face had still faded from her mind.

His voice.

His laughter.

She wanted to hold on to those things. She did, but they were slipping away, and it seemed like there was nothing she could do about it. No amount of reading journal entries or staring at old photos could bring her the clear, sharp image she wanted.

"Let's go see them," Moisey said enthusiastically, jumping off the fence and sprinting through tender stalks of new field grass.

"Moisey! Wait," Sunday cried, jumping after her.

But, of course, she had a bad leg.

It gave out as she landed, her ankle twisting, her knee caving. She flew forward, landing hard and skidding across grass and dirt.

"Mom!" Twila cried, rushing to her side.

The boys were there too. And Moisey. Thank God.

Horses were beautiful animals, but they could be finicky during moves, nipping, biting, and kicking.

Funny how she remembered that, but she couldn't remember how Matt's voice had sounded when he'd said, "I do."

"Are you crying, Mom?" Moisey asked, her palms pressed to Sunday's cheeks. "Does it hurt so much your tears can't be held back?"

"I'm not crying," she replied. "And it doesn't hurt."

Much.

"How about your pride? Is that hurt?" Twila asked solemnly.

"As a matter of fact, it is. Help your old mom up, will you?" She held out her hand, and all four kids tugged her to her feet.

Brown hands and tan hands and ivory hands.

Dirty fingernails and painted ones.

Scuffed sneakers and shiny patent leather.

Her children. The way they were today. Not the way they'd been in some distant memory.

And this was what she'd wanted all those years ago. When she'd stood in front of most of the town, holding Matt's hands and looking into his eyes. Wearing the dress that had been passed down in her family for three generations. Speaking vows she couldn't remember.

She'd tried to find them, hoping she'd saved them in the box of wedding memorabilia or glued them into the scrapbook that contained pressed flowers from her bouquet. The only thing she'd found was a poem Matt had written. Cheesy and long, filled with rhyming words and metaphors, it had made her smile, but it hadn't said one word about what they had promised each other the day they married.

She knew, of course. She'd been to other weddings, and she'd heard enough vows to know they were all pretty much the same—to love until death, to honor always, to stay faithful.

Tires rolled across grass, the quiet purr of an engine growing louder as the truck approached. White exhaust floated into the purple-gray morning, puffing out into the chilly air. Fall was approaching rapidly. Soon the mountains would be tipped with snow, and the air would be cold with winter. The kids would be back in school, and she'd be puttering around the house trying to help Rosie keep order.

It would be a good life without Matt in it. Just as it had been good while he was there. Despite his infidelity, despite their financial problems, despite all the things that should have been right and weren't, she'd been content with what she'd had.

And that had been enough.

The kids had been enough.

The farm and the blue sky and the predictable way the days had unfolded—one after another in perfect order in time—had been enough.

That she knew, because she still felt it.

When she lay in bed, wide awake, trying to grasp memories that shouldn't matter so much, when she listened to the puppy snoring or the girls giggling when they should be sleeping, or nodded her head to Heavenly's music as it drifted through the walls. When she crept through the hall to peek in on Oya, to make certain the twins were sound asleep. To just run her hand along framed photos of her parents and her grandparents and think about the lives that had played out before hers, she felt the peace of the place, the connection to the past that had always held her there. She felt the opposite of the thing that she'd written in one of her notebooks, the word she scrawled on the inside of her forearm every morning, because as soon as she'd heard Flynn say it, she'd known she didn't want to forget.

Discontentment.

She didn't need to roll up her sleeve and check her memory the way she had a few dozen times before. She remembered the word, but she still wrote it every day, whispered it during her prayers at night, because it was the great destroyer of life and of love. It was the thing that stole people away from homes and families and jobs they were meant to have.

It had taken Matt, years before he'd died.

It had taken Flynn's wife.

And Sunday knew if she wasn't careful, it could take her, too.

The truck parked a hundred yards away, the trailer right behind it, pulled by a large pickup that glowed silver in the rising sun.

Sunday grabbed the back of Moisey's shirt before she could dart toward the vehicles. Somehow managed to snag Milo at the same time.

"You'll wait on the fence, or you'll have to go home," she announced, and the kids dutifully returned to their spots, climbing onto the railing and waiting expectantly as Flynn jumped out of the truck, jogged around the side of it, and opened the door for Heavenly.

She climbed out, all arms and legs and gangly body. Not as graceful as she'd be, but getting there, her long legs covered in denim, a plaid shirt buttoned and hanging down to her hips. No flesh peeking out anywhere. She had a cowboy hat in one hand and Rembrandt in the other, and Sunday's heart stopped at the picture she made—confident and lovely.

Instead of running to the back of the trailer, Heavenly set the puppy down and sprinted toward Sunday, her smile broad and bright. No hint of the taciturn teen she usually presented to the world.

"Come on, Sunday!" she called. "We're going to get the ramp and let them out of the trailer."

"Go ahead, sweetheart," Sunday replied, not wanting to slow things down or put a crimp in the joyful morning.

But Heavenly had already reached her side, slowed her pace, and taken Sunday's hand.

"I still can't believe you let me get a horse," the teen said, walking beside Sunday, still holding her hand. They were nearly the same height now, Heavenly sprouting like a well-tended field of wheat.

She'd have hated the comparison.

"You've earned the right to have a horse," Sunday explained.

"By what? Having a bad attitude and picking on the little kids?"

"Things have been tough since the accident, and you've stepped up and helped out. I know you've given up a lot of time to be here when I couldn't. I appreciate that, Heavenly. I hope you know it. Plus, you don't pick on your siblings. Much."

Heavenly grinned. "Well, I try not to be as much of a bi—witch as I used to be. Sometimes, it's hard."

"And sometimes we get the prize. Just for trying."

"Yeah." Heavenly stopped. They were halfway between the fence and the trailer, halfway between where they'd been and where they needed to be.

Halfway to the horses that Heavenly had been talking about from the first day they'd met.

Had it been three years?

Four?

Halfway to Heavenly's nearly fulfilled dream.

But she stopped, looked into Sunday's face, her eyes rimmed with dark shadows and filled with memories of things no child should ever experience. "Can I tell you something, Sunday?"

"You know you can tell me anything," she replied, her heart thumping madly, because she didn't want to say the wrong thing, make this moment something it shouldn't be or keep it from being what it should.

"I didn't believe in you and Matt when you brought me here. You were like Santa Claus." She glanced at her siblings, who were sitting in a row on the fence. "Great until Christmas morning when there are no presents under the tree."

"You've had a lot of disappointments in your life," Sunday assured her. "We understood that."

"No, *you* understood it. Matt liked the idea of being a savior, but he didn't really like the work involved. Like, he wanted people to think he was a good guy . . ."

"He was a good guy."

Heavenly shrugged. "He was a nice guy. He did things for people. He treated me really well, and I appreciated it. But good guys don't cheat. Good guys don't go off for weeks and leave their kids and their wives, so they can be with other women."

"Did you read my journals while I was in the hospital?" Sunday asked, shocked by Heavenly's words.

"I didn't have to. I lived with you. I saw stuff, and I heard stuff, and I know who wanted me here and who just liked the idea of it. If I could give you a prize, Sunday, it wouldn't just be for trying. It would be for being the mother I never had. For sticking with me when I was a pain in the ass."

"Language," Sunday said automatically, and Heavenly smiled.

"See? That's what I love about you. You always want me to be my best. That's what a mom does, right? Come on. I can't wait to see Early again."

She could have sprinted on ahead.

Sunday would have understood.

But she stayed. Talking about the red horse and the gray one, and the beautiful filly that she'd ride one day.

And Sunday let her, because life was about *this* moment, and every moment like it. It was about living and breathing and enjoying things like slow walks across newly sprouted fields.

She'd think about Heavenly's words later. After the horses were in the fields, and the kids were back at the house, and the sun wasn't quite so beautiful.

Or maybe she wouldn't.

Maybe she'd just let them be what they were—a truthful statement about the way things had been.

But weren't any longer.

Flynn had to give Sunday credit. She was great at avoiding things without being obvious.

If she was asked a question she couldn't remember the answer to, she sidestepped and shifted the conversation.

If she greeted someone whose name she'd forgotten, she filled in the blank with *sweetheart, honey,* or *friend.*

And when she didn't want to ride a horse, because she was afraid of falling?

She'd give every one of her kids an opportunity, cheering them on from her seat on the fence or gently leading the horse by the reins as Moisey or Twila or one of the twins held on to the saddle horn.

He'd been watching her for three days.

Three days of horse rides for the kids and smiles from Sunday, and excuses about why it was always someone else's turn to ride.

Now, the kids had returned to the house, and Heavenly was in Early's stall, brushing her the way she'd been taught, whispering secrets in the mare's ear about life and about what she loved.

Flynn didn't listen as he replaced horse tack and swept the small office that he didn't think had ever been used when Matt was alive. It had been furnished with a desk, a chair, and an old file cabinet that had been empty except for a few rogue spiders. Now it was filled with files and paperwork. Eventually, Heavenly wanted to board horses for other people in town. The barn had ten stalls, and four were being used, so it made sense.

It was expensive, though, and a lot of work.

Flynn had decided to let her prove she could care for their horses before he broached the subject with Sunday.

So far, she was doing great.

But, then, everything was easy for a few days.

It was the marathon he wanted to see her run. Not the sprint.

"I'm finished, Uncle Flynn," Heavenly called, and he stepped out of the office, watching as she stepped out of Early's stall and secured the door.

"You'd better go on back to the house, then. Rosie probably has dinner waiting. You've got your first choir rehearsal tonight, right?"

"I'd rather stay here," she muttered, but she took off her hat and hung it on a peg near the tack.

"Don't give up one dream for another when you can have them both," he responded, and she scowled.

"You always say things like that."

"Because one day, when you're my age, you'll remember them and smile."

"Or roll my eyes," she replied.

"You already do that," he said, and she smiled.

"Clementine and Porter are taking me to practice tonight. They're bringing all the kids for ice cream while I'm there. It's a long trip out there, you know."

"Forty minutes?" he said, wondering why she was bringing it up. The drive had been discussed plenty of times. Flynn, Porter, and Sullivan agreed it was worth the effort. Sunday had agreed. Heavenly had seemed excited and willing to sacrifice a few hours twice a week for the chance to be part of the county's junior choir.

"There and back. Plus, a two-hour practice."

"Are you wishing you weren't chosen to be part of the county choir?" he asked, trying to keep his tone neutral, because he, his brothers, and Sunday had also agreed that if Heavenly changed her mind about wanting to be in the choir, they weren't going to force her to do it.

"No! I'm excited. We'll be singing at some fancy party at the children's hospital in Spokane next month. Did I tell you that?"

"I don't think so."

"Well, we will be. I'll have to have a blue dress. That's what all the girls are supposed to wear. Long sleeves."

"We'll find you one," he assured her, still not sure what the conversation was about.

"Mom and Rumer are taking me before school starts. Next week. Can you believe that? Just one week, and I'm starting eighth grade. Next year is high school."

"That's a big deal. Is that why you're worried about the forty-minute drive to practice? You think this last year of middle school is going to be too busy?"

"I'm not worried. I was just mentioning it, because it's Friday night."

"And?" he prodded, because the clock in the office was ticking loudly. He could hear it, and he knew that if Heavenly didn't get moving, she'd be running late for dinner and for practice.

"Rosie always goes home for the weekend Friday night. After she cleans up the dinner dishes."

"Okay."

"And Sullivan and Rumer are in Portland until tomorrow night."

"I'm aware of the schedule, Heavenly," he reminded her, and she sighed. Loudly. Deeply. With every bit of the teenage attitude he'd come to expect from her.

"You and Sunday are going to be here. Alone."

He'd been aware of that, too, but he didn't bother mentioning it.

"And it's a gorgeous evening. You can feel fall in the air, right?"

“Sure.”

“That’s Sunday’s favorite time of year. Did you know that?”

“No. I didn’t.”

“It is. She told me that the first year I lived here. Just like she told me that she loved horses, and that when she was a kid, she used to ride her dad’s old gelding. He was a roan. Just like Chance. Did you know that?”

“No.”

“Damn, Uncle, you really need to be more informed.”

“Language,” he chided, and she grinned.

“Sorry, but you do. So I’ll tell you one more thing, and then I need to run, because Rosie made fried chicken tonight, and that’s my favorite.”

“Go ahead,” he said, curious because he’d been spending a lot of time with Heavenly, and she almost never mentioned Sunday.

“In biblical times, if a man died and left a widow, his unmarried brother was required to marry her. So they could, you know, carry on the family line.”

“What?!” he sputtered, and her grin broadened.

“It’s true. It’s in Deuteronomy.”

“Heavenly, I don’t know what you’re getting at,” he began, but her smile had faded, the happy kid replaced by a serious young woman.

“I’m not getting at anything. I’m just stating a fact. Sunday deserves to be happy. She deserves to have a man in her life who likes what she likes, who supports her dreams, who makes her feel like she's enough."

"Heavenly." *I'm not going to be that man,* he was going to say, but she was still talking, ignoring his effort to cut her off.

"Twila and I have discussed the issue," she announced as if there'd been a board meeting and a PowerPoint presentation listing pros and cons. "And neither of us thinks it would be weird if you and Sunday fell in love. But even if you're not planning to do that, tonight is a perfect night to take Chance and Whisper to the river and watch the sun set. Don't you think?"

"I've already put up the tack."

"And you're smart enough to know how to take it down again," she said, sounding just like Emmerson had all those many years ago when he'd been teaching Flynn the ropes.

Just like Flynn did when he was working with Heavenly.

The old man would be proud to know his legacy was living on.

"She's got to get up on a horse eventually," Heavenly prodded, obviously sensing his weakness and going in for the kill.

"If I take her riding, it's not going to be because I need to fulfill some archaic biblical law," he growled, snatching his cowboy hat from its peg, annoyed that he was verbally sparring with a thirteen-year-old and that she was winning.

"Oh. I know that," Heavenly said. "The Deuteronomy thing is just a point of interest. Not a call to action."

"Where in the heck did you learn to talk like that?" he demanded.

"Didn't I tell you I was on the middle school debate team last year?" she asked, shooting a jaunty smile over her shoulder as she walked out of the barn.

CHAPTER TEN

They were gone.

All of them.

The kids and Rembrandt accompanying Heavenly to her practice.

State choir? County?

Sunday still couldn't get it right, but she knew that's where they were headed. To choir practice and ice cream.

Rosie had left for the weekend.

Clementine and Sullivan were with the kids.

Flynn had gone with them.

Sunday was alone.

Finally.

Thank God.

With school looming and a wedding and fall festival being planned, life had been moving at a frantic pace.

Sunday had been trying to keep up.

Dear God, had she been trying!

Throwing herself into the midst of things, messing up, forgetting, trying to be kind to herself and to the kids and not get in the way but not step out of it, either.

It was a balancing act that took more energy than she had, but she didn't dare think about that. Not when the kids needed her to keep going.

They'd been happier these past few weeks, walking through the fields beside her, working in the kitchen while she washed dishes, sitting cross-legged while she did her daily physical therapy exercises, chattering endlessly about all the things they loved.

It was true, she didn't remember most of what they said. She'd retired the notebooks and only journaled now, jotting down what she could remember at the end of the day, when the kids were in bed.

So she lost a lot, but she retained some, and the kids? They were retaining a lot. They'd bring up things she'd said or flower crowns she'd made or stories she'd told, and maybe she didn't remember, but they did, and that was what mattered.

She hoped.

Because it was all she had.

God, she was tired.

But now the house was quiet, and she was alone and could do what she'd been wanting to for days. Sit in the recliner and stare at the wall and let herself drift.

She must have closed her eyes, because she was suddenly in the car, speeding along the highway, the windows open to let in the cold autumn breeze.

And Matt was beside her. Clear as day. Light brown hair whipping in the wind, hands loose on the steering wheel.

"Pull over," she said, but the words were carried away by the wind.

"Matt! Pull over," she screamed, because she knew what was coming.

Headlights swerving toward them.

Matt's quiet curse.

Glass shattering and metal bending.

"Matt! Please," she yelled, and he seemed to finally hear, because he turned and looked straight into her eyes the way he had when they were kids. Before they'd married and gone through years of infertility and learned each other's flaws as well as their strengths.

When he'd still looked at her as if she were the sun and the moon and every star.

"You deserved better than me," he said.

"No," she replied, but it was too late.

The lights were there.

Flashing across his face, highlighting the charming, handsome man he'd been.

And then the glass and metal and the darkness.

"It's okay, Sunday. You're okay," someone said, running warm palms down her cold cheeks.

For a moment, she thought she was in the hospital again, hooked to machines and trying to free herself from the darkness she'd fallen into.

She sat bolt upright, pushing the hands away, heart galloping, pulse racing, breath heaving.

"Sunday?"

She blinked.

She wasn't in the hospital. Or the car. Or rehab.

She was home, sitting in the easy chair, Flynn crouched beside her.

"I thought you were gone," she managed to say, her voice thick with tears she hadn't realized she was shedding.

She touched her cheek. It was still damp.

"I was out in the barn, fixing one of the stalls."

"Oh. I thought you went with the kids, and . . ." Her mind was blank, and she stood, something clattering across the floor as she moved.

"Porter and Clementine?" he provided, reaching for the thing that had dropped.

"Right."

"I'm driving on Wednesday. Twila made the schedule, and we've all been schooled on the importance of sticking to it. Is this yours?" He dropped a rock into her hand. Smooth. Light pink. Heart-shaped.

"I . . . the boys must have given it to me. Maddox gave me one a few weeks ago, and they've been bringing them to me ever since." But she didn't remember having this one when she sat in the chair, and the boys had been gone before she closed her eyes.

"How many are in your collection?" he asked.

"Twenty-five. Twenty-six now." She tucked the pink rock in her pocket. "Most of them are river rocks."

"That looked like pink onyx."

"Yes. It did," she agreed. Still shaky. Still confused.

You deserved better than me.

"Moisey says they're kisses from heaven," she continued, not wanting to think about the dream. Not wanting to cry over the finality of those words.

Deserved.

Past tense.

Not present.

Because he was gone, and there was nothing that could be done to change the things that had happened while he was alive.

"Your kids have a lot of interesting things to say," Flynn said, smiling gently.

And, God!

She wanted to cry again, because he was there, and Matt wasn't, and somehow that was okay with her. Somehow, it was even nice.

"What have they been saying to you?" she asked, walking past him. Out into the hall. Dust motes danced in the sunlight like tiny ghosts of her forgotten memories.

"According to Milo, his fifth-grade teacher is a hot tamale."

"He did not say that?!" she laughed.

"He did. Maddox doesn't agree. He says she's old."

"Their teacher is . . . Emma Wilkens? Blond? Pretty. Maybe twenty-five?"

"Ella McIntire," he corrected. "But yes to everything else."

"If she's old, I must be ancient."

"If you're ancient, what's that make me?"

She laughed, but didn't respond. The word wasn't there, and she wasn't going to fight for it.

Besides, what she wanted to say was *wonderful*.

Because that's how Moisey described him all the time.

Wonderful Uncle Flynn.

As if it were all part of a very professional title.

"That's better," he said.

"What?"

"Laughter instead of tears."

"I wasn't crying."

"That was just water sliding down your cheeks?"

"Sometimes, I dream about the accident."

"I see," he said, opening the coat closet and pulling out her cowboy boots. "Here."

"What do I need these for?"

"Heavenly says it's the perfect evening for a horse ride."

"I'm not sure what that has to do with me." Because there was no way she planned to climb on a horse's back. Not tonight. Probably not for a very long time.

"You asked what kind of things the kids were saying to me. That's what she said."

"Oh."

"So put on the boots, and let's head out."

"Flynn, you know I can't."

"Why not?"

"Because I can barely walk without tripping. How am I going to stay on a horse?"

"You can worry about that once you're up in the saddle. I've got Chance ready for you, but you can ride the gray if you prefer."

"Is Chance the roan?"

"Yes. I thought about saddling both mares, but Heavenly said your dad used to have a gelding you rode. Apparently, he was just like Chance. Gentle. Older."

"Like us?" she managed to joke even though her heart was slamming against her ribs and her stomach was churning.

She did not want to do this.

She didn't.

And she had a right to say so, to refuse the boots and the saddled gelding and the evening ride.

"There's not much gentle about me, and there's nothing old about you," he said, opening the front door and letting cool air drift inside. "And, it is a beautiful night. Why let fear keep you from enjoying it?"

"I can enjoy it from the easy chair. Or the porch swing. Or the back stoop," she responded, but she found herself slipping into the boots and following him outside.

Fall was there. Skimming the surface of the air, and she lifted her face to it, closed her eyes.

Saw Matt again.

You deserved better than me.

Her heart thudded, and her eyes flew open.

Flynn was standing near the porch railing, arms crossed, cowboy hat shading his face.

"We can ride another night," he said. "How about a walk instead?"

"No. Heavenly was right. It's a good night for a ride."

"You don't have to do this for your daughter," he responded.

"I have to do it for me," she replied, forcing herself to walk down the stairs and around the side of the house. The barn was in the distance, dark red against the purple-blue sky, surrounded by fields of golden cornstalks and lush green fields. This was the patchwork quilt of color she remembered from her childhood. The hallmark of a working farm. The earmark of a well-tended property.

That should make her happy, but it only made her sad.

For all the lost years.

All the time she'd stepped back and let Matt do his thing while the colorful world she loved faded into grays and browns and dusty tans.

She might have forgotten a lot.

But she remembered that.

• • •

Sunday looked like she was walking to the gallows, head down, feet dragging, arms hanging stiffly at her sides.

Flynn almost told her again that she didn't need to ride to enjoy the evening.

Almost.

But this was a part of a life she'd loved and recalled fondly before the accident. A part that she'd described so clearly and so exuberantly to her daughter, Heavenly could recall the details without being prodded.

The roan gelding.

The love of fall.

Flynn would have liked to have seen Sunday when she was a kid, riding through the fields she helped her parents tend, her arms brown from the sun, her face glowing with health and happiness.

He could, if he let himself, picture her as a teenager, galloping across the river, hair flying out behind her.

Because, of course, she'd have been galloping.

No easy trot for the Sunday who'd existed before she'd nearly lost her life.

The horses were tied to a post outside the barn, heads down, munching straggly grass that grew in the shade. The gray mare and the roan were saddled and ready. Both were gentle, but the roan had easy manners that made riding him a pleasure. At fifteen, he was young enough to still be ridden hard and old enough to enjoy a peaceful walk.

If Flynn were going to choose a mount for Sunday, he'd have chosen Chance. But he let her decide, leaning against a fence post as she approached the gray mare and scratched her between the ears.

"She's a pretty horse," she said.

"Yes. She is."

"And you look great riding her."

"I'm flattered you think so," he responded, smiling as her cheeks went bright pink.

"What I mean is, that you seem really comfortable on her, and you should probably ride her tonight. Because that makes sense."

"I kind of figured that was what you meant."

"Okay. Good, because I wasn't saying you look great." Her blush deepened. "Not that you don't."

She stopped. Took a breath. Shook her head, her flyaway hair catching rays of sunlight.

"I'm done now." She pressed her lips together, and he laughed.

"No need to be so disgusted with things, Sunday."

"I'm not used to opening my mouth and putting my foot in it."

"It wasn't a foot. Maybe just a big toe."

"Well, whatever it was, it didn't taste good." She approached the roan and ran a hand over his black mane.

He turned his head, nuzzling her cheek with his lips, probably looking for a handout, but Sunday seemed pleased. "You're a nice old boy, aren't you? I guess if I'm getting back in the saddle, you're the one I should ride. I hope you don't mind an off-balance jockey."

"He's a steady fellow, and he'll move as slowly as you want him to."

"Right. Well, we'll see how it goes." She reached for the saddle horn, her shirt riding up her side, revealing creamy flesh and white scars.

Instead of pulling herself up, she leaned her forehead against Chance's shoulder.

"Sunday," Flynn began.

"Don't. Okay? If you tell me I don't have to do this again, I'll decide you're right, and then we'll have to spend another evening trying to get me up in the saddle." She glanced around, found the mounting block that Heavenly used, and pulled it into position.

Then she grabbed the saddle horn again.

This time she seemed ready. Muscles straining, she put her foot in the stirrup and tried to throw her leg over the horse's back.

He gave her a quick boost, and she was up, wobbling a little as she settled into the leather.

He almost told her to be careful, but she wasn't a child. She knew the dangers. She'd ridden before. Many times.

And riding horses was like riding a bike.

Once you learned, you never forgot.

At least, that's what Emmerson had always said.

"Have you ever ridden a bicycle?" he asked casually as he adjusted the stirrups straps.

"Yes."

"Since the accident?"

Her soft laugh surprised him, and he looked up, realized she was smiling down at him, sunlight kissing her cheeks, humor dancing in her eyes. "You're more afraid than I am, Flynn. Admit it."

"If you break your neck, your kids will have my head on a platter."

"What about your brothers?"

"They'll take care of the rest of me," he admitted, and she laughed again.

"Well, at least I'm not alone in my terror. It's good to have company."

"It'll be better once we're out of the barnyard." He hoped.

He was more worried about her than he'd been about Heavenly or any of the other kids.

But, then, *they* were kids.

They fell. They got back up.

If Sunday fell, she might shatter, all the pieces the doctors had so carefully knit together coming apart again.

"I'm going to be fine," she assured him, and he realized he'd been standing there too long, staring up at her.

“Right.” He untied the reins and handed them to her, then mounted Whisper. The mare pranced sideways excitedly, and he reined her in, set the pace slow and steady. Out of the barnyard, across the grassy field. Trying not to glance back too often to assure himself that Sunday hadn’t slipped from the saddle or lost control of Chance.

He’d been on the farm for over a month now, and he knew it well. He led Sunday through a small copse of trees and out into another field. Beyond it, the river flowed languidly, still low from the early summer drought. A shallow slope led to its banks, and the horses easily navigated it, splashing through knee-high water and out onto the other side.

They were close to Emmerson’s land now, and he could see the old farmhouse, boarded up and abandoned, the old oak that Emmerson had planted for his late wife, dropping early fall leaves onto the ground.

There was no fence here. It was beyond the horse pasture Flynn had created, but several signs marked the boundaries of the land.

FOR SALE. FIVE HUNDRED ACRES.

He’d had no idea that Emmerson’s property was so large.

“It’s a shame what his son let happen,” Sunday said, riding up beside him with a confidence that surprised him.

She looked good, straight-backed and strong,

some of the frailty that was obvious when she was walking hidden when she rode.

"His son never cared about farming or equestrian pursuits. He wanted an easy life, and this"—he waved a hand at the overgrown land—"isn't it."

"It's a shame Emmerson didn't leave the property to you," she said, clicking softly and turning Chance to the right, heading toward the stables. Gray with age, they stood as a testimony to Emmerson's skill. He'd built them himself, and even now, they stood sturdy and strong, the wood weathered but uncompromised.

"He left me his life insurance policy," he responded, following her lead across a crumbling asphalt driveway and into a weed-choked field.

"Really?" She reined Chance in, stopping a few feet from the old stables. Her arms were shaking, and he thought the ride was taking more out of her than she would ever admit. It took stamina and strength to control a horse. Even a docile one.

"Yes. And it was enough to get me and my brothers through college. Two of them, anyway," he said, wishing he hadn't brought that up. Not wanting to get her thinking about Matt or the past. "And for me to put a down payment on my ranch."

"That's interesting." She dismounted messily, legs bumping, arms grabbing. Chance didn't even swish his tail or twitch his ear. Just turned his head and nuzzled her hair once she was finally down.

"I worked for him for five years, and sometimes he couldn't pay me. Heck, most of the time he couldn't. I'd get ten dollars here and there. Maybe fifty in a week."

"What I meant," she said, the reins in her hand as she walked to the stables, "is that it's interesting that you had money to help your brothers. Matt told me that the reason he wasn't going to college was because he didn't have the funds, and he wasn't going to ask your father."

Dang. He knew he shouldn't have taken a walk down memory lane.

"He probably didn't want to ask me, either," he muttered.

"Don't lie for him, Flynn."

He didn't respond. Out of respect for her and for his brother.

"I'll take your silence to mean you offered him the money, and he didn't accept." She didn't sound angry. She didn't sound sad. She sounded worn out, exhausted, ready for all the crap that had come before to be out in the open so she could move on from it.

"That was a long time ago, Sunday."

"And he was lying to me from the beginning. I've read through my journals so many times, and I've tried to tell myself that the suspicions

I jotted down in them were unfounded." She shrugged, pushing open a stall door and glancing inside. "It's a shame no one has purchased this property. It's a lovely piece of land. Quiet. With a gorgeous view."

"You're changing the subject," he pointed out. There was more that needed to be said. He was certain of that.

"We're supposed to be enjoying an evening ride," she responded. "Not rehashing the past."

"Sometimes it helps to talk about things."

"Sometimes, it helps to be quiet."

She reached for the saddle horn, no mounting block in place, and somehow boosted herself up. By the time she did, she was breathing hard, her face pink from effort, sweat beading her brow.

But she looked triumphant sitting there, the fading sun shimmering on her skin, the stables behind her. The world at her feet.

If she'd been someone else, if he'd been someone else, he'd have leaned over and kissed her, because everything about her was natural and organic and sincere.

He respected that, admired it, would have wanted to learn more about it and about her.

If they were different people.

But they weren't, so he kept his distance, following as she and Chance led the way back to the river.

CHAPTER ELEVEN

First horse ride in years? Done.

Sunday could check that off her list.

And not only had she ridden a horse, she'd brushed him, put up his tack, and stabled him. Sure, it had taken her forever. Sure, Flynn had finished with Whisper twenty minutes ago. Sure, the barn was quiet and empty and she was alone, because everything took her so dang long to do. Her arms felt like jelly. Her legs were shaking.

But she'd done it.

All of it.

Herself.

And that felt good.

Good enough to celebrate if she hadn't been so tired, and if she'd actually had someone to celebrate with.

She could call a friend, but most of them had families, and they all had lives, and, really, she couldn't remember whom she'd been closest to before the accident.

Or even if she'd been close to anyone.

Aside from Beatrice, she couldn't think of one person who stopped by recently just to see how she was doing or to offer a ride or a willing ear.

And even Beatrice had things to do on Friday nights.

Like dating a guy she'd met at a wedding a few weeks ago. She'd texted Sunday about it that morning, sending pictures of different outfits and asking for opinions.

It seemed odd that they were the same age, and that most of the people Sunday knew from high school were either just getting married, or just starting families, or still swimming around in the dating pool.

"And here I am, a widow with six kids." She stepped out of Chance's stall, offering him one last scratch on the nose before she latched the gate.

He didn't seem to mind that she fumbled with the latch or that she bumped the door a half dozen times while she was trying to get it to close properly.

He hadn't minded her sloppy riding, mounting, dismounting, or even the fact that she'd turned him in the wrong direction when it was time to go home.

As Flynn had said, he was a gentle horse, sweet and docile and engaging with a funny way of nibbling ears every time they were close. She thought she could get used to riding him, and that maybe, in time, it wouldn't seem so foreign to her.

"Baby steps," she whispered as she walked through the barn and out into the yard. The sun had just set, the last rays of it glinting above the mountains. To the east, storm clouds were moving in, but to the west, the sky was indigo blue and calm.

She still had time before the rain came, and she was just wound up enough from the ride to think a walk might be nice.

The orchard wasn't far, and the apples were beginning to ripen. Soon, there'd be people combing through the branches, filling baskets with ripe fruit, paying for the privilege and, hopefully, having a blast while they were doing it.

She was looking forward to the noisy families and happy kids. To the sweet sound of laughter drifting across the farm. The place had been dead for many years, and it was coming back to life again.

Too late for Matt to see it.

Not that he'd cared.

And that was probably the hardest part. Knowing that the thing she'd loved so much was the thing he could have easily done without.

She walked through the barnyard, dusky silence enveloping her, the dream in her mind again. The lights. The knowing that it was going to happen. That they were going to be hit head-on, and that Matt would die. That everything they had been and might have been would end on the road just minutes after their tenth anniversary dinner.

If she'd known, would she have done things differently?

Would she have traveled the world with him? Given up the farm to go to Africa and Asia and Europe? Forgotten about all the kids she'd wanted to have and turned her love more fully on Matt?

Would that have kept him closer?

Would it have kept him home?

She couldn't know the answers to those questions. Not really, but she wanted them, because she wanted a reason for what he'd done. For the dying farm he'd left behind, the broken relationship, the women living in other places who might still wonder what had happened to him.

Or maybe they knew.

It's possible they'd tried to contact him and reached one of his brothers, or that thcy'd read about the accident on the news. From what Sunday had been told, it had made national news because the truck driver who'd hit them was working on a suspended license.

Suspended because of three previous DUIs.

If the company he drove for had bothered checking, they'd have known.

And Matt might still be alive while the farm continued to die, and Sunday paced the house at night, wondering when he'd come home.

She shoved the memory away, the sharp, clear pictures of herself, pacing through the hall, glancing at the clock, peeking out the window.

Waiting and waiting.

And suddenly, she wasn't walking any longer, strolling to the orchard to enjoy the remainder of the evening light. She was running, or trying. Tripping over gnarled roots, falling, getting up again. Through the orchard resplendent in fading-summer light.

She tripped again, and this time, went down so hard she should have stayed down. It would have been the smart thing to do, to lie there in the twilight catching her breath and letting her thoughts fade with the daylight.

The thing was, she'd always been intelligent, but she wasn't sure she'd ever been smart. Not in a way that mattered. In a way that kept farms going and relationships strong.

She'd memorized a million facts and juggled a half dozen schedules and kept the farm limping along, but she hadn't put her foot down and told Matt he needed to stay home.

Although, that one, she wasn't sure about. Maybe, at the end, she had put her foot down.

She could remember the accident, and the dinner, but she couldn't remember the words they'd spoken as they'd sat across the table from each other. Lifetime friends who's suddenly seemed like strangers.

She limped out of the orchard, walking down the slope that led to the river. It was silvery black this time of day, the water burbling over the rocks in a joyful melody she'd once loved.

The dock was in this section. The old boathouse that Matt had let fall to ruin.

That she'd allowed him to let fall to ruin.

She'd been raising the kids, working in the home, doing as much as she could outside. He'd been puttering around pretending to be a gentleman farmer. She'd known that was what he was doing. Pretending. Playing a part.

Yes. She'd known, but she hadn't wanted to nag. She hadn't wanted to be the discontented wife, the one who drove her husband away with her constant demands. She'd wanted to support his dreams, encourage his happiness, help him find his way in life, because they'd been growing up together, learning how to be adults.

Only, she'd been the only one learning. He'd just continued to play the part.

She stepped onto the deck. Someone had fixed it, replacing rotting boards with new ones, fixing the rail that ran on either side. A fishing platform had been added to one side, a tackle box lying forgotten in the shadow of a wooden bench. The boathouse had been reborn, as well, fresh white paint gleaming on newly hung siding.

Her brothers-in-law had been busy.

But she'd known that.

The strange thing was, Matt had been the golden Bradshaw brother, the one admired by the town. She'd read the tributes people had written on the online memorial page one of their high school friends had created. *You were the good one, Bradshaw. The best of the bunch. One good egg in a carton of rotten ones.*

For a while, she'd jotted notes in a notebook to remind herself of Matt's good qualities.

And maybe to make herself feel better about his bad ones.

But, of course, the town hadn't known how bad things were getting. Most of the people who lived there saw Sunday and her family at church or at the kids' sports functions.

They hadn't been to the farm in years, and they had no idea that the land had gone fallow, the crops had died, the bank was threatening to foreclose. They didn't know how often Matt slipped out of the house in the middle of the night or made up some faux business trip that would give him a reason to be gone for three or four or five days in a row.

Yeah. Sunday had grown up. She'd learned how to juggle bills until she was dizzy from it, how to scrape the last drop of peanut butter from the bottom of the jar and tell her kids it was a feast. She'd learned to make bread without sugar, to create a meal from a quarter of a box of pasta and a can of tomatoes.

She'd learned to be hungry so the kids could eat, and to dig through Matt's things to find credit cards he hid just so she could buy a loaf of bread and a pound of bologna.

She'd learned to lie to herself and to her children and to her friends, because she'd learned to protect Matt even when he wasn't protecting her.

If that was growing up, she'd done more than her fair share.

And if it was love?

She wanted no part of it.

Dear God! She wished she'd tossed her journals.

Or better yet, never written in them. She'd have no record of what her marriage had been, and only whatever memories had been left after the accident.

Maybe the tough things would have gone and the good things would have stayed, and she wouldn't be standing on a dock that her brothers-in-law had fixed, wondering how her life had gone so wrong.

"Damn you, Matt," she shouted, surprising herself and a bird that was sitting on the dock railing.

It fluttered away, but she was still there, shouting at someone who couldn't hear.

Had never, she didn't think, been able to.

"Damn you!" she yelled again, the words echoing through the silence.

She didn't care that she was cursing, or that

her kids would be appalled if they heard her, or that the blue-haired ladies would wince and click their tongues and worry that the brain injury had stolen her memories and her salvation.

She didn't care that her mother wouldn't have approved or that her father might have applauded or that Matt might be standing at the pearly gates, listening to the curse ricocheting through the universe.

And she didn't care that she was crying, tears sliding down her cheeks and neck, pooling in the hollow of her throat where the dark purple scar told the story of her survival.

She didn't care, and she didn't wipe the tears away.

"Damn you," she said one more time, the words a broken whisper that reflected the state of her heart.

Because she had loved Matt.

She still loved him, and if he'd lived, she'd have forgiven him.

Again.

"So, damn me, too," she said, digging into her pocket and pulling out the heart-shaped rock that had fallen from her lap after the dream.

"Because I did deserve better. I did. So you can keep your kisses, Matt. Maybe you'll find someone in Heaven to give them to."

She tossed the rock with all her strength, but she didn't see it fly. Her eyes were too filled with tears, her head pulsing with the kind of pain she hadn't felt in months.

She swung around, ready to go home, to climb into bed before the kids returned. She didn't want them to know she'd been crying. She didn't want them to think she was upset.

She did care about that.

Her foot caught on a boat tie coiled near the edge of the dock, and she sprawled forward, landing with a thud that shook the platform and made her tears come even faster.

She couldn't even do this right, for God's sake. Throw her fit and scream to the universe and then march home and tuck herself in bed.

She lay where she was, head cradled in her arms, the river swishing beneath her, the dock shifting subtly. She thought she heard footsteps, but she didn't lift her head. She was too tired, and she didn't care enough.

"Sunday?" Flynn said, because of course it would be him. Every time she failed, he was there to see it. When she forgot names or dates or which kid needed to be where. When she burned bacon and ruined pancake batter and struggled to open canteens.

Every time. Every failure.

There he was.

And she was as tired of that as she was of the rest.

"Go away," she responded, not bothering to lift her head.

"It's a supermoon tonight," he responded, and she felt him stretching out beside her.

Side by side. Arms touching. Legs touching.

And it shouldn't have made her feel less alone, but it did.

"Good for it," she replied, and he chuckled, his body vibrating with amusement.

If she hadn't been so pissed off, so upset, she might have chuckled too.

"You'd have a better view of it if you rolled over," he suggested, a note of humor still in his voice.

"My life situation is not funny," she replied, but she rolled to her left, away from him, stopping short when his arm clamped around her waist.

"Other way, Sunday. Unless you want to take a dip in the river."

"Probably not tonight," she managed to say as she rolled toward him, elbows and knees bumping his solid frame.

She took too long to find her place, to finally lie still, to see what he had—the giant white orb that was just drifting above the mountains.

"Wow!" she breathed, and felt his fingers curl through hers, his palm pressed warm and calloused against her chilled skin.

"God knew what He was doing when He made the mountains to frame the moon," he said. "And the stars to glitter in the dark night sky. Emmerson used to say that when I'd had a rough day, and I didn't want to go home. We'd sit on his back porch watching the moon rise. He'd never ask me why I didn't want to leave. He'd just let me be until I was ready to go."

"You can ask, if you want," she said, because her brain might not work as quickly as it once had, but she knew what he was telling her. That she could keep her silence and her peace.

"I'm pretty sure I know," he said, shifting so that he was lying on his side, propped up on his elbow, staring into her face. "You're angry at Matt for letting the farm fail. You're angry at him for failing you and the kids. You're angry because he cheated, and because you still loved him. You're angry at yourself for not taking control when you could have, for not telling him the truth and making him own up to his problems and his responsibility. You're angry at God for leaving you in a mess that a bunch of people you barely knew had to help you out of. And, you're angry at life, because it's not the pretty little picture you thought it would be."

"That about sums it up," she admitted, because she wasn't going to pretend. Not like she had before the accident. She knew where all the pretending led, and it wasn't a place she wanted to be.

He nodded and squeezed her hand, his thumb running across the base of her thumb. It was a friendly caress, a reminder that she wasn't in this alone. That he was there with her, living in the aftermath of his own mistakes.

"What was your wife's name?" she asked, and he smiled.

"Patricia. I'm surprised you remember that I was married."

"I wrote it down. It seemed important."

"Did it?" There was something warm in those words, something inviting. Something that might have been flirtation or invitation, but she'd never been with anyone but Matt. She'd never had any reason to learn the rules of romantic relationships. She'd grown into love the same way she'd grown into adulthood—slowly and easily.

And, if flirtation were going on, she had no real idea how to recognize it.

"You're a big part of the kids' lives," she said, knowing there was more to it than that. Knowing that if she'd lived another life and met him in another place, they'd be doing more than lying on the dock, looking into each other's eyes.

"I hope so. I don't want to be the uncle they barely remember. Not anymore."

"You'll be the uncle who taught them about building fences and making paddocks and riding horses. The one who helped their mother find her way back home."

"You've always been home."

"Not really." She shook her head, the aching

pain behind her eyes still there and still insistent, but the tears were gone, and the anger. "I've been living in my house for months, but I haven't been home."

"Then I'm glad I helped you find your way." His lips brushed her cheek, and her pulse jumped, a million butterflies flittering in her stomach.

And, God! He must have felt it too.

He'd stopped talking, stopped moving, his lips just a millimeter away from her skin. Just inches away from her mouth.

And she knew he hadn't meant for this to happen, the spark of heat that arched between them, the rapid rise and fall of her chest and his. The way their bodies seemed to want to find each other, to roll closer and fit curves to hollows.

He hadn't meant it, but it had happened, and when he pulled her into a sitting position, when his palms cupped her cheeks, when his hand brushed hair from her face, she didn't tell him he should stop.

No.

Of course she didn't.

She leaned forward when he probably would have moved away, because she wanted to know what it was like to be in someone else's arms. She wanted to know how it felt to want someone besides Matt, and to be wanted by someone other than him.

She kissed Flynn, because he was there, and

because every day she'd spent with him had been a day when she'd remembered why she was alive, why she had to try, who she should become rather than who she'd once been. She kissed him, because he'd finished the barn and created a horse pasture and urged her to ride again.

She kissed him, and she couldn't say she planned it, but she wouldn't say she hadn't. She *could* say that it was a clumsy attempt, her body off balance, her hands slapping against his chest as she nearly fell into his lap.

And that should have been it.

He should have laughed her off like she was a desperate housewife drunk at a party and coming on to him, and she should have apologized a million times and prayed to God that they'd both forget how stupid she'd been.

But his lips were gentle, his hands warm as he smoothed them up her back, settled them on her shoulders, held her steady beneath the bright moon and shimmering stars.

And something that should have been nothing seared itself into her soul. She knew, without even remembering, that Matt's first kiss had been nothing like this. That what they'd had together, what they'd believed would carry them through from childhood to old age, had been a faint reflection of what real love should be.

When he pulled her closer, when he deepened the kiss, when all the thoughts in her head flew away and there was only Flynn, she wasn't afraid. She wasn't worried.

She was with him.

And, right now, that felt an awful lot like home.

She tasted like honeysuckle and fresh spring water.

Like long summer mornings and lazy winter nights.

And having her in his arms?

It was the best thing that had happened to him in a very long time.

But God! She was his brother's widow. A woman who'd been through hell and had lived to tell about it.

She didn't need more heartache, more trouble, or more drama.

And she sure as heck didn't need to be kissing Flynn in the moonlight.

He told himself to let her go, to move back, to walk away.

But her body was warm and pliant, her lips soft and welcoming, and he couldn't make himself do anything but pull her closer.

"Wow, Uncle Flynn, I know I told you Twila and I wouldn't think it was weird, but I didn't expect you to move so fast," Heavenly said, her voice pouring over him like arctic water.

He jerked back but didn't release Sunday.

He was afraid she'd fall backward and land in the river.

She shifted away, one jerky movement that gave him room to think.

And what he was thinking wasn't good, because what he was thinking was that he wanted to pull her into his arms again.

"Heavenly," Sunday said, whirling to face her daughter, silky strands of hair slapping his face.

Maybe he deserved more than that for overstepping his place, for reaching for something that didn't belong to him.

But, he wasn't sorry. Not even a little.

He'd heard her cursing his brother. He'd seen her toss the pink heart into the river. He knew what Matt had done. And if Matt had been alive, he'd have pounded some sense into him and then gone back to Texas to live his life.

But Matt was gone, leaving Sunday with more baggage than any woman her age should carry.

How many times had Matt cheated?

That's what he wanted to know, but he wouldn't ask. He wasn't even sure she'd remember if he did.

"It's okay, Sunday," Heavenly said. She was standing just a few feet away, Rembrandt on a leash at her side. "You don't have to explain."

"That's good, because I don't think I could," Sunday responded.

"From what I've heard, that's how these kinds of things work." Heavenly took her arm, pulling her farther away from Flynn.

As if he were a villain and a cad, someone who planned to take advantage of a woman who couldn't protect herself.

"What things?" Sunday asked. She didn't look in Flynn's direction. He hadn't expected her to.

The kiss . . .

Maybe it had been the moonlight or the water or the stars in the navy sky, but it had taken on a life of its own. If Heavenly hadn't arrived, he didn't know where it would have led. Or when it would have ended.

"Lust. Love. Whatever you want to call it."

"Sweetheart—"

"Like I said, you don't have to explain," she continued, ushering her mother away. "My friends all think he's irresistible too."

"What?!" Flynn nearly shouted, and Heavenly met his eyes. "Your friends are kids."

"And they're boy crazy. I find it annoying, but they have pretty good taste. It's not like you're hideous."

"Thanks," he said wryly, and she shrugged.

"I'm just stating the facts. You're not hideous, but I still don't want to hear them talk about you all the time. It's embarrassing."

"Now, hold on," he said, following them off the dock. "What do you mean 'embarrassing'?"

"You're old. They're stupid."

"And I guess I am too?" Sunday offered.

"You're not old or stupid. You're a woman who

found a nice guy to kiss beneath the stars. It's romantic. If you're into that kind of thing."

Obviously, Heavenly was not.

"Sweetie," Sunday began again, but Heavenly patted her shoulder.

"Look, I didn't mean to interrupt your fun. Clementine was looking for you. She's trying to pick colors for the wedding, and she says she needs your keen eye. I figured you might be out in the barn, but Rembrandt had other ideas. I guess he's not as dumb as he was pretending to be when he snatched the ice cream cone Moisey saved for me."

"She saved you a cone?" Sunday asked, looking relieved to be able to change the focus of the conversation.

"With ice cream in it. Clementine and Porter tried to tell her it was going to melt before I got out of practice, but she insisted that she could freeze it with her mind. I think she's been reading too many sci-fi books."

"So it melted? And then the dog ate it?"

"Pretty much. I thanked Moisey anyway. I figured you'd think it was the right thing to do. Now, if you don't mind, I'm going to leave you here with Uncle Flynn, because I'm about ready to starve to death. I'll tell Clementine you're on the way, but I'll leave out the kiss. Unless you'd like me—"

"No!" he and Sunday shouted in unison, and Heavenly had the nerve to smirk.

“That’s what I kind of thought. See you back at the house,” she said, walking off with a bounce in her step and the dog by her side.

“Well,” Sunday murmured. “That was awkward.”

“She’s a teenager. They like to make people uncomfortable.”

“I meant the kiss.”

“*Awkward* is not the word I’d use for it.” He cupped her elbow, making sure to keep his grip light.

Because what he really wanted to do was take up where they’d left off when Heavenly had arrived—Sunday’s soft, pliant body pressed against his.

“No?”

“I’m pretty certain you know it’s not,” he replied. “But if you want me to use a few adjectives, incredible, life-changing, and not-even-close-to-enough come to mind.”

“I don’t think that last one is an adjective,” she said, and he thought he heard a smile in her voice.

“How about soul-searing? Mind-blowing?”

“A mistake?”

She said what he’d been thinking, but that didn’t mean he liked it. “That’s not an adjective either.”

She sighed.

“I know, but it was the only thing I could think of that didn’t make me want to . . .”

“Kiss me again?”

“Dang, Flynn. One kiss, and now you’re reading

my mind?" She was trying to make light of it.

Which was what he should want but, like her description of the kiss as a mistake, it bothered him.

"What I'm doing is thinking that my brother has been gone for nearly a year, and that even when he was here, he was a piss-poor excuse for a spouse."

She stiffened. "I told you. He was good to me."

Stop! His brain shouted. *Do not proceed.*

But, of course, his mouth just kept moving. "Right. He bought you flowers from the same florist he used for his girlfriends. He spent thousands of dollars going on business trips that were really just for pleasure."

"Don't," she said, and her voice was so small, her muscles so taut, it finally got through to him.

What he was doing.

Beating her over the head with the truth wasn't going to make the kiss any more, or less, meaningful, and it sure as heck wasn't going to make a relationship with her a possibility.

If they wanted each other, that was their decision to make, and it should have nothing to do with the past or with Matt.

"I'm sorry." He ran his knuckles down Sunday's cheek. A gentle caress followed by a gentler kiss. His lips touching hers for just long enough to let them both know how much he meant it.

"It *was* a mistake, Flynn," she said, her voice

gritty and hot. "I shouldn't have thrown myself at you."

"Is that what you call what you did?"

"What would you call it?"

"Taking what you wanted, giving what you could, allowing us both to see if the friendship we have could be more."

"That's a pretty way to say it, and a pretty way to see it, but when I wake up in the middle of the night remembering the feel of your lips on mine, I'm going to wonder why I didn't just leave things be. I need to go back to the house. Clementine is waiting for me."

He let her go, because there was nothing more to say.

Not tonight.

Maybe not ever.

But the line had already been crossed. He'd already done what he thought he never would—kissed a woman whom one of his brothers loved. It was a taboo they'd never discussed, because it was a betrayal none of them could have conceived of.

A good guy didn't date his brother's ex, steal his brother's girlfriend, fall for his brother's wife.

A good guy didn't lust for someone who didn't belong to him.

Flynn liked to think of himself as a good guy.

But he wanted Sunday in a way he couldn't remember ever wanting another woman.

Which shouldn't matter, because she wasn't Matt's wife, she was his widow. She didn't belong to anyone but herself.

She'd been a kid when she'd married. One Flynn could honestly say he'd barely paid attention to. Aside from thinking that she and his brother were making a colossal mistake, thinking they'd be better off going to college, prepping for life, not getting hitched and settling down, he hadn't spent a whole heck of a lot of time thinking about Sunday.

Until now. Now, he seemed to spend four out of every five minutes of his day thinking about her, wondering if she was doing okay, wishing he could make things easier on her.

She was becoming more than a project to him, more than a sister-in-law he had to convince to step back into her life.

And the more time he spent with her, the more time he wanted to spend. One horseback ride to the river wouldn't be enough. Not two or three, either. He wanted to fly her and the kids to his ranch and let the kids drive his housekeeper crazy while he and Sunday explored the land.

He wanted to return here and help her prune the orchards and plow the fields and ready the land for next year's crop.

He wanted to hear her laugh a thousand times, and he wanted to be the one to make her do it.

That shouldn't make him feel guilty.

But it did.

"Damn you, Matt," he muttered, repeating the phrase he'd heard Sunday say three times while she was standing on the dock.

He could have sworn he heard his brother laugh in response.

CHAPTER TWELVE

The funny thing about life was that it just kept going on. No matter a person's struggles, no matter her heartache, no matter how tough things got, time marched forward. One day into the next. One season into the next.

Sunday was thinking about that as she packed lunches for the first day of school, the food spreadsheet Twila had made taped to the front of the fridge. A year ago, on this date, she'd been six weeks away from the car accident that had changed her life forever. She'd probably been puttering around in the kitchen, just like she was now. Putting together lunches. Albeit a lot more easily.

She frowned, glancing at the spreadsheet, two pretzel rods in her hand.

Moisey liked them.

Or was it Twila?

She walked to the fridge, stepping over Rembrandt on the way, and stared at the spreadsheet, trying to make sense of it. If a ten-year-old could create it, she should be able to read it.

But, of course, the words went from her eyes to her brain and right back out of her head. She'd look at the food that each child liked, walk to the counter, and forget.

Again.

"This shouldn't be so hard," she muttered, walking to Moisey's pink lunch box and dropping the bagged pretzel rods into it.

"I'd be happy to do it for you, Sunday," Rosie offered, her head bent over the morning edition of the *Benevolence Times*, as if she were paying more attention to it than the epic struggle going on in the kitchen.

"No. It's okay. I'm fine," Sunday lied.

Rosie looked up from the paper. Her salt-and-pepper hair was still in curlers, her housecoat pulled tight around her plump figure. She'd been hired before Sunday's release from the rehab facility, and there was no doubt she'd been a godsend, cooking meals, corralling children, helping Sullivan's wife, Rumer, with all the chores that went along with raising six children.

"Are you sure you don't want me to take over, dear?" Rosie asked, tapping her fingers restlessly on the tabletop. She'd have had all the lunches packed by now, the counter clean, breakfast on the table.

But Sunday had wanted to do this for herself and for the kids.

She still wanted to do it.

Herself.

Without anyone rushing in to save the day.

They were getting close to the wire, though, the timer on the microwave ticking down the minutes until Twila ushered her siblings downstairs. All of them dressed in the outfits she'd made them lay out the previous night.

Twila was like that.

A little mother hen.

Maybe Sunday had known that before the accident. Maybe she hadn't. She knew it now, though, and she was starting to accept that what she knew right in the moment she was living was enough.

"Everything is under control, Rosie," Sunday lied, grabbing snack packs of cookies from the pantry and dropping one into each of the four lunch boxes and one into Heavenly's lunch sack.

"She won't eat those," Rosie commented, lowering her gaze to the paper again. "Says they make her face break out."

"Oh. Okay. Sure. So"—she ran back to the fridge, scanned it for Heavenly's name—"cheese cubes."

"In the fridge. Bottom shelf. Already in baggies. Thanks to Twila. That girl is quite an organizer. And"—Rosie waved toward a calendar that had been tacked to the wall next to the back door—"it seems to me, she's going to be right on time. Marching down those steps, cracking the whip to get the crew going in about three minutes."

"Right." Sunday yanked open the fridge, pulled out a small bag of cheese cubes, and tossed them in the pink lunch box.

“The bag. Remember?” Rosie said.

“Right. Again.” She dropped the cheese in the bag.

Done.

With a minute to spare.

“ ’Course, they’ll be wanting breakfast. I made cinnamon rolls yesterday. You just toss a few on a plate and throw them in the microwave. I’ll put out the cereal bowls and milk. We’d better hurry, because the troops are on the move.”

Rosie stood and was bustling around with purpose, plopping plastic bowls on the table, placing cereal boxes and a gallon of milk on the counter.

Sunday managed to find the cinnamon rolls and plop them on a plate before the sound of footsteps on the back stairs reached her ears. She punched in the cooking time and turned to the stairway just as Twila bounced into view.

“Mom! You’re awake!”

“Aren’t I always awake on your first day of school?”

“Well, every other year you have been, but this year is different.” Twila poured cereal into a bowl, grabbed a spoon, and sat at the table. She’d dressed in a flowered skirt and light blue T-shirt, her dark hair pulled back in a matching headband. She’d packed her things the night before, and her backpack was in the mudroom, sitting beside the back door.

Sunday knew because she’d almost tripped over

it when she'd gone outside to get the paper. She'd been trying to start a routine that might work for the rest of the year.

Start the coffee, get the paper, pack the lunches.

Except she'd forgotten to start the coffee.

Rosie had done that.

And it had taken Sunday nearly an hour to pack the lunches.

But she wasn't going to beat herself up over it.

Not like she had over the kiss.

She winced away from the thought, because the kiss had happened nearly a week ago, and it hadn't been repeated.

She and Flynn saw each other every day. Most evenings they rode down to the river and watched the sun set. He hadn't mentioned the supermoon or the dock, her tears or the kiss.

And she hadn't either.

It was water under the bridge, and the way she saw things, not worth spending time dwelling on.

But, of course, she had been dwelling on it. Wondering what she'd been thinking. What he had. Why they'd embraced in the moonlight and were now pretending it hadn't happened.

Although, she really shouldn't be wondering that.

She knew Flynn was letting her lead the way.

And she knew if she brought it up, he'd be happy to discuss it, but she hadn't.

"Mom!" Moisey hollered, barreling into the

room, her hair styled in perfect glossy ringlets. Heavenly's handiwork. So were the bright pink fingernails Moisey sported. "What are you doing awake already?"

"That seems to be the question of the hour, and I'll give you the same answer I gave your sister: It's the first day of school. I always see you off on the first day."

"And every day afterward, dweebs," Heavenly said as she walked into the kitchen, Oya on her hip.

She handed Sunday the baby. "I hope she does okay today. We've spent a lot of time together this summer. She might miss me."

"I'll make sure she's happy," Sunday assured her, kissing Oya's chubby cheek.

The baby giggled.

"Okay. I mean, I know you're her mom, but I'm her big sister, and I kind of feel like she needs me."

"She does, but she'll be fine while you're gone," Rosie said as she stepped in and took the baby from Sunday's arms. "So don't even worry. Not one bit. Your mom and I know how to handle things."

Heavenly nodded, running a hand down her knee-length denim skirt in a nervous gesture that drew Sunday's attention to the skirt. The shirt. The makeup-free face.

"Do I look okay, Sunday? I'm wondering

if I should change," the teen said. Maybe because she wasn't wearing too-tight clothes that revealed more than they covered. Instead, she'd chosen a knee-length skirt and a fitted T-shirt, wedge heels, and a few silver bracelets. No black eyeliner. No blue lipstick. No brightly colored eye shadow. Her short hair was cut in a shaggy pixie style, her face free of makeup except for a sweep of light-pink lip gloss. She looked young and beautiful, friendly and approachable.

She looked like a girl who felt good about herself and about her place in the world.

"Heavenly, you're beautiful," Sunday said. "Don't change a thing. I love your new style."

"Well, it's a new school year. I wanted to start it off as a new person, someone different than the girl who came to Benevolence a few years ago."

"You should always be yourself," Maddox shouted, racing into the room with a backpack over his shoulder and skidding to a stop next to Heavenly.

His mouth opened, his eyes widened, and he shook his head. "But new and different look good on you. Me and Milo are going to have to get the baseball bats to beat all the boys away. Milo!" he yelled. "Bring the bats."

"No bats!" Sunday said, and Maddox frowned.

"Never mind," he hollered, "bring the hockey sticks instead."

"What for?" Milo entered the room, dragging his backpack behind him.

"Heavenly needs protection."

"I don't need protection. I need to make sure I don't miss the bus. There's an honor's choir breakfast this morning, and I was invited. I don't want to miss out because one of my siblings was running behind, and I had to wait for him. Eat." She pointed at the boys, and both dropped into chairs and poured cereal for themselves.

"*We're* all going to be ready, but *you* should have gotten up earlier," Moisey said, her mouth filled with food.

"That's gross. Swallow before you talk," Twila said.

And Sunday could feel a headache starting to pound behind her eyes. She'd forgotten how exhausting the early-morning routine was.

"Why should I have to get up earlier? We all ride the same bus."

"Yeah, but we don't have to feed and water the horses," Moisey pointed out, shoveling in another mouthful of cereal.

"Dang!" Heavenly said, and she sounded so much like Flynn, Sunday smiled. "I was so busy worrying about what I was going to wear, I forgot all about that. You're right. I should have gotten up earlier."

"I'll take care of it for you, sweetheart," Sunday offered, but Heavenly shook her head.

"It's my chore. My responsibility. A person who doesn't take those things seriously isn't going to get far in life."

"You really do sound like your uncle," Sunday murmured, and Heavenly shot her a sly smile.

"I bet you two are going to have fun today," she said as she kicked off her wedge heels and shoved her feet into boots that she kept beside the back door.

"I don't know about Flynn, but I'm planning to do some laundry," Sunday responded. "There's not a whole lot of fun to be had there."

"No, you're not doing laundry. You're going to town to taste a new chocolate ganache Mr. Lamont is making for Clementine's wedding. She was going to do it, but she and Uncle Porter have to go to Spokane to shop for his tux. Remember?" Heavenly said.

Sunday thought she might. Vaguely.

"I . . . guess I do."

"If you don't, look at your calendar. I wrote it in for you. Ten o'clock. Maybe you guys can grab breakfast at the diner beforehand." She grinned and dashed outside.

The next few minutes passed in a blur. Kids eating. Kids spilling. Kids chatting and bickering and grabbing lunch boxes and backpacks. At some point during the chaos, Heavenly reappeared, kicked off the hay-flecked boots, and slid into the heels.

"Oh my gosh!" she panted. "We are going to miss the bus, if we don't get out of here right now!"

"I've been trying to tell everyone that," Twila agreed, kissing Sunday's cheek. "Have a good day, Mom. And don't eat too much chocolate. You'll get a stomachache. Oh. And bring an umbrella when you go out. It's supposed to storm today."

She skipped outside.

The other kids followed, offering hugs and kisses and words of advice until, finally, the kitchen was quiet except for the sound of Oya babbling happily as she tried to feed herself cereal from a bowl Rosie had set on the high chair tray.

"Well," Rosie said, grabbing dirty bowls from the table and putting them in the sink. "That went very well. Don't you think?"

"I can't remember how it usually goes, so I have nothing to compare it to."

"In that case, it went exceptionally well," Rosie said, pouring two cups of coffee and handing one to her.

"I've been thinking about things," she continued in a tone of voice that made Sunday's heart sink.

"Have you?"

"Yes. Thinking about how this is your house, and I tend to do things my way. The cleaning, the cooking, the packing lunches. All the things that the woman of the house should decide about.

I'm sure you had a routine before the accident. I'm sure I've messed it up something awful." She spooned three scoops of sugar into her coffee and stirred. "My sister has a nice room at her place. Even has a bathroom attached to it. She said I could stay with her after I've outstayed my welcome here."

"Are you quitting on us, Rosie?" Sunday asked, because that's what she thought she was hearing, but she wanted to be sure.

"That's not what I'm saying at all, dear," Rosie replied, her dark eyes focused on the newspaper again. "It's just that, I see you're improving every day now, taking over more of the daily chores. Look what you've done this morning, packing lunches and getting the children off to school."

"I screwed up the lunches, and Twila and Heavenly got the others off to school."

"That's the way you see it, but the way the kids see it, you're their mother again. Doing all the things a mother should do. And I'm an interloper. Keeping all of you from being the family you once were."

"Rosie," Sunday said, reaching for her hand and squeezing it gently. "Did one of the kids say something to you that made you think you're not wanted?"

"I have eyes in my head, and I can see that I'm in the way. No one has to say a word about it."

"You're not in the way," Sunday assured her,

taking Rembrandt's leash from the hook near the back door. "As a matter of fact, I don't know what I'd do if you weren't around."

"Well, for one, you wouldn't have an old lady micromanaging you while you're trying to take care of your children."

"You don't micromanage, and if you did, I wouldn't remember it."

Rosie let out a bark of laughter and shook her head. "That's a pretty good one. I've got to admit it."

"Thank you. But I'm serious. Who would watch Oya while I took the dog for a walk, if you weren't around?" Sunday asked. "She's too little to walk very far, and strollers aren't good off paved paths. I'd have to carry her in the pack, but I'm not strong enough for that yet."

"I hadn't thought of that. I'd just been thinking you probably weren't going to need my help anymore what with the kids back in school."

"I haven't been cleared to drive yet, and I'll need someone to bring me shopping and to appointments and to the school, because I'm sure the boys' antics will mean a couple of visits there a week."

"Clementine is always willing to lend a hand," Rosie said, but she was starting to look . . . hopeful.

"She's getting married in a couple of weeks. She's busy. Plus, fall harvest and the festival the farm is hosting. She won't have time for anything else."

"You do have a point," Rosie said with a nod, setting her cup down and straightening her shoulders. "So that settles it. I'll stay until Christmas, and we'll discuss things again then."

"Great. Wonderful," Sunday said.

"And, since I'm staying, don't mind if I tell you that you're looking a wee bit pale and a lot too thin. You grab one of those cinnamon rolls I made and go on outside. Get yourself some sun."

"But the laundry needs—"

"What are you paying me for, if not to wash the clothes? Out. Now. Go on. Take the puppy for a walk, but make sure you're back before ten." She opened the door, letting bright sunlight and chilly air in.

"Okay. Fine. I get it. You want me out of the kitchen." Sunday kissed Oya, tickled her bare feet. "I'll be back soon, sweetie."

She hooked Rembrandt to his leash, grabbed the plate Rosie thrust into her hands, and walked outside.

Sunday was asleep on the tree swing when Flynn walked around the side of the house, lying with her head on one end of the bench, her feet dangling off the other.

An empty plate sat on the ground nearby, Rembrandt lying beside it, attached to a leash that was wrapped around Sunday's wrist.

His tail thumped languidly as Flynn approached, his mouth opening in what could only be a smile.

"Hey, boy. Having fun?" Flynn crouched near the dog, scratching him behind his ears.

"He'd be having more fun if I were actually walking him instead of pretending to," Sunday said sleepily, her eyes still closed.

She looked beautiful there, sunlight dappling her arms and cheeks, her body long and lean, relaxed in the late-summer warmth. Today was the kids' first day back at school, and he'd thought about being at the house to see them off, but he hadn't wanted to be in the way or to make Sunday uncomfortable.

Doing things right had been a big deal to her, looming in her mind and taking up a lot of their conversations. Her plan to get up two hours early so that she could pack lunch bags and make breakfast and be sure that all the kids made it onto the bus was something she'd plotted out carefully, going through every step out loud, asking him again and again if he thought she could do it.

And, of course, he'd told her he did.

That she could.

He figured she could do just about anything she set her mind to, and he'd told her so. Enough times that he hoped she'd begun to believe it.

"How'd it go?" he asked, and she sighed, finally opening her eyes and meeting his gaze.

"It was a total disaster."

"Impossible," he said. "There's no way you made a disaster of your kids' first day back at school."

"You know that plaque on my wall? The one that says that nothing is impossible, because the very word says I'm possible?"

"Yes."

"It lies." She closed her eyes again, and he laughed, grabbing her hand and tugging her to her feet.

"I'm pretty sure the situation wasn't as dire as you're making it out to be."

"It took me an hour to make their lunches," she responded. "And I never cooked breakfast. They had to have cold cereal and reheated cinnamon rolls. I'm not even sure Heavenly ate."

"That doesn't sound like a disaster."

"Twila gave me instructions before she left the house. I should have been giving her a pep talk or telling her she was going to be awesome, but no. I was standing there with my mouth closed while she reminded me to bring an umbrella when I go out, because it's going to rain."

"Still not disaster," he said, dropping an arm around her shoulder, because she was there and he was, and they'd become friends.

But, of course, it felt like more.

Everything felt like more with Sunday.

"Rosie tried to quit."

That got his attention.

In a big way.

Because Rosie ran the kitchen and the kids, and Flynn didn't worry as much when she was there.

"That could be a disaster," he admitted.

"I explained that to her. Told her how much we needed her and how things are really busy, and how there's no way I could ever do this on my own."

"Yet. Eventually, you'll be able to."

"Maybe. Maybe not. We have to be realistic, Flynn. I'm not the person I was, and I'll never be her again."

"Thank God for that." The words slipped out, and she frowned.

"What's that supposed to mean?"

"The person you were was married to my brother, and if that were still the case, things would be a heck of a lot more awkward than they are now."

There. He'd tossed it out on the table. Left it there for both of them to see, because he was tired of pretending the kiss hadn't happened or that he didn't want it to happen again.

"Things aren't awkward," she protested.

"Good. Then you won't have a problem coming to town with me today. Doing the ganache tasting for my brother and Clementine. Maybe getting something to eat afterward."

"Why would I have a problem with that?"

“Because people are going to see us together, Sunday,” he replied. “And you’re not going to be in a wheelchair or using a cane. You’re not going to be limping much, and you’re going to have some color in your cheeks.”

“So what?”

“We’re talking about Benevolence. We’re talking about an entire town that knows you and that knew my brother, and that is going to wonder why the two of us seem so close.”

“Because we are close. We’re family.”

“Don’t be obtuse,” he said, using the word Twila had texted him.

She’d be proud to know he’d used it before he’d had his first cup of coffee.

Sunday scowled. “Don’t use the word of the day on me this early in the morning. My brain isn’t prepared for it.”

“Now you’re trying to change the subject.”

“Would you rather I pretend I’ve forgotten what happened the other night?” she asked.

“It might be preferable to the song and dance we go through every time I mention it,” he responded.

“Fine,” she snapped. “Have it your way. As far as the other night is concerned, I have no idea what you’re talking about. It’s gone. Slipped out of my head like water off a window, like mist off a lake, like butter off a hot roll, like sweat off an overheated brow.”

“Sweat off an overheated brow?”

"I ran out of similes," she said.

He laughed, and she joined him, leaning her head into his shoulder as if it had always been this way—the two of them, walking beside each other, bickering and laughing like a couple who'd been together forever and who knew each other to the deepest part of their souls.

Maybe that was why he kissed her.

There in the morning sun, dark clouds rolling in from the south and a chilly wind blowing from the north. Maybe it was why he cradled her face in his hands and then let his finger trail from her jaw to the hollow of her throat, let it rest on the scar there.

Maybe it was why he shifted his lips from her mouth to her forehead, why he whispered, "I'm glad you're still around, Sunday," against her skin.

Maybe it was why, when he looked into her eyes, he forgot that he had a ranch and a life to return to. Why he forgot everything but her.

"Yooohooo!" someone called, and Sunday jerked back, her lips still pink from his kiss, her eyes wide with surprise as she turned to face the house.

Rosie was standing on the porch, Oya in her arms, a broad smile on her wrinkled face.

She'd seen the kiss.

There was no doubt about that.

But she had the good grace not to mention it.

"I'm sorry, Rosie. I meant to come right back

in, but I fell asleep on the swing, and I lost track of time," Sunday said, the words rushing out in a jumble.

"Honey, there was no hurry. I just wanted to make certain you two weren't late for the chocolate tasting. I wouldn't want anyone to be disappointed. Most especially not Heavenly. She did make a special effort to remind you."

"Right. Of course. Let me just run and get changed and brush my hair and make myself presentable." She was moving as she spoke, jogging to the house, with the disjointed, hitched stride that had been hers since the accident.

She made it to the door without falling and slipped inside.

Which left Flynn standing in the yard, Rosie still smiling broadly in his direction.

"I should probably get ready too," he said, offering a quick wave.

"Before you go, I just wanted to mention one thing," she said, and he braced himself, certain he was about to get lectured on common sense and decency, on etiquette, and the amount of time a man should wait before he kissed a widow.

"What's that?"

"I agree with the girls."

"About?"

"It's not weird."

With that, she turned and sashayed back into the house like she'd won the day.

CHAPTER THIRTEEN

The ganache was delicious.

Of course.

It had been made by Byron Lamont himself. Proprietor of Chocolate Haven, Benevolence, Washington's one claim to fame, he'd been making the best fudge on this side of the Mississippi for more years than Sunday had been alive.

She hadn't remembered the last part.

She'd read it on a sign that hung near the cash register. It listed awards the shop has received as well as the date Byron had taken over running the place.

Nearly a decade before she was born.

"So what do you think?" Byron asked, standing beside the table as she took another forkful of dense yellow cake covered in gooey chocolate.

"I think it's delicious," she said.

"You?" Byron asked, spearing Flynn with a hard look. "What's your palate saying?"

"It's saying I could eat a gallon of this stuff, but the horse I've been riding might not be too pleased if I did."

"Humph," Byron responded, apparently not impressed with Flynn's attempt at humor.

That surprised her.

She'd known Byron her whole life.

She might have forgotten a lot about him, but she hadn't forgotten how kind he'd always been.

Gruff but kind.

That's how she'd have described him.

Now he just seemed grumpy, his green eyes shooting fire in Flynn's direction.

"Is something wrong?" Flynn asked, apparently not bothered enough to lose his appetite. He'd finished off an entire piece of yellow cake and was reaching for a slice of chocolate.

"Wrong? You bet your life there's something wrong." Byron pulled up a chair and sat down, elbows on the table, green eyes flashing. "Some damn developer is sniffing around at Emmerson Riley's property."

"It's for sale, right?" Flynn asked reasonably.

Which obviously wasn't the response Byron wanted.

"What's that got to do with the price of tea in China?" he demanded, and Flynn set down his fork, pushed the slice of cake away.

"The chocolate is good. The yellow is better. I think Porter and Clementine will be happy with it," he said, obviously trying to change the subject.

"This is not the time to talk about cake, son," Byron replied, lifting the tray of samples and setting it on the next table over. "You want a Walmart going up right next to Sunday's property?"

"I don't," Sunday replied, the thought of someone buying out the land adjacent to hers and building a shopping center making her feel physically ill.

She pushed aside her slice of cake.

"What makes you think the developer is going to build a Walmart?" Flynn asked.

Byron leaned close, glancing around the empty shop as if he thought a spy might be hiding in their midst.

"He's from California," he whispered. "And don't you be breathing a word of that to anyone. I got the information from my daughter-in-law. She's a Realtor, so she's in the know."

"I understand your concern, Byron," Flynn assured him. "I really do, but progress happens. Small towns grow into bigger ones."

"That's all you've got to say?"

"I don't know what else I *can* say," Flynn responded. "Emmerson left the land to his son, and his son can sell it to whomever he wants."

"Bull," Byron spat. "That boy hasn't set foot in this town in ten years. He doesn't get to decide anything."

"The law would probably say something different," Flynn reminded him, but Byron was on a roll.

He stood, pacing to a wall nearly covered with old black-and-white photos. "See that?" he asked, jabbing at a picture of an old milk wagon being pulled by horses. “That milk came from Sunday’s farm. Those horses came from Emmerson’s. They delivered it to this shop three times a week. Gallons of sweet cream and farm-fresh milk. That was and is the backbone of this business. Good product sourced locally.”

“I understand your passion—” Flynn began, but Byron raised his hand.

“No. You don’t, because you haven’t watched towns like this one die. You haven’t seen them overrun by city folk who don’t care about local business and who worship the damn almighty dollar more than they do the God who gave it to them. You’ve got yourself a nice setup in Texas, I hear.”

“I do.”

“So you’re not invested in your hometown. I get that. But the next time you come home? When you see the clouds of smog sitting heavy in the air because dozens of tractors and bulldozers are tearing up the land and pouring concrete on our heritage? You remember we had this talk.” He stood, met Sunday’s eyes. “I’m sorry, honey. I didn’t mean to ruin your morning.”

“You didn’t,” she lied, and he nodded.

“I did. Forgive an old fool, okay? I love this town a little too much, I guess. I don’t want it to change.” He stepped behind the counter, grabbing a small white box from a shelf and putting two large squares of peanut butter fudge in it.

He handed it to her, smiling kindly. “It’s been a long time since I’ve sent any of this home for you.”

“Sent it home?” she repeated, the sick feeling that had settled in the pit of her stomach when he’d mentioned the developer growing.

“Sure. That husband of yours liked to buy himself a pound of chocolate. Every so often, he’d come in and pick out the fancy stuff, fill an entire box with nougats and caramels and bonbons. Said I shouldn’t tell you because his sugar levels were too high, and he wasn’t supposed to be eating sweets.”

He paused, and she thought he might be waiting for her to agree, to tell him that Matt had been prediabetic.

She didn’t, because it wouldn’t have been true.

“Anyways,” he continued, “he’d buy the chocolate, and I’d always throw in the fudge for free. I know how much you love it.”

“I do,” she said, surprised that she sounded normal, that her words hadn’t been strangled out by her rage.

Matt had never been a sweet eater. She knew that. He didn’t like candy and hated fudge. He preferred salty food. But he’d bought pounds of chocolates enough times that Byron remembered.

He hadn’t given it to Sunday.

She’d gotten the free fudge that Byron had sent for her.

The knowledge was a knife to the back after she'd already been stabbed in the heart.

Her love for Matt had started dying the first time she'd suspected he was cheating.

This?

It had killed it completely.

She stood, the box of fudge in her hand, a smile on her face, her heart pounding crazily, because she was that angry, that disappointed.

In herself.

In Matt.

"Thank you for thinking of me, Byron," she said.

"Anytime, hun. It's great to see you out and about. How about you bring the kids when you're in town next? I'll let them choose a bonbon or a caramel."

"They'd like that," she responded as if lava weren't trying to flow up her throat and explode out her head. "I'll see you soon."

That was it. All she could manage.

And then she was out of there, rushing to the door and stepping outside. Clouds had drifted across the sun, and the sky matched her mood—ominous and heavy.

She kicked something as she walked, and it skittered across the cobblestone sidewalk. A purple rock. Shiny and smooth. Shaped like a heart.

She left it where it was.

She wasn't surprised when Flynn appeared at

her side, matching his long steps to her shorter stride, not touching her, but close enough that she could have touched him.

If she'd wanted to.

All she wanted right then was to be alone, to find her way back to the farm and sit in the living room and try to forget the ganache and the cake and the candy that had never made it home.

For a moment, they walked in silence, the distant rumble of thunder and the quiet sounds of town life filling the space between them.

When Flynn finally spoke, she could feel his words as much as she could hear them, the cadence of his voice as familiar as the melody of the river and the whisper of grass behind the farmhouse.

"He was a bastard," he said quietly. "I hate saying that about my brother, but it's true."

She didn't respond.

She didn't suppose he expected her to.

After all, what could she say? That he was right? That the man she'd married had been a liar, a cheat, a charlatan?

"He was a bastard, but he loved you, Sunday. I know he did. You. The kids. The life you had together."

"What kind of love buys chocolates for another woman? What kind of love orders flowers for his wife with one hand and for his mistress with another? What kind of love leaves debt and destruction and unhappiness? What kind, Flynn? I really want to know."

"The kind that isn't mature enough to value what it has," he said.

"Love doesn't have to be mature to value what it has," she said. "Just look at the charts and calendars and lists the kids make me. Look at all the attention and time they've expended trying to keep me from failing. Not because they need me to succeed, but because they don't want me to be hurt again, and they know that disappointing them upsets me."

"They learned their hearts from you," he said, the words simple and eloquent and, probably, true.

He reached for her hand. She let him take it.

Let him weave his finger through hers, because she liked the raspy feel of his calloused palm against hers, and because Matt didn't deserve her loyalty.

He never had.

The first raindrops fell as they reached the truck, bouncing off dry earth and pinging against the pavement.

"I should have listened to Twila," she said as Flynn opened the door and helped her in. "She said I should bring an umbrella."

He called Porter and Clementine on the way back to the house, using his handless phone to give a report on the ganache and cake.

He thought Sunday might chime in with her opinion, but she was staring out the window, watching as the landscape flew past.

"Is Sunday there?" Clementine asked, her voice muffled by the rain. "I'd like to hear her opinion."

"She's here," he responded.

"It was good," Sunday offered.

Good.

As if that were going to help Porter and Clementine decide.

"Which one did you like best?" Clementine asked. "We've got to order today. The baker is making a big stink about not being the one to provide the frosting. I keep trying to explain to her that Byron's ganache is going to enhance her cake, but she's not having any of it, so she's being a pain in the butt about the deadline. We either tell her what we want today, or she won't have the cake ready for the wedding."

"There are other bakers," Sunday offered.

Again. Not helpful.

"True, but she makes the best marble cake I've ever had."

"Then order that," Sunday said. "It will be great with the ganache."

She sounded as enthusiastic as a dead man at the gates of hell.

He wanted to disconnect the call, remind her that Clementine and Porter were a little excited about getting married, and tell her to turn up the enthusiasm.

But she must have realized how she sounded.

She rubbed her palms over her thighs, cleared her throat. “What I mean is, the ganache is to die for. I don’t even like chocolate, and I could have eaten a cup of the stuff. You could slather it on anchovies and people would eat it.”

“Really?”

“Absolutely. Do the marble cake with the ganache. We’re having the ceremony and reception at the farm, right? Rosie and I can make apple pies and cider. The kids can make cookies.”

“That’s too much work, Sunday,” Porter cut in. “You have enough on your plate with the fall festival coming up. We just thought we’d do the ceremony at the chapel and then have some cake and punch.”

“The festival is a month away, and we’ve got everything under control. Besides, your wedding is just as important. What if we drag out the smoker I saw in the garage? We can have pulled pork and chicken sandwiches. Chips. A dessert bar. And that delicious cake.” She was on a roll now, tossing out ideas like a Google search engine.

“That sounds like fun,” Clementine said. “A nice barbeque at the end of summer.”

“I bet some of the women from church would be willing to bring side dishes. Salads and pastas. You know how the community is. Always happy to have something to celebrate." Her voice broke, but she was in it for the long haul, chatting with Clementine until Flynn pulled up to the house.

"Hey, Clementine?" he said, interrupting her description of flowers she was planning to order for the ceremony. "We're back at the house, and we've got some work to do. We'll talk later, okay?"

"Sure! I'll take a picture of your brother in his tux and send it to you so that you can laugh at him."

"There's not going to be anything to laugh about," Porter said. "I wear tuxes all the time, and I look pretty damn good in one. If I do say so myself."

"Nothing like a big head to get a guy noticed," Clementine responded, her laughter ringing through the truck as Flynn ended the call.

He turned off the engine and clapped.

"What's that for?" Sunday asked, her face gaunt, her eyes deeply shadowed.

"That was a stellar performance. You deserve a standing ovation, but I can't make it work while we're in the truck."

She smiled. "In that case, I'll take the applause and be happy with it."

"Of course, your performance has created a problem."

"What kind of problem?"

"Clementine and Porter like your ideas. Now

we have to pull them off. The smoker. The food. The decorated tables and little twinkly lights."

"Fairy lights," she corrected, opening her purse and frowning. "I forgot I'm not taking notes anymore."

"Since when?"

"Since the day you told me I needed to be there for my kids."

"I don't remember saying that."

"I'm paraphrasing, and you had a point. I was spending so much time worrying about forgetting that I wasn't living. Not the way the kids needed me to."

"What about the way you needed?" he asked, tucking a strand of hair behind her ear.

"One of the things I know that your brother didn't is that it isn't all about me. Not this life. Not this house. Not this land." She waved toward the landscape, the rain pouring down onto green grass and golden fields. "I'm doing this for the kids. All of it, because I want them to have it when I'm gone."

"And what do you want them to have when you're here?"

"Me. My presence. My involvement. I want them to know that if they wake up afraid in the middle of the night, they can climb into bed with me. I want them to understand that they can tell me the truth about anything, and I'll still love them. I might not remember to take them shopping for clothes, and I might put the wrong snack in their lunch boxes, but I want them to remember that I was always there for them."

"That's quite a legacy," he said, oddly touched by her words.

He'd never thought about having kids.

It hadn't even occurred to him to want them.

He'd planned his life around ranching, and he'd figured that would be enough. He'd passed his knowledge on to ranch hands as eager to learn as he'd been, and that legacy was one that he knew would stick.

But children?

No. He'd never planned them. He'd never wanted them.

Now, though, he thought it might be nice to stick around after the wedding, to keep teaching Heavenly about horses and the boys about being young men. To keep listening to Moisey's endless chatter and marveling at Twila's organized planning.

He thought it might be nice to be around when Oya said her first word and when she rode her first bike.

He thought it might be nice to watch Sunday grow older, her hair turning white, her skin more transparent.

And it might be nice to hold her hand as the sun set on their final days.

Whoa!

He pulled himself up short. In his world of right and wrong and good and bad, he could fathom falling in love with Sunday, and he could also imagine hurting her.

He could imagine stepping in and being a father to his nieces and nephews, and he could also imagine failing them. Disappointing them.

Teaching them what not to be.

Just like his father had done.

He opened the door, letting rain splash into the truck.

It splattered his face but did nothing to clear his thoughts.

"We'd better go inside," he said, not looking at Sunday, because he was afraid he'd see his future in her eyes, and he was even more afraid of what that future would be.

"What are you running away from, Flynn?" she asked.

"I'm not running away," he said, and felt her stiffen.

"I thought you were different," she said, and he finally met her eyes.

He expected anger, but all he saw was disappointment, sadness. Maybe a little relief.

"I thought you were a straight shooter."

"I am."

"And yet, you just lied."

"I didn't lie. I'm not running away," he repeated, and this time anger flared in her eyes.

"And now you did it again."

"Sunday," he began, wanting to explain the unexplainable. Wanting to tell her that he wasn't running away, he was leaving, because he never wanted to hurt her or the kids, and he was afraid he couldn't trust himself not to.

"You're the one who made me look at the moon when I wanted to close my eyes. You're the one who made me laugh when all I wanted to do was cry. You're the one who told me I could when I thought I couldn't, and I believed you, because I never thought you would lie. But I was wrong about you. Just like I was wrong about your brother, and I'm glad I figured it out now, because I don't want to be standing on the dock in ten years, tossing heart-shaped rocks into the river and cursing your name." Her voice broke, and he reached for her.

But she stepped out into the rain, falling as her feet slipped out from under her. She landed in a puddle of mud, and he bolted from the truck.

But she was up before he reached her side, hobbling toward the house, her soaked hair stuck to her scalp. He could see the scar, snaking around the curve of her skull, and he could remember how she'd looked, lying helpless in the hospital bed.

And he knew he'd failed her without even meaning to.

He waited where he was until she was inside, his clothes heavy with rain, his body chilled.

Twila had been right.

They should have brought umbrellas.

CHAPTER FOURTEEN

He woke to a hand on his shoulder, the pitch-black house pulsing around him.

"Uncle Flynn," Moisey said, her face so close to his, she could see the whites of his eyes through the darkness. "We have a problem."

"We do?" he asked, a rumble of thunder and a blast of wind nearly drowning out his words.

"Yes," she responded, her breath fanning his face. Froot Loops and milk with a hint of mint.

"Have you been eating cereal?" he asked.

"I told her not to. She dropped some on the floor, and I couldn't find them. I would have turned on the lights, but the electricity is out," Twila responded, and he realized it was her hand on his shoulder.

"What's going on, girls?" he said, sitting up.

The boys were a few feet away, their hair glowing white in the darkness. "And boys?"

"I told you, we have a problem," Moisey repeated.

"The electricity will come back on soon. How about we all just go back to sleep before we wake up the rest of the house?" he suggested.

"That's the problem. The rest of the house isn't here," Milo replied.

At least, Flynn thought it was Milo, his voice a little higher-pitched than his brother's.

"What do you mean, it's not here?"

"The rest of the house isn't here," Milo repeated, as if that made perfect sense. As if, somehow, part of a house could disappear.

The wind howled again, rattling the windows, and Flynn thought he finally understood.

"Did a tree fall on the house?" he asked. "Is there a hole in the roof?"

"No," Moisey said, and he could hear tears in her voice. When he leaned closer, he could see them tracking down her face.

"Honey, what's wrong?" He pulled her into his arms, surprised when she burrowed against him, her hands clamped around his waist.

Something inside him melted.

This must be what it felt like to be a parent. This soul-deep love that sprang out of nowhere and made a guy like him go soft. He could imagine it would be enough to keep a temper in check, to keep fists relaxed. To keep any normal person from harming his child.

Because it didn't just feel like love.

It felt like a fierce need to protect and comfort and provide for.

He'd always thought his father was a bastard.

Now, he realized he'd been a monster, too.

"Mommy is gone," Moisey wailed, her voice rivaling the storm raging outside.

"What do you mean 'gone'?" he asked, turning his head so he could see Twila. She was the calm one. The organized one. The one who should be able to help him figure this out.

Even in the darkness, he could see that she was crying, too, her shoulders shaking with the force of her tears. He reached for her hand, tugged her closer.

"Hey," he murmured, keeping one arm around Moisey and throwing the other around her. "It's going to be okay."

"No, it's not," she said, her voice so clear and precise, he wouldn't have known she was crying if he hadn't seen her shoulders heaving.

"Tell me what's going on? Okay? Because there's nothing in this world that we can't fix together."

"We can't fix the fact that Daddy is dead," she said.

"Right. There aren't many things," he corrected. "So tell me what's going on. Why do you think your mother is missing?"

"Because she was looking for me." Heavenly stepped into the room, a white wraith moving toward him through the shadows.

Her hair was wet.

Soaked.

And she was wrapped in the terry-cloth robe that usually hung on the back of the bathroom door.

"Looking for you where?"

"I didn't latch one of the stalls properly this morning, and when I went to feed the horses this evening, Chance was gone." Her voice broke, and if he'd had an extra arm, she'd have been in it.

"Why didn't you tell me?" He stood, easing the younger girls from his arms and grabbing his shirt from the back of the chair.

"You were out all night. Probably having beers with your buddies."

He didn't like her tone or her implication, but he didn't have time to deal with a teenage attitude, so he ignored both. "I was out with my brothers, touring the property next door to yours. After that, we went to dinner," he corrected.

"Why would you tour property for six hours?" she demanded.

"Two. And then I had dinner, and then I drove around for a while."

Because he hadn't wanted to return until he knew what to say to Sunday, knew how to make it right.

But the words hadn't come to him, and he'd finally driven back to the house, the wind just beginning to howl as he'd walked inside.

"Men are all liars and pigs," she spat, and he'd finally had enough.

"Wrong, but we don't have time to discuss it. Chance got out of the stable, and you could have reached me, if you'd wanted to. You have a cell phone. You have my number. Why didn't you call?"

"Because it was my fault," she admitted. "And

I didn't want to get in trouble. I figured I could find him and bring him back, dry him off and give him some good feed, and everything would be all right."

"Okay, so how did this turn into your mother missing?" He opened his suitcase and used his Maglite to find his emergency pack. He knew what it contained. He checked it before he traveled. First aid kit. Compass. Emergency phone zipped into a waterproof bag. Flare gun. Fire starter. Mylar blanket. MREs.

He grabbed his duster and slid into it, then put on the pack.

"Hurry up, Heavenly. Every minute I'm in here, I'm not out searching for your mother," he said, because the teen had fallen silent, and he didn't have time to coax the answer out of her.

"I waited until everyone was asleep. Which took forever, because Sunday didn't stop pacing her room until you returned from whatever happy little jaunt you'd been on."

"Stay on track," he cautioned.

"Sorry," she muttered. "Once everyone was asleep, I used the fire escape ladder to climb down from my window, and I went looking for Chance. But one of the dweebs heard me, and went and got Sunday."

"I am not a dweeb," Twila said, her voice thick with tears.

"Okay. You're not. So stop crying."

"I have to cry. This is my fault. If Mom dies, it will be because of me."

"It's my fault," Heavenly corrected. "And Sunday isn't going to die. Is she, Uncle Flynn?" she asked, obviously looking for and needing reassurance.

"No. How long were you outside?" he asked, trying to get a time frame because that would help him figure out how far Sunday might have gone.

"An hour."

"You're sure?"

"Yes. I set the alarm on my phone so I wouldn't stay out any longer than that. I didn't want to get hypothermia. When I got home, the kids were waiting in my room, and Sunday was gone."

"And how long did you wait before you came to get me?"

"I sent them to get you right away. I figured you would know what to do." She said it without any attitude, without any particular tone. She said it like she meant it. Like she'd really believed he was the solution to their problem.

God, he hoped she was right.

He'd been involved in plenty of searches. Sometimes, things worked out and the missing were reunited with their loved ones.

But only sometimes.

Other times, all the hard work and dedication led to heartache.

"Heavenly, I want you to wake Rosie. Have her

call the sheriff. He can get some men together to help with the search. Milo, you call Uncle Porter. Maddox, you call Sullivan. You have their numbers, right?"

"Yes," the boys responded.

"Once you've finished that, come back in here and sit with your sisters. No lighting candles unless Rosie is supervising, and no leaving the house. Understood?"

"Yes," all five replied.

"Good. Where's Rembrandt?"

"Sunday's room. I'll get him." Heavenly sprinted away.

"You're not going to take Rembrandt out in the storm, are you?" Moisey asked. "He might get scared."

"He won't. He's a brave guy, and he loves to play games. So we're going to make a game of finding your mother."

And the sooner they got started, the better. With the storm raging, flash floods were a danger. Sunday had lived in the area long enough to know that, but that didn't mean she'd remember.

He could hear Rembrandt racing through the upstairs hall, and he called to him as he stepped outside and into the downpour.

Sunday figured she'd done a lot of stupid things in her life. She might not remember them, but she was sure she'd kept a list when she was a kid.

A nicely typed homage to her childish exploits. A written testimony of all the things that she'd done that were a lot stupider than going to church the day she'd turned eighteen and speaking vows that committed her to someone for a lifetime.

She'd probably jumped into shallow pools without checking the depth of the water, or gone to the river without her parents' permission, or snuck out of the house late at night just to say she'd done it.

Yes. Sunday was absolutely convinced that she'd done stupid things during the nearly thirty years she'd been alive, but this?

It took the cake.

It raised the standard.

And if she wasn't careful, it was going to earn her a Darwin Award for the stupidest way to die.

She picked her way along the bank of the overflowing river, looking for a place to cross. The footbridge was underwater, all the shallow areas now deep. The wind gusted, slapping wet hair against her cheeks and plastering her soaked pajamas to her skin.

Because, of course, she hadn't bothered getting dressed.

She hadn't bothered grabbing a coat.

She'd figured she'd be fast enough to climb down the ladder and nab her escapee child before a drop of rain touched either of their heads.

She had also grossly overestimated her ability to keep up with a thirteen-year-old.

By the time she'd reached the ground, Heavenly had disappeared into the storm, searching for a horse that, according to Twila, had escaped his stall.

Sunday had gone to the barn first, hoping to find Heavenly hunkered down with Chance. She'd found the horse, munching hay, damp but seemingly happy.

Had she bothered to saddle him up so that she could cover ground more quickly? Had she grabbed a blanket from the tack room or a jacket from the office? Had she gone back to the house to alert Rosie and Flynn?

Of course she hadn't.

She'd run from the barn pell-mell into the granddaddy of all storms, screaming for Heavenly until she lost her voice.

And then, to compound the matter, she'd crossed the footbridge, knowing darn well that it washed out during storms like this.

So she was stranded and frantic to find her daughter, but she didn't want to be stupid, because stupidity in situations like this meant you died.

"Heavenly!" she tried to shout, but all that emerged was a raspy croak.

"Heavenly," she tried again, her bare feet sinking into muck and slipping on moss-covered rocks.

She hadn't bothered with shoes, either, because she hadn't imagined that she'd walk more than a few feet from the house.

But here she was, walking the riverbank, her feet stone-cold.

Her teeth chattered, and she was tempted to stop for a while, maybe find a little cubbyhole to hide away in until the storm passed.

She had to find Heavenly first.

She had to make sure she was okay.

Right now, nothing else mattered.

Her legs felt heavy, but she continued to move, trudging around the bend in the river that marked the end of her property and the beginning of Emmerson Riley's.

Strange how she could remember that, but she couldn't remember what she'd eaten on her wedding day or where she and Matt had honey-mooned.

Had they gone somewhere?

Or had they hidden away in the little rancher on her parents' property, pretending they were in some exotic location because they couldn't afford to visit one?

She didn't know.

It didn't matter.

But she'd been thinking about Matt a lot recently. Tonight even more.

Because of Flynn. Because of the conversation they'd had and the things she'd said.

That he was a liar, and that she was glad she'd found out now rather than later.

She'd meant it, but after she'd gone in the

house, she'd realized that she hadn't really been speaking to Flynn. She'd been speaking to Matt. Just like she had been on the dock, shouting her accusations to the universe in some vain hope that he would hear.

Because she knew Flynn wasn't a liar, and if she hadn't been such a coward she would have found him and told him that.

Instead, she'd wasted time, pacing her room and trying to pinpoint the exact moment she'd known Matt had been deceiving her.

After their first anniversary when he'd said he couldn't buy her a gift because they didn't have the money? A few weeks later, she'd seen the receipt for a hunting rifle he'd bought. Seven hundred dollars. But Matt didn't hunt, and he hadn't wanted to learn.

He'd never even bought ammunition.

He'd hung the rifle above the fireplace mantel and bragged about his marksmanship skills when friends came to visit.

Those memories were as clear and crisp as the lightning that flashed across the sky.

"Flynn was right. You were a bastard," she said, water streaming into her mouth as she opened it.

She was shaking violently.

She needed to find shelter, and she needed to get warm.

God, she hoped Heavenly had done the same.

"Please," she whispered, the word torn from

her mouth and tossed into the whirling storm. "Keep her safe."

She didn't know if she was talking to God, or praying to Him, or trying, once again, to send a message to Matt.

She was too cold and too tired to care.

She just wanted someone to hear and save her daughter.

"Please," she murmured again, her lips numb with cold, her pulse sloshing loudly in her ears. She stumbled, her foot slipping between two river rocks.

She tried to yank free, but she was stuck tight, water swirling around her ankle and then her calf, and then her knee.

She pulled desperately, imagining her name at the top of the Darwin Award list. Imagining her kids telling the story of how their mother had survived a horrible car wreck only to die because she'd gone out in a raging storm in the middle of the night.

She yanked with renewed energy, determined to *not* die.

Not here anyway. Not so close to home. To her kids. To Flynn.

To all the things and people she loved.

One of the rocks gave, and she was free, flying backward and landing hard. Water flooding her nose and mouth, stealing the air from her lungs.

She tried to right herself, but the rocks were

slippery, her perpetually clumsy movement clumsier from cold.

Darkness edged in as her body shouted that she needed to inhale, and her brain shouted that if she did, she'd die. Something grabbed the back of her pajama top, pulling and tugging and yanking until she was flat on her back in shallow water, staring up at the rain-filled sky.

She lay there stunned, something wet and velvety tickling her cheek.

She reached for it, touched the soaked muzzle of a dog.

"Rembrandt?" she said, her voice raspy and raw.

He licked her cheek again. Then her nose and chin.

It didn't do much to warm her, but it sure made her feel better.

"Thanks, buddy," she said, pulling him into her lap. He was still small enough to fit, and she had no idea how he'd managed to drag her from the river.

Somehow, he had, and she was alive, and the best way to thank him was to get up and keep moving.

"Okay," she rasped, standing unsteadily. "Want to go home?"

He barked happily and darted away.

"Rembrandt!" she called, terrified that they'd be separated in the storm, and she'd be alone again.

He returned seconds later, nudging her calves,

trying to get her to move away from the water. She was too tired to fight him, so she went, moving away from the rolling waves and overflowing banks and into a field of grass.

She was on Emmerson's property.

She could see his house in the distance, and that's where Rembrandt seemed to want her to go. He ran in that direction, disappeared for a few seconds, and raced back, circling her legs until he was sure she was heading the right way.

She reached the crumbled asphalt, rivulets of rainwater rushing through its cracks. The house was just ahead, boarded up, the FOR SALE sign hanging listlessly from a post in the yard.

Only, it didn't say FOR SALE.

It said SOLD.

Byron had been right.

An investor had purchased it.

She tried not to think about the house being torn down and a Walmart going up. She was soaked to the skin and cold to the bone, and she didn't have time to wax nostalgic about a house she'd never even been inside.

"We need to find a way inside, Rembrandt," she shouted above the howling wind.

But the puppy had disappeared as quickly as he'd arrived, and she was alone again. Standing on the porch of someone else's house, shivering.

She knocked on the door, because that seemed like the right thing to do.

To her surprise, it swung open.

She stepped inside and was surprised again.

It didn't have the musty scent old houses tended to acquire. The floor felt solid beneath her feet, and she moved cautiously, walking through a foyer and into a room to the right of the door.

There were shadowy pieces of furniture in the corners. Table. Chairs.

This had to have been the dining room.

She stepped through another doorway and into a kitchen, the cupboards black in the dim light.

"I bet the living room is next," she commented.

"He called it the study," a man said.

She screamed, running for the back door. She could see it just ahead, boarded up, letting in no light.

She pivoted, racing back the way she'd come.

And straight into a hard chest.

Familiar arms.

And the sweet touch of lips against her forehead.

Flynn.

She threw her arms around him, buried her face in the warmth of his neck.

And she wondered how she hadn't known the moment he'd spoken that it was him.

CHAPTER FIFTEEN

"Flynn," she cried, her arms wrapping around his waist, her hands clutching his sides. "Thank God! I thought I was going to be spending the night alone in this house."

"That would have been a heck of a lot better than spending it out in the rain and wind," he replied. "What were you thinking running out of the house on a night like this? No shoes. No coat. You could have frozen to death."

"No need for a lecture," she responded, her teeth chattering. "I was following Heavenly. She snuck out of the house to find—"

"Chance. I know. I heard the entire sordid tale."

"Did Twila tell you?"

"Heavenly. She made it home just fine."

"Thank God for that, too," she whispered, letting her head drop to his chest.

She could hear his heart thumping, the slow, steady beat as soothing as firelight on a winter morning.

She shivered, and it had nothing to do with the cold and everything to do with a soul-deep longing for this. For him. For endless moments standing in the warmth of his embrace.

"You're freezing," he said, dragging a sheet off one of the chairs and tucking the edges beneath her chin, his hands so gentle, she wanted to cry.

"I'm sorry," she said, her teeth chattering.

"For what? Running out in the rain to find your daughter? I'd have done the same." He turned on a flashlight and set it in the center of the table. It didn't illuminate everything, but she could see his face, the deep circles beneath his eyes, the dark stubble on his chin.

God, he looked good, and she wanted to run her hands through his wet hair, tell him a million times how wrong she'd been.

"Not for that. For calling you a liar."

"You didn't call me a liar." He slipped out of a backpack and set it next to the light.

"I implied that you were one."

"Maybe, but I understand why you'd have a hang-up about lying men."

"Not you, Flynn. I don't have a hang-up about you."

"No?" He met her eyes, offering the slow, gentle smile she'd come to know so well. If she lived a thousand years and never saw him again, she would still remember the way his lips curved, and his face softened, and all the things he didn't say shone in his eyes.

"At least not a bad one," she added, and his smile broadened.

"That's good to know, Sunday, because I've kind of got a hang-up about you."

"You do?"

"Sure." He took a small silver square from the

pack and unfolded a Mylar blanket, wrapping it around her shoulders.

Then he shrugged out of his coat and dropped it on top, tugging it close under her chin, before pulling her back into his arms.

"There," he said. "That's better."

"For which one of us? Because from where I'm standing, it looks like you got the short end of the stick. I've got the sheet, the blanket, and your coat, and you've got nothing but a plaid shirt and jeans."

"I've got you, so I think things are working out pretty nicely."

"Because you have a hang-up about me?"

"Because I missed you tonight. We usually take a ride down by the river."

"It was raining."

"And you were angry," he pointed out.

"And confused about who I was angry with. I know you're not your brother, Flynn."

"That's good, because I'd like to take a lot more rides with you. I'd like to bring you and the kids to Texas and let you see the ranch. I'd like to show you the old shed behind this house that contains all Emmerson's work tools. And I'd like you to help me find and revive the rosebushes that boarder this yard."

"Rosebushes?"

"One for every year Emmerson was married to his wife."

"He gave her a rosebush every year?" she asked, still standing in his arms and looking into his face. And it felt so right and so good, she didn't think she'd ever be able to make herself move away.

"No. He was a cheapskate. Frugal to a fault. He always gave her practical things. Vacuums and new dishes and mops and brooms."

"Ouch," she said, and he chuckled.

"Yeah. That's what I thought when he told me, and I was only twelve or thirteen. So he'd given her all those practical gifts, and then she got sick. Cancer. It was in her pancreas and liver. The doctor said she might have a year to live, if she was lucky. She made it two, and every month for two years, on the date of their anniversary, Emmerson brought her a rosebush. Twenty-four for their twenty-four years, and she'd lie on the couch in their living room watching as he planted them for her. Didn't matter if it was raining or snowing or hot as hell. On the twentieth of every month, he planted the rosebush. She died on their twenty-fifth anniversary, and after the coffin was in the grave, Emmerson planted a rosebush in front of the marker. He said those roses bloomed in every color. Red. Yellow. Pale peach. All her favorites."

"That is probably the most romantic story I've ever heard," she said, caught up in it and in him.

"Romantic, yes. But he didn't share it with me because of that. I was a kid. I didn't care squat about romance."

"So why did he tell you?"

"My mother was sick. She was dying, and I spent a lot of time away, because I couldn't stand to see her suffer or to watch the way my father treated her. Emmerson wanted me to know the truth about love before it was too late. It's not about the romantic gestures. It's about the sacrifice. The work. The going out in every kind of weather, because you want to make another person happy."

"Wow."

"Yeah. He was a smart guy, and he gave me something my father never could or would."

"Respect?"

"That, but he also gave me the second chance so few of us have. He told me that story, and I started going home every night and sitting beside my mom, reading her passages from the books she loved. I made a lot of memories that way, and I like to think, I made her happy."

You did, she wanted to say, but she was crying, salty tears stinging the corner of her eyes.

"I didn't mean to make you cry," he said, wiping them away.

"You didn't. Your story did."

"I think that might be the same," he said, offering a wry smile.

"Maybe," she admitted. "But I'd rather cry for beauty than for sorrow. I wish I could see the roses in the spring. I bet they're lovely."

"Once we free them from weeds, they will be," he agreed.

"I'm sure whoever bought the property will take care of it," she said, not sure why the thought of that made her so sad.

Maybe because the house might be torn down, the roses plowed, the life Emmerson and his wife had lived buried under asphalt and dirt-cheap prices.

"I'm the new owner," Flynn said. "Or I will be as soon as the paperwork is done. I offered a cash deal, because I knew Emmerson's son couldn't resist."

"You're the owner?" she repeated, because the rain was clattering on the tin roof, and she wasn't sure she'd heard him right.

"Like I said, I will be."

"But . . . why?"

"Because I realized Byron was right. A Walmart would change the town more than it needed to be. Plus, the acreage is attached to yours, and I can see us expanding in a few years. Either moving more toward equestrian pursuits or raising cattle."

"You own a ranch. In Texas," she pointed out, but her hands were on his shoulder and she'd levered up on her toes.

She was looking into his face and into his eyes, and she was trying to read the truth there, because she needed to know that he meant what he said, that the future he was describing was a possibility.

"I'm very aware of that," he said. "I'm also aware that I have a ranch manager who is great at his job. He can handle things for me when I'm here."

"Flynn, I don't want you to give up your dreams."

"I have my dreams, and I'm continuing to pursue them. But I'm making new dreams, too. That's part of life, right? Looking up at the starlit sky and realizing where you are is exactly where you want to be?"

"There are stars in Texas," she said, because she was so afraid that he'd regret buying Emmerson's farm and devoting a part of himself to a place that he'd once fled.

"But there's not you," he whispered against her lips. "The thing is, it wasn't the stars, Sunday. It wasn't the giant moon rising above the mountains. None of those things were home until you were in my arms."

He kissed her then, and she could see it—the starlit sky and the giant moon, and the two of them, wrapped in each other's arms.

"I like your new dreams," she murmured, and felt him smile.

"Will you write about them in your journal?"

"I won't have to. They're already written on my heart."

EPILOGUE

This wedding was going to go off without a hitch.

Even if it killed her!

Sunday lifted the hem of her tea-length skirt and tried to jump over the wagon filled with flowers. The one that she was *supposed* to be bringing to the chapel.

She'd been waylaid by a massive, curly-haired beast.

She tripped, of course, missing the dog by a hair's breadth. He darted away, head held high, tail wagging, a silky piece of purple fabric in his mouth.

"Rembrandt!" she shouted. "Come back here with that cummerbund!"

She tried to give chase, but the darn dress tangled around her legs and she pitched forward again.

And probably would have face-planted if someone hadn't grabbed her by the waist and hauled her to her feet.

"Thanks," she managed to say as she turned to face her rescuer.

Not that she needed to look.

She knew it was Flynn.

She knew the feel of his hands, the gentleness of his grip, the easy way he moved.

Even on the worst days, on the days when she couldn't remember dates or times or appointments, when she struggled to find words and remember names, she knew those things.

"You're welcome," he replied, stealing a kiss.

"I've been thinking. You know that dream you were talking about a few weeks ago? The one with starlight and the moon and us?" she asked.

"Yeah?"

"You forgot to mention six kids, a dog, a horse that likes to escape, and a housekeeper who has made it her life's mission to make sure every one of my children is starched and pressed before your brother's ceremony."

"I guess I did forget to mention those things," he said, chuckling as he signaled for the dog.

Rembrandt came, prancing along with that piece of fabric still dangling from his mouth.

"Off," Flynn said, and Rembrandt dropped it right into his waiting palm.

"You're a pest," Sunday said to the dog, but she patted his head because he was a cute one.

"Doesn't look like this is any worse for wear," Flynn said, handing her the cummerbund.

"Right. As long as no one notices the fang marks and slobber."

"Mom! Are the flowers coming?" Moisey called, whirling into view, her violet dress swirling around her legs as she twirled toward them. "Because Clementine is at the chapel, and she's looking beautiful but worried. On account of you not being there, and the flowers missing."

"We're on the way," Flynn assured her, grabbing the handle of the wagon and pulling. "You two go on ahead, and let her know I'm coming."

"I can help, Uncle Flynn," Milo offered, rushing to the back of the wagon, ready to push it up the hill. They'd transported the flowers from Clementine's fall garden. All of them picked by the bride that morning. Reds and oranges and deep pinks, the hues reflecting the beauty of the fall sky and the setting sun.

"Put this on first." She handed Milo the cummerbund.

He sighed deeply but didn't complain.

They'd had the discussion, she and the kids, about how important this day was, how special it needed to be for Porter and Clementine.

"Mom!" Twila rushed toward her, her dress bouncing as she moved. She had a clipboard in her hand and pencil behind her ear. "You're running three minutes behind."

"Sorry, I'm not as fast as I used to be."

"Yes, well, that's why you should have started sooner," Twila chided, brushing a fleck of dirt from Sunday's dress.

"The way you talk, sweetheart, one might think you were the adult, and I was the child."

Twila cocked her head to the side, her silky braid sliding across her shoulder. "No one would think that, because everyone would be able to see that you're older than I am."

"True."

"Come on. We've got to move. Uncle Porter will be here any minute. All the guests have arrived, and we want Clementine walking in the chapel exactly when the sun goes down." She grabbed Sunday's hand, dragging her up the hill.

The chapel was gleaming in the fading sun, the mountains behind it glittering with gold. The air had the crisp cold sting of fall and the sweet fragrance of fresh-cut grass.

Clementine was waiting near the door, wearing an ivory dress woven from alpaca fleece. She'd made it herself, and it was gorgeous, hugging her curves and floating languidly to the ground.

"You're stunning," Sunday said, hugging her friend.

"I'm nervous," she replied, twisting a curl that had fallen from her long braid.

"Don't be nervous, Clementine," Heavenly stepped around the corner of the building. "You and Porter are meant to be."

"Says a thirteen-year-old who's never been in love."

"I've been in love plenty. With the sky and the clouds and the grass under my feet."

"Hanging out with your uncle is turning you into a philosopher," Sunday said, and Heavenly smiled.

"No. It's just making me appreciate the things I have. Like you. You're beautiful. And when I'm grown, I want to be just like you."

"Heavenly . . ." She wanted to say something clever and meaningful, lovely and right, but music drifted from inside the chapel, Rosie playing the first strains of the wedding march on the keyboard set up at the back of the room.

"That's it! That means Uncle Porter is here!" Twila yelled. "Hide."

She grabbed Clementine and Sunday by the arms and dragged them around the side of the building.

"Five minutes," she announced. "Four. You know when to come, right? Because I have to walk in with Oya and the flowers and thc other girls."

"We know," Sunday assured her.

Clementine was mute, staring at the façade of the chapel as if the secrets of the universe were written there.

"It's going to be okay," Sunday assured her friend as the girls disappeared and the music swelled.

It was time.

And she took Clementine's hand. "It really is going to be okay."

"Neither of us knows that. Not for certain."

"I guess we don't. But we have this day, and this place," she said, gesturing to the silver-blue sky and the lush fields, thc horses grazing in the distant pasture. "And we have each other."

"And the men we love," Clementine said, finally smiling.

"And a bunch of crazy kids and animals, and so much love, the hill seems to be singing with it."

"That's Moisey," Flynn said, stepping around the corner.

And Sunday's breath caught, her heart jumped.

"She's decided she needs to sing the song of her people."

"People?" Clementine asked.

"Yesterday, she decided she might be a princess mermaid from Atlantis," Flynn explained. "Because she can hold her breath for so long."

"Holy cow!" Sunday said. "Did she tell me this?"

"Yes," he said, a smile tugging at the corner of his lips.

"And what did I tell her?"

"That she should feel free to embrace the princess inside herself."

"Oh. Dear. God. I should have written that down, looked it over, and come up with a better answer."

"She'd still be singing," Clementine said, all the tension gone from her face. "And I love it. This is going to make the best wedding story ever."

"If we ever get you down the aisle," Flynn said.

"Right." She raised her chin, lifted the hem of her skirt, and marched to the door of the chapel.

"You two first," Twila hissed, darting out of the

building and gesturing for Sunday and Flynn to enter.

He took Sunday's arm, his fingers curving neatly around her elbow. The music swelled, Moisey's wobbly tribute pealing out loud and clear.

Twirling through the chapel and the sky and spinning out into the universe. And it wasn't about mermaids, princesses, or underwater worlds.

It was about love.

That thing that stayed even when everything else was gone.

The thing that had pulled Sunday from a coma, back into the world, brought her back to her children, back to her friends.

Back to her home.

And the song was every word of a young girl's heart and a family's healing, and there wasn't a person in the chapel who didn't know it.

Sunday could hear them sniffling as she and Flynn walked past. She could see the tissues and the handkerchiefs. The hands dabbing at eyes.

She could see Porter waiting for his bride, his stance relaxed, his expression somber, his hand resting lightly on Moisey's back.

Sullivan was there too. Holding Oya, swaying to the music, his gaze on his wife.

And then she and Flynn were at the front of the chapel, his hand slipping from her arm as he went to stand by his brother.

And she could see the future as it was going to be—bright with the joy of family and love.

She stepped to the side, standing next to Twila and Heavenly, waiting as the keyboard music swelled and the bridal march began.

Clementine appeared, resplendent in the light of the setting sun, beautiful in a way only love could make a person.

Sunday's eyes filled with tears as she watched her friend walk up the aisle.

This was a memory she'd hold on to, one that she'd carry deep in her heart, where nothing could touch it or change it or take it away.

Her gaze was drawn to Flynn, tall and confident beside his brother.

He must have felt her gaze, because he met her eyes, smiled the smile that always made her soul sing.

"I love you," he mouthed, and she knew it was as true as dawn or dusk or the rising of the tide. She knew it was more than words or promises or sweet kisses.

It was what happened when two people wandered off and then found their way back home.

"I love you, too," she mouthed back.

And Heavenly leaned against her, wrapped her arm around her waist.

"See, Mom?" she whispered. "It's not weird at all."

Books are produced in the United States using U.S.-based materials

Books are printed using a revolutionary new process called THINKtech™ that lowers energy usage by 70% and increases overall quality

Books are durable and flexible because of Smyth-sewing

Paper is sourced using environmentally responsible foresting methods and the paper is acid-free

Center Point Large Print
600 Brooks Road / PO Box 1
Thorndike, ME 04986-0001 USA

(207) 568-3717

US & Canada:
1 800 929-9108
www.centerpointlargeprint.com